The Holy Thief

The Holy Thief

The Nineteenth Chronicle of Brother Cadfael

Ellis Peters

GENERAL
P·U·B·L·I·S·H·I·N·G

This edition published by General Publishing,
30 Lesmill Road, Toronto, Canada M3B 2T6 in 1994

**Canadian Cataloguing in Publication Data
available National Library of Canada**
Peters, Ellis, 1913–
    The Holy Thief: the nineteenth chronicle
of Brother Cadfael

ISBN 1-55144-008-3

Printed in Great Britain

The Holy Thief

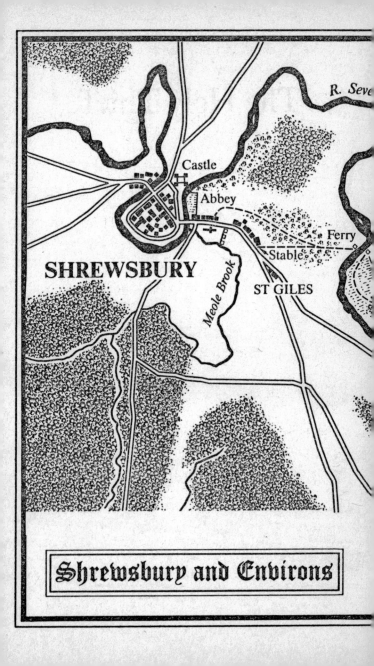

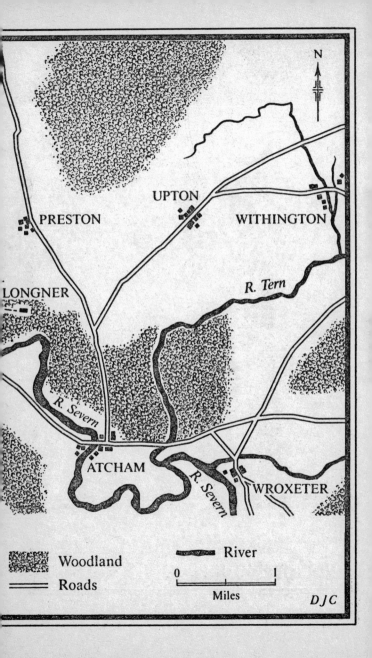

Prologue

N THE height of a hot summer, in late August of 1144, Geoffrey de Mandeville, Earl of Essex, deferred to the heat of the sun, and made the final, fatal mistake of his long and opportunist career. He was engaged, at the time, in planning the destruction by siege of one of the circle of improvised but effective fortresses King Stephen had thrown up to contain and compress the depredations of Geoffrey's host of outlaws, rebels and predators in the Fen country. For more than a year, from his elusive bases in the Fens, Geoffrey had so devastated the countryside as to ensure that not a field should be safely planted or reaped, not a manor properly tended, not a man with anything of value to lose should be left in possession of it, and not one who refused to surrender it should be left with even a life to lose. As the king had wrested from him all his own relatively legitimate castles and lands and titles, none too legally if the truth be told, so Geoffrey had set to work in defiance to do as much to every man, poor or

1

rich, who got in his way. For a year, from the borders of Huntingdon to Mildenhall in Suffolk and over much of Cambridgeshire, the Fens had become an enclosed robber kingdom in spite of King Stephen's head, and though his hasty ring of castles had done something to prevent its further enlargement, it had not hampered the earl's movements greatly, or brought him to the battle he was expert at avoiding.

But this strong-point of Burwell, north-east of Cambridge, irritated him because it was beginning to interfere with his supply lines, almost the only thing vulnerable about him. And on one of the hottest days of August he was riding round the offending castle to view the best possibilities for attack. Because of the heat he had discarded his helmet and the curtain of fine chain mail that guarded his neck. An ordinary bowman on the wall loosed a shot at him, and struck him in the head.

Geoffrey laughed at it, the wound seemed so slight; he withdrew to allow a few days for healing. And in a few days he was burning with a fevered infection that pared the flesh from his bones and brought him to his bed. They carried him as far as Mildenhall in Suffolk, and there awoke to the knowledge that he was dying. The sun had done what all King Stephen's armies could not do.

What was impossible was that he should die in peace. He was an unabsolved excommunicate; not even a priest could help him, for in the mid-Lent council called the previous year by Henry of Blois, bishop of Winchester, the king's brother and at that time papal legate, it had been decreed that no man who did violence to a cleric could be absolved by anyone but the Pope himself, and that not by any distant decree, but in the Pope's veritable presence. A long way from

2

Mildenhall to Rome for a dying man in terror of hell-fire. For Geoffrey's excommunication had been earned by his seizure by violence of the abbey of Ramsey, and his expulsion of the monks and their abbot, to turn the convent into the capital of his kingdom of thieves, torturers and murderers. For him there was no possible absolution, no hope of burial. The earth would not have him.

There were those who did their best for him, frantic in defence of his soul, if they could not help his body. When he grew so weak that he ceased to rave and sank into stupor, his officials and men of law began feverishly issuing charters in his name, restoring to the Church various properties he had seized from her, including the abbey of Ramsey. Whether with his good-will or not, no one stopped to ask, and no one ever knew. The orders were carried out, and respected, but they did not avail him. His body was refused Christian burial, his earldom was abolished, his lands and offices remained forfeit, and his family disinherited. His eldest son was excommunicate with him, and partner in his rebellion. A younger, and his namesake, was already with the Empress Maud, and recognized by her as earl of Essex, for what such an acknowledgement was worth without lands or status.

On the sixteenth day of September Geoffrey de Mandeville died, still excommunicate, still unabsolved. The only remaining mercy was shown to him by certain Knights Templar who were in Mildenhall at the time, and took his coffined body back with them to London, where for want of any Christian relenting they were forced to let him lie in a pit outside the churchyard of the Temple, in unhallowed ground, and even so a step beyond what was permitted by canon law, for by the strict letter he should not have been laid in the earth at all.

In the ranks of his motley army there was no one strong enough to take his place. The only thing that held them together was mutual self-interest and greed, and without him their dubious alliance began to fall apart, as the encouraged forces of the king moved in upon them with renewed resolution. Parties of outlaws withdrew discreetly in all directions to look for less frequented pastures and more impenetrable solitudes, where they could hope to continue their lives as beasts of prey. The more reputable, or those of more regarded birth and with more to proffer, went roundabout to make their peace and retire into safer alliances.

To everyone else the news of Geoffrey's death gave universal satisfaction. It reached the king quickly, relieved him of the most dangerous and implacable of his enemies, and instantly eased him of the necessity of immobilizing the greater part of his forces in one region. It was carried from village to village through the Fen country as the raggle-taggle marauders withdrew, and people who had lived in terror emerged cautiously to retrieve what they could of a plundered harvest, rebuild their burned homes and reassemble their families and kinships. Also, for death had been more than usually busy in those parts, to bury their dead decently. It would take more than a year for life to get back into any kind of normality, but at least now it could take the first wary steps.

And before the year's end it reached Abbot Walter of Ramsey, with the deathbed charter that gave his monastery back to him, and he gave due thanks to God, and set about sending the word on to his prior and sub-prior and all his scattered brothers, who had been forced out penniless and homeless to find shelter where

4

they could, some with their kin, some in other hospitable Benedictine houses. The first and nearest hurried to answer the summons home, and entered a total desolation. The monastic buildings were a mere shell, the lands untilled, the manors the house had formerly possessed handed out to thieves and vagabonds, all its treasures stripped away. The walls, they said, bled for very grief. Nevertheless, Abbot Walter and his brothers set to work to restore their house and their church, and sent out the news of their return to all those monks and novices who had had to go long distances to find a shelter during their exile. Being members of a wider brotherhood, having all the Benedictine Order as kin, they also sent out an urgent appeal for help in alms, material and labour to speed the work of rebuilding and refurnishing the sacred place.

In due time the news, the invitation and the need arrived at the gatehouse of the abbey of Saint Peter and Saint Paul, at Shrewsbury.

Chapter One

THE MESSENGERS arrived during the halfhour of chapter, and would not eat, drink or rest, or wash the mud of the roads from their feet, until they had made their way in to the assembly in the chapterhouse, and delivered their charge. If the suppliants failed in zeal, so would the givers.

They stood with every eye upon them, refusing to sit until the message was proclaimed. Sub-Prior Herluin, long in experience and authority, a man of impressive presence, stood fronting the lord abbot, his lean hands folded at his girdle. The young novice who had walked with him all the way from Ramsey stood modestly a pace or two behind, devoutly copying his superior's pose and stillness. Three lay servants of their house, escort on the journey, they had left with the porter at the gatehouse.

'Father Abbot, you know, as all men know, our lamentable history. It is now two months since our house and estates were restored to us. Abbot Walter is now calling back to their vocation all those brothers who were forced to disperse and find shelter wherever they could, when the rebels and outlaws took everything from us, and drove us out at sword-point. Those of us who remained close returned with our abbot as soon as we were permitted. To an utter desolation. By right we were possessed of many manors, but after the dispossession all were handed out to such lawless villains as would support de Mandeville, and to declare them restored to us avails us nothing, since we have no force to recover them from the robber lords except by law, and the law will take years to justify us. Also, such as we do recover will have been plundered and stripped of everything of value, half-ruined, possibly burned. And within the pale . . .'

He had a clear, confident voice which had proceeded thus far with considered force, but without passion, but throbbing indignation robbed him of utterance for a moment when he reached the day of the return.

'I was there. I saw what they had made of the holy place. An abomination! A midden! The church defiled, the cloisters an uncleansed stable, dortoir and frater stripped of woodwork to feed fires, all provisions taken away, all those valuables we had no time or warning to remove, stolen. Lead stripped from roofs, rooms left open to the weather, to rain and frost. Not so much as a pot for cooking, or a service book or a slip of vellum. Ruinous walls, an emptiness, a barren void. All this we have undertaken to rebuild and make more glorious than before, but we cannot do it alone. Abbot Walter has even given up much of his own wealth to buy food for the people of our villages, for harvest there has been none. Who could till the fields with death for ever at his heels? Even from the poorest of the poor those malefactors extorted the last wretched possession, and if there was nothing left to steal, they killed.'

'We have heard, all too truly, of the terror let loose on all your countryside,' said Abbot Radulfus. 'With grief we have heard it, and prayed an end to it. Now that that end is come, there is no house of our Order that can refuse all possible help to restore what was despoiled. Ask of us what can best serve Ramsey's needs. For I think you are sent as a brother to brothers, and within this family of ours injury to one is injury to all.'

'I am sent to ask help from this house and from any among the laity who may be moved to do a deed of grace, in alms, in skills, if there are any in Shrewsbury experienced in building and willing to work for some weeks far from home, in materials, in whatever aids may avail for our restoration and the benefit of the souls of the generous. For every penny and every prayer Ramsey will be grateful. To that end, I ask leave to preach once here in your church, and once, with the permission of sheriff and clergy, at the High Cross in Shrewsbury, so that every goodman of the town may search his heart and give what he is moved to give.'

'We will confer with Father Boniface,' said Radulfus, 'and he will surely agree to have you speak at a parish service. Of the sympathy of this house you may already be assured.'

'On brotherly love,' said Herluin graciously, 'I knew we could rely. Others, like Brother Tutilo here and myself, have gone forth to pray the aid of other Benedictine houses in other shires. We are charged, also, with carrying the news to all those brothers who were forced to scatter to save their lives when our troubles began, to call them home again, where they are sorely needed. For some of them cannot yet even know that

8

Abbot Walter is back within the enclave, and has need of every son's labour and faith to bring about the great work of restoration. There is one of our number, I believe,' he said, earnestly watching the abbot's face, 'came here to Shrewsbury, to the home of his family. I must see him, and exhort him to return with me.'

'That is true,' Radulfus allowed. 'Sulien Blount, of the manor of Longner. He came here to us, with Abbot Walter's countenance. The young man had not taken his final vows. He was approaching the end of his novitiate, and was in some doubt of his vocation. He came here upon terms, with his abbot's full leave, to consider on his future. It was his own decision to leave this house, and return to his family, and I absolved him accordingly. In my view he had entered the Order mistakenly. Nevertheless, he must and will answer for himself. I will have one of the brothers show you the way to his elder brother's manor.'

'I shall do my best to recall him to his better self,' Herluin stated, with a distinct implication in his tone that he would enjoy hounding back to the fold a reluctant but out-argued penitent.

Brother Cadfael, studying this formidable personage from his retired corner, and his long years of secular and monastic experience of all sorts and conditions of men, reflected that the sub-prior would probably make a very good preacher at the High Cross, and exact donations from a great many guilty consciences; for he was voluble enough, even capable of passion in the service of Ramsey. But over his chances of shifting young Sulien Blount's mind, as against the fine girl he was shortly to marry, Cadfael shook his head. If he could do it, he was a miracle-worker, and on his way to sainthood. There were uncomfortable saints in Cadfael's hagiology, whom he personally would have

9

consigned to a less reverend status, but whose aggravating rectitude he could not deny. On the whole, he could even feel a little sorry for Sub-Prior Herluin, who was about to blunt all his weapons against the impregnable shield of love. Try and get Sulien Blount away from Pernel Otmere now! He had learned to know the pair of them too well to be in doubt.

He found that he was not, so far, greatly attracted to Sub-Prior Herluin, though he could respect the man's toughness on this long journey afoot, and his determination to replenish Ramsey's plundered coffers and rebuild its ruined halls. They were a pair very oddly assorted, these itinerant brothers from the Fens. The sub-prior was a big man, long-boned, wide-shouldered, carrying flesh once ample, perhaps even excessive, but shrunken and a little flabby now. Certainly no reproach to him; he had shared, it seemed, the short commons on which the unfortunate fen-dwellers had had to survive during this harvestless year of oppression. His uncovered head showed a pale tonsure encircled with grizzled, springy hair more brown than grey, and a long, lantern face, austere of feature, deep-set and stern of eye, with a long straight stroke of a mouth, almost lipless in repose, as though totally stranger to smiling. Such lines as his countenance had acquired, during a lifetime Cadfael judged at about fifty years, all bore heavily downward, repressed and forbidding.

Not a very amiable companion on a long journey, unless his looks belied him. Brother Tutilo, who stood modestly a little behind his superior, following with rapt attention every word Herluin said, looked about twenty years old, perhaps even less; a lightly built lad, notably lissome and graceful in movement, a model of disciplined composure in stillness. His crown only just topped Herluin's shoulder, and was ringed with a

10

profusion of light brown curls, the crop grown during a lengthy journey. No doubt they would be clipped austerely close when Herluin got him back to Ramsey, but now they would have done credit to a painted seraph in a missal, though the face beneath this aureole was scarcely seraphic, in spite of its air of radiant devotion. At first glance a lovely innocent, as open as his wide eyes, and with the silken pink and whiteness of a girl, but a more penetrating study revealed that this childlike colouring was imposed upon an oval face of classic symmetry and sharp and incisive moulding. The colouring of roses on those pure marble lines had almost the air of a disguise, behind which an engaging but slightly perilous creature lurked in possibly mischievous ambush.

Tutilo – a strange name for an English youth; for there was nothing of the Norman or the Celtic about this young man. Perhaps the name chosen for him when he entered his novitiate. He must ask Brother Anselm what it signified, and where the authorities in Ramsey could have found it. Cadfael turned his attention once again to what was being discussed between host and guests.

'While you are in these parts,' said the abbot, 'I take it you may wish to visit other Benedictine houses. We will provide horses, if you so please. The season is not the most favourable for travelling. The rivers are running high, some of the fords will be impassable, you will be better mounted. We will hasten whatever arrangements you may choose to make, confer with Father Boniface about the use of the church, for he has the cure of souls in the parish of Holy Cross, and with Hugh Beringar as sheriff and the provost and Guild Merchant of the town concerning your gathering at the

High Cross in Shrewsbury. If there is anything more we can do to be of service, you need but state it.'

'We shall be grateful indeed to go mounted a while,' agreed Herluin, coming as near to smiling as his features would permit, 'for we intend to go on at least to our brothers at Worcester, perhaps also to Evesham and Pershore, and it would be simple to return by Shrewsbury and bring back your horses. Ours were taken, every one, by the outlaws before they departed. But first, even this day if possible, we would wish to go and speak with Brother Sulien.'

'As you think best,' said Radulfus simply. 'Brother Cadfael, I think, is best acquainted with the way – there is a ferry to be crossed – and also with the household of the lord of Longner. It may be well if he accompanies you.'

'Brother Sulien,' remarked Cadfael, crossing the court afterwards with Brother Anselm the precentor and librarian, 'has not been called by that title for some while, and is hardly likely to take kindly to it again now. And so Radulfus could have told him, for he knows the whole story of that young man as well as I do. But if he had said as much, this Herluin would not have listened, I suppose. "Brother" means his own brother Eudo now to Sulien. He's in training for arms, and will be one of Hugh's young men of the garrison up there in the castle as soon as his mother dies, and they tell me that's very close now. And a married man, very likely, even before that happens. There'll be no going back to Ramsey.'

'If his abbot sent the boy home to come to his own decision,' said Anselm reasonably, 'the sub-prior can hardly be empowered to bring too severe pressure on him to return. Argue and exhort as he may, he's

12

helpless, and must know it, if the young man stands fast. It may well be,' he added drily, 'that what he hopes for from that quarter is a conscience fee in silver.'

'Likely enough. And he may very well get it, too. There's more than one conscience in that house,' agreed Cadfael, 'feels a debt towards Ramsey. And what,' he asked, 'do you make of the other?'

'The young one? An enthusiast, with grace and fervour shining out of his creamy cheeks. Chosen to go with Herluin to temper the chill, would you say?'

'And where did he get that outlandish name of his?'

'Tutilo! Yes,' said Anselm, musing. 'Not at his baptism! There must be a reason why they chose that for him. Tutilo you'll find among the March saints, though we don't pay him much attention here. He was a monk of Saint Gall, two hundred years and more ago since he died, and by all accounts he was a master of all the arts, painter, poet, musician and all. Perhaps we have a gifted lad among us. I must get him to try his hand on rebec or organetto, and see what he can do. We had the roving singer here once, do you remember? The little tumbler who got himself a wife out of the goldsmith's scullery before he left us. I mended his rebec for him. If this one can do better, maybe he has some small claim to the name they've given him. Sound him out, Cadfael, if you're to be their guide out to Longner this afternoon. Herluin will be hot on the heels of his strayed novice. Try your hand with Tutilo.'

The path to the manor of Longner set off northeastward from the lanes of the Foregate, threaded a short, dense patch of woodland, and climbed over a low crest of heath and meadow to look down upon the winding course of the Severn, downstream from the town. The

13

river was running high and turgid, rolling fallen branches and clumps of turf from the banks down in its currents. There had been ample snows in the winter, without any great gales or frosts. The thaw still filled the valleys everywhere with the soft rippling of water, even the meadows by the river and the brook whispered constantly and shimmered with lingering silver among the grass. The ford a short way upstream was already impassable, the island that helped foot traffic across at normal times was under water. But the ferryman poled his passengers across sturdily, so familiar and at ease with his troubled waters that storm, flood and calm were all one to him.

On the further side of the Severn the path threaded wet water-meadows, the river lipping the bleached winter grass a yard inland already. If heavy spring rains came on the hills of Wales, to follow the thaw-water, there would be flooding under the walls of Shrewsbury, and the Meole Brook and the mill pond would back up strongly and threaten even the nave of the abbey church. It had happened twice since Cadfael entered the Order. And westward the sky hung ponderous and grey, leaning upon the distant mountains.

They skirted the encroaching waters, below the dark ploughland of the Potter's Field, climbed thankfully inland up the gentle slope beyond, into the well kept woodlands of the manor of Longner, and came to the clearing where the house backed snugly into the hillside, sheltered from the prevailing winds, and surrounded by its high stockade and the encrustation of demesne buildings within.

As they entered at the gate Sulien Blount came out from the stables to cross to the house. He wore leather jerkin and the working cotte and hose becoming a younger brother doing his share on his elder's estate until he could find occasion to carve out his own holding, as surely he would. At the sight of the trio entering he halted, stiffly at gaze, instantly recognizing his former spiritual superior, and startled to see him here so far from home. But at once he came to meet them, with reverent and perhaps slightly apprehensive courtesy. The stresses of the past year had removed him so far from the cloister and the tonsure that the reappearance so close to home of what was past and done seemed for a moment to offer a threat to his new and hard-earned composure, and the future he had chosen. Only for a moment. Sulien was in no doubt now of where he was going.

'Father Herluin, welcome to my home! I rejoice to see you well, and to know that Ramsey is restored to the Order. Will you not come within, and let us know in what particular we of Longner can serve you?'

'You cannot but understand,' said Herluin, addressing himself warily to possible battle ahead, 'in what state we have regained our abbey. For a year it has been the den of a rogue army, pillaged and stripped of everything burnable, even the walls defiled, where they did not shatter them before they departed. We have need of every son of the house, and every friend to the Order, to make good before God what has been desecrated. It is to you I come, and with you I wish to speak.'

'A friend to the Order,' said Sulien, 'I hope I am. A son of Ramsey and a brother of its brothers I no longer am. Abbot Walter sent me back here, very fairly, to consider my vocation, which he knew to be dubious, and committed my probation to Abbot Radulfus, who has absolved me. But come within, and we can confer as friends. I will listen reverently, Father, and respect all you may have to say.'

15

And so he would, for he was a young man brought up to observe all the duties of youth towards his elders; all the more as a younger son with no inheritance and his own way to make, and therefore all the greater need to please those who had power and authority, and could advance his career. He would listen and defer, but he would not be shifted. Nor did he need any friendly witness to support his side of the case, and why should Herluin's side of it be weighted even by a devout and silent young acolyte, imposing on an ex-brother by his very presence a duty he no longer owed, and had undertaken mistakenly and for the wrong reasons in the first place?

'You will wish to confer strictly in private,' said Cadfael, following the sub-prior up the stone steps to the hall door. 'With your leave, Sulien, this young brother and I will look in upon your mother. If, of course, she is well enough and willing to receive visits.'

'Yours, always!' said Sulien, with a brief, flashing smile over his shoulder. 'And a new face will refresh her. You know how she views life and the world now, very peacefully.'

It had not always been so. Donata Blount had suffered years of some consuming and incurable disease that devoured her substance slowly and with intense pain. Only with the last stages of her bodily weakness had she almost outlived pain itself, and grown reconciled to the world she was leaving as she drew nearer to the door opening upon another.

'It will be very soon,' said Sulien simply. He halted in the high dim hall. 'Father Herluin, be pleased to enter the solar with me, and I will send for some refreshment for you. My brother is at the farm. I am sorry he is not here to greet you, but we had no prior word. You will excuse him. If your errand is to me, it may be better

16

so.' And to Cadfael: 'Go in to my mother's chamber. I know she is awake, and never doubt but you are always welcome to her.'

The Lady Donata, confined to her bed at last, lay propped on pillows in her small bedchamber, her window unshuttered, a little brazier burning in one corner on the bare stone of the floor. She was nothing but fine bones and translucent skin, the hands quiet on her coverlet like fallen petals of lilies in their transparent emaciation. Her face was honed into a fragile mask of silver bones, and the deep pits of her eyes were filled with ice-blue shadow round the startling, imperishable beauty of the eyes themselves, still clear and intelligent, and the darkest and most luminous of blues. The spirit encased in this frail shell was still alert, indomitable, and sharply interested in the world about her, without any fear of leaving it, or any reluctance to depart.

She looked up at her visitors, and greeted Cadfael in a low voice that had lost none of its quality. 'Brother Cadfael, this is a pleasure! I've hardly seen you through the winter. I should not have liked to leave without your valediction.'

'You could have sent for me,' he said, and went to set a stool by her bedside. 'I am biddable. And Radulfus would not refuse you.'

'He came himself,' said Donata, 'to take my confession at Christmas. I am an adopted ewe of his flock. He does not forget me.'

'And how do your affairs stand?' he asked, studying the serenity of her face. There was never need to go round-about with Donata, she understood him as he meant, and preferred it so.

'In the matter of life and death,' she said, 'excellently well. In the matter of pain . . . I have gone beyond

17

pain, there is not enough of me to feel it, or regard it if it could make itself felt. I take that as the sign I've looked for.' She spoke without apprehension or regret, or even impatience now, perfectly content to wait the short while longer. And she lifted her dark eyes to the young man standing apart.

'And who is this you have brought to see me? A new acolyte of yours in the herb garden?'

Tutilo came nearer. rightly interpreting this as an invitation. His eyes were large and round, beholding her condition, youth and abundant life confronted with death, but he did not seem at all dismayed, nor pitying. Donata did not invite pity The boy was very quick and accurate of apprehension.

'Not mine,' said Cadfael, measuring the slight figure consideringly, and warily approving a bright pupil he certainly would not have refused. 'No, this young brother is come with his sub-prior from the abbey of Ramsey. Abbot Walter is back in his monastery, and calling home all the brothers to the work of rebuilding, for Geoffrey de Mandeville and his brigands have left an empty shell. And to let you know the whole of it. Sub-Prior Herluin is in the solar this moment. trying what he can do with Sulien.'

'That is one he will never reclaim,' said Donata with certainty. 'My sorrow that ever he was driven to mistake himself so grossly, and if Geoffrey de Mandeville did nothing of good besides, among his much evil, at least his onslaught drove Sulien back to his proper self. My younger son,' she said, meeting Tutilo's wide golden eyes with a thoughtful and appreciative smile, 'was never cut out to be a monk.'

'So an emperor said, I believe,' remarked Cadfael, recalling what Anselm had said of the saint of Saint Gall, 'about the first Tutilo, after whom this young brother is named. For this is Brother Tutilo, a novice of Ramsey, and close to the end of his novitiate, as I hear from his superior. And if he takes after his namesake he should be painter, carver, singer and musician. Great pity, said King Charles – Charles the Fat, they called him – that ever such a genius should be made a monk. He called down a malediction on the man that did it. So Anselm tells me, at least.'

'Some day,' said Donata, looking this very comely and graceful young man over from head to foot, and recording with detached admiration what she saw, 'some king may say as much of this one. Or some woman, of course! Are you such a paragon, Tutilo?'

'It is why they gave me the name,' said the boy honestly, and a faint rosy blush surged out of the coils of his cowl and climbed his sturdy throat into the suave cheeks, but apparently without causing him the slightest discomfort. He did not lower his eyes, which dwelt with fascination upon her face. In its final tranquillity something of its long-departed beauty had returned, to render Donata even more formidable and admirable. 'I have some skill,' he said, 'in music.' It was stated with the certainty of one capable of detached judgement, without either boasting or deprecating his powers. Small flames of interest and liking kindled in Donata's hollow eyes.

'Good! So you should lay claim to what you know you do well,' she said approvingly. 'Music has been my easiest way to sleep, many a night. My consolation, too, when the devils were too active. Now they spend their time sleeping, and I lie awake.' She moved a frail hand upon the coverlet, indicating a chest that sat remote in a corner of the room. 'There is a psaltery in there, though it has not been touched for a long time. If you care to try it? No doubt it would be grateful to be given a voice again. There is a harp in the hall, but no one now to play it.'

Tutilo went readily to lift the heavy lid and peer down at the stored valuables within. He lifted out the instrument, not a large one, meant to be played on the knees, and shaped like the broad snout of a pig. The manner in which he handled it was eloquent of interest and affection, and if he frowned, it was at the sight of a broken course among the strings. He peered deeper into the chest for quills to play it, but found none, and frowned again.

'Time was,' said Donata, 'when I cut quills new every week or so. I am sorry we have neglected our duty.'

That brought her a brief, preoccupied smile, but his attention went back at once to the psaltery. 'I can use my nails,' he said, and brought the instrument with him to the bedside, and without ceremony or hesitation sat down on the edge of the bed, straightened the psaltery on his knees, and passed a stroking hand over the strings, raising a soft, quivering murmur.

'Your nails are too short,' said Donata. 'You will flay your finger-ends.'

Her voice could still evoke colours and tones that made the simplest utterance eloquent. What Cadfael heard was a mother, between indulgence and impatience, warning youth of venturing an undertaking possibly painful. No, perhaps not a mother, nor even an elder sister; something more distant than a blood relative with rights, and yet closer. For those contacts free of all duty and responsibility are also free of all restraints, and may approach as rapidly and as close as they will. And she had very little time left, to submit to limitations now. What the boy heard there was no knowing, but he flashed up at her a bright, naked glance, not so much surprised as alerted, and his hands were abruptly still for an instant, and he smiled.

'My finger-ends are leather – see!' He spread his palms, and flexed his long fingers. 'I was harper to my father's lord at the manor of Berton for a year and more before I entered Ramsey. Hush, now, let me try! But it lacks one course, you must hold me excused for the flaws.' There was something of indulgence in his voice, too, a soft amusement, as if to a needlessly solicitous elder who must be reassured of his competence.

He had found the tuning key lying in the chest with the instrument, and he began to test the gut strings and tighten busily at the pegs that anchored them. The singing murmur rose like a chorus of insects in a summer meadow, and Tutilo's tonsured head stooped over his work in total absorption, while Donata from her pillows watched him from under half-closed eyelids, the more intently because he was now paying no heed to her. Yet some intense intimacy bound them, for as he softened into a passionate private smile over his work, so did she over his concentration and pleasure.

'Wait, one of the strings in this broken course is long enough to serve. Better one than none, though you'll notice when the tone thins.'

His fingers, if toughened by the harp, were very nimble and neat as he attached the single string and tightened it gingerly. 'There! Now!' He passed a light hand over the strings, and produced a shimmering rill of soft notes. 'Wire strings would be louder and brighter than gut, but this will do very well.'

And he bent his head over the instrument, and plunged like a hawk stooping, and began to play, flexed fingers dancing. The old soundboard seemed to swell and throb with the tension of notes, too full to find adequate release through the fretted rose in the centre.

Cadfael withdrew his stool a little from the bedside, to have them both in plain view, for they made an interesting study. The boy was undoubtedly hugely gifted. There was something almost alarming in the passion of the assault. It was as if a bird had been muted for a long time, and suddenly found his muffled throat regain its eloquence.

In a little while his first hunger was slaked, and he could soften into moderation, and savour all the more gratefully the sweetness of this indulgence. The sparkling, whirling dance measure, light as thistledown for all its passion, eased into a gentle air, better adapted to an instrument so soft. Even a little melancholy, some kind of virelai, rhythmic and rueful. Where had he learned that? Certainly not at Ramsey; Cadfael doubted if it would have been welcome there.

And the Lady Donata, world-weary and closely acquainted with the ironies of life and death, lay still in her pillows, never taking her eyes from the boy who had forgotten her existence. She was not the audience to which he played, but she was the profound intelligence that heard him. She drew him in with her great bruised eyes, and his music she drank, and it was wine to her thirst. Crossing the half of Europe overland, long ago, Cadfael had seen gentians in the grass of the mountain meadows, bluer than blue, of the same profound beyond-blue of her eyes. The set of her lips, wryly smiling, told a slightly different story. Tutilo was already crystal to her, she knew more of him than he himself knew.

The affectionate, sceptical twist of her mouth vanished when he began to sing. The tune was at once simple and subtle, playing with no more than half a dozen notes, and his voice, pitched higher than in speech, and very soft and suave, had the same qualities, innocent as childhood, piercing as a wholly adult grief. And he was singing not in English, not even in Norman-French as England knew it, but in the *langue d'oc* Cadfael remembered imperfectly from long ago. Where had this cloister novice heard the melodies of the Provençal troubadours, and learned their songs? In the lord's hall where he had been a harper? Donata knew no southern French, Cadfael had long forgotten it, but they knew a love song when they heard it. Rueful, unfulfilled, eternally hopeful, an *amour de loin*, never to come face to face.

The cadence changed in an instant, the secret words passed magically into: 'Ave mater salvatoris . . . ' and they were back with the liturgy of Saint Martial before they realized, as Tutilo had realized with the wild perceptions of a fox, that the door of the room had opened. He was taking no chances. The door had actually opened on the harmless person of Sulien Blount, but Sub-Prior Herluin was there at his shoulder, looming like a cloud.

Donata lay smiling, approving the lightning wit that could change course so smoothly, without a break, without a blush. True, Herluin drew his austere brows into a displeased frown at the sight of his novice seated upon the edge of a woman's bed and plainly singing for her pleasure; but a glance at the woman herself, in her wasted and daunting dignity, disarmed him at once She came as a shock, all the more because she was not old, but withered in her prime.

Tutilo arose modestly, clasping the psaltery to his breast, and withdrew himself dutifully into a corner of the room, his eyes lowered. When he was not looking at her, Cadfael suspected, he was seeing her all the more clearly.

'Mother,' said Sulien, grave and a little stiff from his small battlefield, 'here is Sub-Prior Herluin, sometime my instructor in Ramsey, willing you well and promising you his prayers. In my brother's name, as I do, make him welcome.'

In the absence of son and daughter-in-law she spoke authoritatively for both. 'Father, use our house as your own. Your visit does us honour. It was welcome news to every soul among us that Ramsey is again delivered to the service of God.'

'God has indeed regarded us,' said Herluin, a little cautiously and with less than his usual assurance, for the sight of her had shaken him. 'But there is much to be done to restore our dwelling, and we have need of every hand that can be brought to our aid. I had hoped to take your son back with me, but it seems I may no longer call him brother. Nevertheless, be sure both he and you will be in my prayers.'

'I will remember Ramsey,' said Donata, 'in mine. But if the house of Blount has denied you a brother, we may still be of help in other ways.'

'We are seeking the charity of all good men,' agreed Herluin fervently, 'in whatever form. Our house is destitute, they left us nothing but the fabric of the walls, and that defaced, and stripped of all that could be carted away.'

'I have promised,' said Sulien, 'to return to Ramsey and work there with my hands for one month, when the time is right.' He had never rid himself completely of a feeling of guilt for abandoning a vocation he had been foolish and mistaken ever to undertake. He would be glad to pay his ransom with hard labour, and free his conscience before he took a bride. And Pernel Otmere would approve him, and give him leave to go.

Herluin thanked him for the offer, but with no very great enthusiasm, perhaps doubtful how much work Ramsey was likely to get out of this recusant youth.

'I will also speak to my brother,' Sulien pursued earnestly, 'and see what more we may be able to do. They are cutting coppice-wood, there will be older stands well seasoned. And they are taking out some well grown trees from the woodland. I will ask him for a load of timber for your rebuilding, and I think he will let me have it. I am asking no other portion before I go into the king's service at Shrewsbury. If the abbey can supply a cart to transport it, or one can be hired? Eudo's carts cannot be spared for so long.'

This practical offer Herluin received with more warmth. He was still resentful, Cadfael thought, of his failure to overwhelm all argument and take the back-slider home with him, not for the promised month, but for life. Not that Sulien himself was of such great value, but Herluin was not accustomed to being so stoutly resisted. All barricades should have fallen like the walls of Jericho at the blast of his trumpet.

Still, he had extracted all he could, and prepared to take his leave. Tutilo, all attentive ears and modestly lowered eyes in his corner, opened the chest quietly, and laid away the psaltery he had been clasping to his heart. The very gentleness with which he laid it within and slowly closed the lid over it brought a small, thoughtful twist to Donata's ashen mouth.

'I have a favour to ask,' she said, 'if you will hear it. Your songbird here has given me delight and ease. If I am sometimes sleepless and in pain, will you lend me that consolation for an hour, while you remain in

Shrewsbury? I will not send unless I need him. Will you let him come?'

If Herluin was taken aback at such a request, he was nevertheless shrewdly aware that she had him at a disadvantage, though in all probability, thought Cadfael, interested, he was hoping that she was less aware of it. In which hope he was certainly deluded. She knew very well he could hardly refuse her. To send a susceptible novice to provide music for a woman, and a woman in her bed, at that, was unthinkable, even scandalous. Except that this woman was now so closely acquainted with death that the subtle creaking of the opening door was present in her voice, and the transparent pallor of the bodyless soul in her face. She was no longer responsive to the proprieties of this world, nor afraid of the dread uncertainties of the next.

'Music medicines me to peace,' she said, and waited patiently for his submission. And the boy in the corner stood mute and passive, but beneath the long, lowered lashes the amber-gold eyes glowed, pleased, serious and wary.

'If you send for him in extreme need,' said Herluin at last, choosing his words with care, 'how can our Order reject such a prayer? If you call, Brother Tutilo shall come.'

Chapter Two

O QUESTION now how he got his name,' said Cadfael, lingering in Brother Anselm's workshop in the cloister after High Mass next morning. 'Sweet as a lark.' They had just heard the lark in full song, and had paused in the precentor's corner carrel to watch the worshippers disperse, the lay visitors from the guesthall among them. For those who sought lodging here it was politic and graceful, if not obligatory, to attend at least the main Mass of the day. February was not a busy month for Brother Denis the hospitaller, but there were always a few travellers in need of shelter.

'The lad's immensely talented,' agreed Anselm. 'A true ear and an instinct for harmony.' And he added, after a moment's consideration: 'Not a voice for choral work, however. Too outstanding. There's no hiding that grain among a bushel.'

No need to stress the point, the justice of that verdict was already proved. Listening to that pure, piercingly sweet thread, delivered so softly, falling on the ear with such astonishment, no one could doubt it. There was no way of subduing that voice into anonymity among the balanced polyphony of a choir. Cadfael wondered if it might not be equally shortsighted to try and groom its owner into a conforming soul in a disciplined brotherhood.

'Brother Denis's Provençal guest pricked up his ears,' remarked Anselm, 'when he heard the lad. Last night he asked Herluin to let the boy join him at practice in the hall. There they go now. I have his rebec in for restringing. I will say for him, he cares for his instruments.'

The trio crossing the cloister from the south door of the church was a cause of considerable curiosity and speculation among the novices. It was not often the convent housed a troubador from the south of France, obviously of some wealth and repute, for he travelled with two servants and lavish baggage. He and his entourage had been here three days, delayed in their journey north to Chester by a horse falling lame. Rémy of Pertuis was a man of fifty or so, of striking appearance, a gentleman who valued himself on his looks and presentation. Cadfael watched him cross towards the guesthall; he had not so far had occasion to pay him much attention, but if Anselm respected him and approved his musical conscience he might be worth studying. A fine, burnished head of russet hair and a clipped beard. Good carriage and a body very handsomely appointed, fur lining his cloak, gold at his belt. And two attendants following close behind him, a tall fellow somewhere in his mid-thirties, all muted brown from head to foot, his good but plain clothing placing him discreetly between squire and groom, and a woman, cloaked and hooded, but by her slender figure and light step young.

28

'What's his need for the girl?' Cadfael wondered.

'Ah, that he has explained to Brother Denis,' said Anselm, and smiled. 'Meticulously! Not his kin . . .'

'I never thought it,' said Cadfael.

'But you may have thought, as I certainly did when first they rode in here, that he had a very particular use for her, as indeed he has, though not as I imagined it.' Brother Anselm, for all he had come early to the cloister, had fathomed most of the byways that were current outside the walls, and had long ago ceased to be either surprised or shocked by them. 'It's the girl who performs most of his songs. She has a lovely voice, and he values her for it, and highly, but for nothing else, so far as I can see. She's an important part of his stock in trade.'

'But what,' wondered Cadfael, 'is a minstrel from the heart of Provence doing here in the heart of England? And plainly no mere jongleur, but a genuine troubadour. He's wandered far from home, surely?'

And yet, he thought, why not? The patrons on whom such artists depend are becoming now as much English as French, or Norman, or Breton, or Angevin. They have estates both here and oversea, as well seek them here as there. And the very nature of the troubadour, after all, is to wander and venture, as the Galician word *trobar*, from which they take their name, though it has come to signify to create poetry and music, literally means to find. Those who *find* – seek and find out the poetry and the music both, these are the troubadours. And if their art is universal, why should they not be found everywhere?

'He's heading for Chester,' said Anselm. 'So his man says – Bénezet, he's called. It may be he hopes to get a place in the earl's household. But he's in no haste, and plainly in no want of money. Three good riding horses and two servants in his following is pretty comfortable travelling.'

'Now I wonder,' said Cadfael, musing darkly, 'why he left his last service? Made himself too agreeable to his lord's lady, perhaps? Something serious, to make it necessary to cross the sea.'

'I am more interested,' said Anselm, undisturbed by such a cynical view of troubadours in general, 'in where he got the girl. For she is not French, not Breton, not from Provence. She speaks the English of these borders, and some Welsh. It would seem she is one property he got this side the ocean. The groom, Bénezet, he's a southerner like his master.'

The trio had vanished into the guesthall by then, their entangled lives still as mysterious as when they had first entered the enclave. And in some few days, if the roads stayed passable and the lame horse mended, they would depart just as enigmatically, like so many who took refuge under that hospitable roof a day, a week, and then passed, leaving nothing of themselves behind. Cadfael shook himself free of vain wondering about souls that passed by as strangers, and sighed, and went back into the church to say a brief word into Saint Winifred's ear before going to his work in the garden.

Someone was before him in needing Saint Winifred's attention, it seemed. Tutilo had something to ask of the saint, for he was kneeling on the lowest step of her altar, sharply outlined against the candlelight. He was so intent upon his prayer that he did not hear Cadfael's steps on the tiles. His face was lifted to the light, eager and vehement, and his lips were moving rapidly and silently in voluble appeal, and by his wide-open eyes and flushed cheeks with every confidence of being heard and having his plea granted. What Tutilo did, he did with his might. For him a simple request to heaven, through the intercession of a kindly disposed saint, was equal to wrestling with angels. and out-arguing doctors of divinity. And when he rose from his knees it was with an exultant spring in his step and tilt to his chin, as though he knew he had carried his point

When he did sense another presence, and turn to face the newcomer, it was with the most demure and modest front. abating his brightness and exuberance as smoothly as he had diverted his love song into liturgical piety for Herluin's benefit in Donata's bedchamber True, when he recognized Cadfael his devout gravity mellowed a little. and a subdued gleam came back cautiously into his amber eyes.

'I was praying her aid for our mission,' he said. 'Today Father Herluin preaches at the High Cross in the town. If Saint Winifred lends us aid we cannot fail.'

His eyes turned again to the reliquary on the altar, and lingered lovingly, wide with wonder.

'She has done miraculous things. Brother Rhun told me how she healed him and took him to be her true servant. And other such marvels   many   . When the day of her translation comes round. every year. there are hundreds of pilgrims, Brother Jerome says so. I have been asking him about all the treasury of relics your house has gathered here. But she is the chief. and incomparable.'

Brother Cadfael certainly had nothing to object to that. Indeed there were some among the treasury of relics amassed by obedientiaries here over the years about which he felt somewhat dubious. Stones from Calvary and the Mount of Olives – well. stones are stones. every hill has a scattering of them. there is only the word of the purveyor as to the origin of any particular specimen. Fragments of bones from saints and martyrs. a drop of the Virgin's milk, a shred of her robe, a

31

little flask of the sweat of Saint John the Baptist, a tress from the red hair of Saint Mary Magdalen . . . all easily portable, and no doubt some of the returning pilgrims from the Holy Land were genuine, and believed in the genuineness of what they offered, but in some cases Cadfael wondered whether they had ever been nearer Acre than Eastcheap. But Saint Winifred he knew well, he had lifted her out of the Welsh earth with his own hands, and with his own hands laid her reverently back into it, and drawn the sweet soil of Gwytherin over her rest. What she had bequeathed to Shrewsbury and to him in absence was the sheltering shadow of her right hand, and a half-guilty, half-sacred memory of an affection and kindness almost personal. When he appealed, she listened. He tried to present her with only reasonable requests. But no doubt she would listen as attentively to this persuasive and enthusiastic youth, and grant him, perhaps not all he demanded, but whatever was good for him.

'If only,' breathed Tutilo, burning up into his brightest and most irresistible radiance, 'if only Ramsey had such a patroness, our future glory would be assured. All our misfortunes would be over. Pilgrims would come by the thousand, their offerings would enrich our house. Why should we not be another Compostela?'

'It may be your duty,' Cadfael reminded him drily, 'to work for the enrichment of your monastery, but that is not the first duty of the saints.'

'No, but that is what happens,' said Tutilo, unabashed. 'And surely Ramsey needs and deserves a particular grace, after all her sufferings. It cannot be wrong to plead for her enrichment. I want nothing for myself.' That he corrected in haste the next moment. 'Yes, I want to excel. I want to be profitable to my brothers and my Order. That I do want.'

'And that,' Cadfael said comfortably, 'she will certainly look upon with favour. And so you are profitable. With gifts like yours you should count yourself blessed. You go and do your best for Ramsey in the town, and give as good when you get to Worcester, or Pershore, or Evesham, and what more can possibly be required of you?'

'What I can, I'll do,' agreed Tutilo, with a great deal of resolution, but decidedly less genuine enthusiasm, and his eyes still dwelling fondly on Winifred's chased reliquary, points of silver shining in the candlelight. 'But such a patroness . . what could she not do to restore our fortunes! Brother Cadfael, can you not tell us where to find such another?'

He took his leave almost reluctantly, looking back from the doorway, before he shook his shoulders firmly, and went off to submit himself to Herluin's orders, and undertake, one way or another, to unloose the purse-strings of the burghers of Shrewsbury.

Cadfael watched the slender, springy figure stride away, and found something slightly equivocal even in the back view of the overlong curls, and the tender, youthful shaping of the nape of the neck. Ah, well! Few people are exactly what they seem on first acquaintance, and he hardly knew the boy at all.

They sallied forth in solemn procession to the town, Prior Robert lending his dignified presence to add to the gravity of the occasion. The sheriff had notified the provost and Guild Merchant of the town, and left it to them to make sure that the whole of Shrewsbury recognized its duty, and would be present. Alms to so eminent a religious house in its persecution and need provided an infallible means of acquiring merit, and there must be many in so large a town willing to pay a

33

modest price to buy off reprobation for minor backslidings.

Herluin returned from his foray so clearly content with himself, and Tutilo bearing so heavy a satchel, that it was plain they had reaped a very satisfactory harvest. The following Sunday's sermon from the parish pulpit added to the spoils. The coffer Radulfus had donated to receive offerings grew heavier still. Moreover, three good craftsmen, master-carpenter and two journeyman masons, proposed to go back with the Ramsey men and seek work in the rebuilding of the gutted barns and storehouses. The mission was proceeding very successfully. Even Rémy of Pertuis had given good silver coin, as became a musician who had composed liturgical works in his time for two churches in Provence.

They were scarcely out of church after the Mass when a groom came riding in from Longner, with a spare pony on a leading rein, to prefer a request from the Lady Donata. Would Sub-Prior Herluin, she entreated, permit Brother Tutilo to visit her? The day being somewhat advanced, she had sent a mount for his journey, and promised a return in time for Compline. Tutilo submitted himself to his superior's will with the utmost humility, but with shining eyes. To return unsupervised to Donata's psaltery, or the neglected harp in the hall at Longner, would be appropriate reward for piping to Herluin's tune with such devotion during the day.

Cadfael saw him ride out from the gatehouse, the childish delight showing through plainly by then; delight at being remembered and needed, delight at riding out when he had expected only a routine evening within the walls. Cadfael could appreciate and excuse that. The indulgent smile was still on his face as he went to tend certain remedies he had working in his

34

herbarium. And there was another creature just as shiningly young, though perhaps not as innocent, hovering at the door of his hut, waiting for him.

'Brother Cadfael?' questioned Rémy of Pertuis' girl singer, surveying him with bold blue eyes just on a level with his own.

Not tall, but above average for a woman, slender almost to leanness, and straight as a lance. 'Brother Edmund sent me to you. My master has a cold, and is croaking like a frog. Brother Edmund says you can help him.'

'God willing!' said Cadfael, returning her scrutiny just as candidly. He had never seen her so close before, nor expected to, for she kept herself apart, taking no risks, perhaps, with an exacting master. Her head was uncovered now, her face, oval, thin and bright, shone lily-pale between wings of black, curling hair.

'Come within,' he said, 'and tell me more of his case. His voice is certainly of importance. A workman who loses his tools has lost his living. What manner of cold is it he's taken? Has he rheumy eyes? A thick head? A stuffed nose?'

She followed him into the workshop, which was already shadowy within, lit only by the glow of the damped-down brazier, until Cadfael lit a sulphur spill and kindled his small lamp. She looked about her with interest at the laden shelves and the herbs dangling from the beams, stirring and rustling faintly in the draught from the door. 'His throat,' she said indifferently. 'Nothing else worries him. He's hoarse and dry. Brother Edmund says you have lozenges and draughts. He's not ill,' she said with tolerant disdain. 'Not hot or fevered. Anything that touches his voice sends him into a sweat. Or mine, for that matter. Another of his tools he can't afford to lose, little as he cares about the rest of me. Brother Cadfael, do you make all these pastes and potions?' She was ranging the shelves of bottles and jars with eyes respectfully rounded.

'I do the brewing and pounding,' said Cadfael, 'the earth supplies the means. I'll send your lord some pastilles for his throat, and a linctus to take every three hours. But that I must mix. A few minutes only. Sit by the brazier, it grows cold here in the evening.'

She thanked him, but did not sit. The array of mysterious containers fascinated her. She continued to prowl and gaze, restless but silent, a feline presence at his back as he selected from among his flasks cinquefoil and horehound, mint and a trace of poppy, and measured them into a green glass bottle. Her hand, slender and long-fingered, stroked along the jars with their Latin inscriptions.

'You need nothing for yourself?' he asked. 'To ward off his infection?'

'I never take cold,' she said, with scorn for the weaknesses of Rémy of Pertuis and all his kind.

'Is he a good master?' Cadfael asked directly.

'He feeds and clothes me,' she said promptly, proof against surprise.

'No more than that? He would owe that to his groom or his scullion. You, I hear, are the prop of his reputation.'

She turned to face him as he filled his bottle to the neck with a honeyed syrup, and stoppered it. Thus eye to eye she showed as experienced and illusionless, not bruised but wary of bruises, and prepared to evade or return them at need; and yet even younger than he had taken her to be, surely no more than eighteen.

'He is a very good poet and minstrel, never think otherwise. What I know, he taught me. What I had from God, yes, that is mine; but he showed me its use.

If there ever was a debt, that and food and clothing would still have paid it, but there is none. He owes me nothing. The price for me he paid when he bought me.'

He turned to stare her in the face, and judge how literally she meant the words she had chosen; and she smiled at him. 'Bought, not hired. I am Rémy's slave, and better his by far than tied to the one he bought me from. Did you not know it still goes on?'

'Bishop Wulstan preached against it years back,' said Cadfael, 'and did his best to shame it out of England, if not out of the world. But though he drove the dealers into cover, yes, I know it still goes on. They trade out of Bristol. Very quietly, but yes, it's known. But that's mainly a matter of shipping Welsh slaves into Ireland, money seldom passes for humankind here.'

'My mother,' said the girl, 'goes to prove the traffic is both ways. In a bad season, with food short, her father sold her, one daughter too many to feed, to a Bristol trader, who sold her again to the lord of a half-waste manor near Gloucester. He used her as his bedmate till she died, but it was not in his bed I was got. She knew how to keep the one by a man she liked, and how to be rid of her master's brood,' said the girl with ruthless simplicity. 'But I was born a slave. There's no appeal.'

'There could be escape,' said Cadfael, though admitting difficulties.

'Escape to what? Another worse bondage? With Rémy at least I am not mauled, I am valued after a fashion, I can sing, and play, if it's another who calls the tune. I own nothing, not even what I wear on my body. Where should I go? What should I do? In whom should I trust? No, I am not a fool. Go I would, if I could see a place for me anywhere, as I am. But risk being brought back, once having fled him? That would be quite another servitude, harder by far than now. He

37

would want me chained. No, I can wait. Things can change,' she said, and shrugged thin, straight shoulders, a little wide and bony for a girl. 'Rémy is not a bad man, as men go. I have known worse. I can wait.'

There was good sense in that, considering her present circumstances. Her Provençal master, apparently, made no demands on her body, and the use he made of her voice provided her considerable pleasure. It is essentially pleasure to exercise the gifts of God. He clothed, warmed and fed her. If she had no love for him, she had no hate, either, she even conceded, very fairly, that his teaching had given her a means to independent life, if ever she could discover a place of safety in which to practise it. And at her age she could afford a few years of waiting. Rémy himself was in search of a powerful patron. In the court of some susbtantial honour she might make a very comfortable place for herself.

But still, Cadfael reflected ruefully at the end of these practical musings, still as a slave.

'I expected you to tell me now,' said the girl, eyeing him curiously, 'that there is one place where I could take refuge and not be pursued. Rémy would never dare follow me into a nunnery.'

'God forbid!' prayed Cadfael with blunt fervour. 'You would turn any convent indoors-outdoors within a month. No, you'll never hear me give you that advice. It is not for you.'

'It was for you,' she pointed out, with mischief in her voice and her eyes. 'And for that lad Tutilo from Ramsey. Or would you have ruled him out, too? His case is much like mine. It irks me to be in bondage, it irked him to be a menial in the same house as a loathsome old satyr who liked him far too well. A third son to a poor man – he had to look out for himself.'

'I trust,' said Cadfael, giving the linctus bottle an experimental shake to ensure the contents should be well mixed, 'I trust that was not his only reason for entering Ramsey.'

'Oh, but I think it was, though he doesn't know it. He thinks he was called to a vocation, out of all the evils of the world.' She herself, Cadfael guessed, had known many of those evils on familiar terms, and yet emerged thus far rather contemptuous of them than either soiled or afraid. 'That is why he works so hard at being holy,' she said seriously. 'Whatever he takes it into his head to do he'll do with all his might. But if he was convinced, he'd be easier about it.'

Cadfael stood staring at her in mild astonishment. 'You seem to know more than I do about this young brother of mine,' he said. 'And yet I've never seen you so much as notice his existence. You move about the enclave, when you're seen at all, like a modest shadow, eyes on the ground. How did you ever come to exchange good-day with him, let alone read the poor lad's mind?'

'Rémy borrowed him to make a third voice in triple organa. But we had no chance to talk then. Of course no one ever sees us look at each other or speak to each other. It would be ill for both of us. He is to be a monk, and should never be private with a woman, and I am a bond-woman, and if I talk with a young man it will be thought I have notions only fit for a free woman, and may try to slip out of my chains. I am accustomed to dissembling, and he is learning. You need not fear any harm. He has his eyes all on sainthood, on service to his monastery. Me, I am a voice. We talk of music, that is the only thing we share.'

True, yet not quite the whole truth, or she could not

39

have learned so much of the boy in one or two brief meetings. She was quite sure of her own judgement.

'Is it ready?' she asked, returning abruptly to her errand. 'He'll be fretting.'

Cadfael surrendered the bottle, and counted out pastilles into a small wooden box. 'A spoonful, smaller than your kitchen kind, night and morning, sipped down slowly, and during the day if he feels the need, but always at least three hours between. And these pastilles he can suck when he will, they'll ease his throat.' And he asked, as she took them from him: 'Does any other know that you have been meeting with Tutilo? For you have observed no caution with me.'

Her shoulders lifted in an untroubled shrug; she was smiling. 'I take as I find. But Tutilo has talked of you. We do no wrong, and you will charge us with none. Where it's needful we take good care.' And she thanked him cheerfully, and was turning to the door when he asked: 'May I know your name?'

She turned back to him in the doorway. 'My name is Daalny. That is how my mother said it, I never saw it written. I cannot read or write. My mother told me that the first hero of her people came into Ireland out of the western seas, from the land of the happy dead, which they call the land of the living. His name was Partholan,' she said, and her voice had taken on for a moment the rhythmic, singing tone of the storyteller. 'And Daalny was his queen. There was a race of monsters then in the land, but Partholan drove them northward into the seas and beyond. But in the end there was a great pestilence, and all the race of Partholan gathered together on the great plain, and died, and the land was left empty for the next people to come out of the western sea. Always from the west. They come from there, and when they die they go back there.'

She was away into the gathering twilight, lissome and straight, leaving the door open behind her. Cadfael watched her until she rounded the box hedge and vanished from his sight. Queen Daalny in slavery, almost a myth like her namesake, and every bit as perilous.

At the end of the hour she had allowed herself, Donata turned the hourglass on the bench beside her bed, and opened her eyes. They had been closed while Tutilo played, to absent herself in some degree from him, to relieve him of the burden of a withered old woman's regard, and leave him free to enjoy his own talent without the need to defer to his audience. Though she might well take pleasure in contemplating his youth and freshness, there could hardly be much joy for him in confronting her emaciation and ruin. She had had the harp moved from the hall into her bedchamber to give him the pleasure of tuning and playing it, and been glad to see that while he stroked and tightened and adjusted, bending his curly head over the work, he had forgotten her very presence. That was as it should be. For her the exquisite anguish of his music was none the less, and his happiness was all the more.

But an hour was all she could ask. She had promised he should return by the hour of Compline. She turned the hourglass, and on the instant he broke off, the strings vibrating at the slight start he made.

'Did I play falsely?' he asked, dismayed.

'No, but you ask falsely,' she said drily. 'You know there was no fault there. But time passes, and you must go back to your duty. You have been kind, and I am grateful, but your sub-prior will want you back as I promised, in time for Compline. If I hope to be able to ask again, I must keep to terms.'

'I could play you to sleep,' he said, 'before I go.'

'I shall sleep. Never fret for me. No, you must go, and there is something I want you to take with you. Open the chest there – beside the psaltery you will find a small leather bag. Bring it to me.'

He set the harp aside, and went to do her bidding. She loosened the cord that drew the neck of the little, worn satchel together, and emptied out upon her coverlet a handful of trinkets, a gold neckchain, twin bracelets, a heavy torque of gold set with roughly cut gemstones, and two rings, one a man's massive seal, the other a broad gold band, deeply engraved. Her own finger showed the shrunken, pallid mark below the swollen knuckle, from which she had removed it. Last came a large and intricate ring brooch, the fastening of a cloak, reddish gold, Saxon work.

'Take these, and add them to whatever you have amassed for Ramsey. My son promises a good load of wood, part coppice wood, part seasoned timber, indeed Eudo will be sending the carts down tomorrow by the evening. But these are my offering. They are my younger son's ransom.' She swept the gold back into the bag, and drew the neck closed. 'Take them!'

Tutilo stood hesitant, eyeing her doubtfully. 'Lady, there needs no ransom. He had not taken final vows. He had the right to choose his own way. He owes nothing.'

'Not Sulien, but I,' she said, and smiled. 'You need not scruple to take them. They are mine to give, not from my husband's family, but my father's.'

'But your son's wife,' he urged, 'and the lady who is to marry your Sulien – have not they some claim? These are of great value, and women like such things.'

'My daughters are in my councils. We are all of one mind. Ramsey may pray for my soul,' she said serenely, 'and that will settle all accounts.'

He gave in then, still in some wonder and doubt, accepted the bag from her, and kissed the hand that bestowed it.

'Go now,' said Donata, stretching back into her pillows with a sigh. 'Edred will ride with you to see you over the ferry, and bring back the pony. You should not go on foot tonight.'

He made his farewells to her, still a little anxious, unsure whether he did right to accept what seemed to him so rich a gift. He turned again in the doorway to look back, and she shook her head at him, and motioned him away with an authority that drove him out in haste, as though he had been scolded.

In the courtyard the groom was waiting with the ponies. It was already night, but clear and moonlit, with scudding clouds high overhead. At the ferry the river was running higher than when they had come, though there had been no rain. Somewhere upstream there was flood water on its way.

He delivered his treasures proudly to Sub-Prior Herluin at the end of Compline. The entire household, and most of the guests, were there to witness the arrival of the worn leather bag, and glimpsed its contents as Tutilo joyfully displayed them. Donata's gifts were bestowed with the alms of the burgesses of Shrewsbury in the wooden coffer that was to carry them back to Ramsey, with the cartload of timber from Longner, while Herluin and Tutilo went on to visit Worcester, and possibly Evesham and Pershore as well, to appeal for further aid.

Herluin turned the key on the treasury, and bestowed the coffer on the altar of Saint Mary until the time should come to commit it to the care of Nicol, his most trusted servant, for the journey home. Two days more, and they would be setting out. The abbey had loaned a large wagon for transport, and the town provided the loan of a team to draw it. Horses from the abbey stable would carry Herluin and Tutilo on their further journey. Shrewsbury had done very well by its sister-house, and Donata's gold was the crown of the effort. Many eyes followed the turning of the key, and the installation of the coffer on the altar, where awe of heaven would keep it from violation. God has a powerful attraction.

Leaving the church, Cadfael halted for a moment to snuff the air and survey the sky, which by this hour hung heavy with dropsical clouds, through which the moon occasionally glared for an instant, and was as quickly obscured again. When he went to close up his workshop for the night he observed that the waters of the brook had laid claim to another yard or so of the lower rim of his peasefields.

All night long from the Matins bell it rained heavily.

In the morning, about Prime, Hugh Beringar, King Stephen's sheriff of Shropshire, came down in haste out of the town to carry the first warning of trouble ahead, sending his officers to cry the news along the Foregate, while he brought it in person to Abbot Radulfus.

'Word from Pool last evening, Severn's well out below the town, and still raining heavily in Wales. Upriver beyond Montford the meadows are under water, and the main bulk still on its way down, and fast. I'd advise moving what's valuable – stores can't be risked, with transport threatened.' In time of flood the town, all but the encrustation of fishermen's and small craft dwellings along the riverside, and the gardens under the wall, would be safe enough, but the Foregate could soon be under water, and parts of the abbey enclave were the lowest ground, threatened on every side by the river itself, the Meole Brook driven backwards by the weight of water, and the mill pond swelled by the pressure from both. 'I'd lend you some men, but we'll need to get some of the waterside dwellers up into the town.'

'We have hands enough, we can shift for ourselves,' said the abbot. 'My thanks for the warning. You think it will be a serious flood?'

'No knowing yet, but you'll have time to prepare. If you mean to load that timber from Longner this evening, better have your wagon round by the Horse Fair. The level there is safe enough, and you can go in and out to your stable and loft by the cemetery gates.'

'Just as well,' said Radulfus, 'if Herluin's men can get their load away tomorrow, and be on their way home.' He rose to go and rally his household to the labour pending, and Hugh, for once, made for the gatehouse without looking up Brother Cadfael on the way. But it happened that Cadfael was rounding the hedge from the garden in considerable haste, just in time to cross his friend's path. The Meole Brook was boiling back upstream, and the mill pool rising.

'Ah!' said Cadfael, pulling up sharply. 'You've been before me, have you? The abbot's warned?'

'He is, and you can pause and draw breath,' said Hugh, checking in his own flight to fling an arm about Cadfael's shoulders. 'Not that we know what we can expect, not yet. It may be less than we fear, but better be armed. The lowest of the town's awash. Bring me to the gate, I've scarcely seen you this side Christmas.'

'It won't last long,' Cadfael assured him breathlessly. 'Soon up, soon down. Two or three days wading, longer to clean up after it, but we've done it all before.'

'Better make sure of what medicines may be wanted,

and get them above-stairs in the infirmary. Too much wading, and you'll be in a sickbed yourself.'

'I've been putting them together already,' Cadfael assured him. 'I'm off to have a word with Edmund now. Thanks be, Aline and Giles are high and dry, up there by Saint Mary's. All's well with them?'

'Very well, but that it's too long since you came to see your godson.' Hugh's horse was hitched by the gatehouse; he reached to the bridle. 'Make it soon, once Severn's back in its bed.'

'I will so. Greet her for me, and make my peace with the lad.'

And Hugh was in the saddle, and away along the highroad to hunt out and confer with the provost of the Foregate; and Cadfael tucked up his habit and made for the infirmary. There would be heavier valuables to move to higher ground later, but his first duty was to make sure he had whatever medicaments might be needed in some readily accessible place, clear of the waters which were slowly creeping up from the thwarted Meole Brook one way, and the congested mill pond another.

High Mass was observed as always, reverently and without haste, that morning, but chapter was a matter of minutes, devoted mainly to allotting all the necessary tasks to appropriate groups of brothers, and ensuring an orderly and decorous move. First to wrap all those valuables that might have to be carried up staircases or lifted into lofts, and for the moment leave them, already protected, where they were. No need to move them before the rising waters made it essential. There were things to be lifted from the lowest points of the enclave long before the flood could lip at the church itself.

The stable-yard lying at a low point of the court, they

46

moved the horses out to the abbey barn and loft by the Horse Fair ground, where there was fodder enough in store without having to cart any from the lofts within the enclave, where stocks were safe enough. Even the Severn in spring flood after heavy snows and torrential rain had never reached the upper storey, and never would; there was more than enough lower ground along its course into which to overflow. In places it would be a mile or more wide, in acres of drowned meadow, before ever it invaded the choir. The nave had been known to float a raft now and again over the years, once even a light boat. That was the most they need fear. So they swathed all the chests and coffers that housed the vestments, the plate, the crosses and candlesticks and furnishings of the altars, and the precious minor relics of the treasury. And Saint Winifred's silver-chased reliquary they wrapped carefully in old, worn hangings and a large brychan, but left her on her altar until it should become clear that she must be carried to a higher refuge. If that became necessary, this would be the worst flood within Cadfael's recollection by at least a foot; and if ever during this day the worst threatened, she would have to be removed, something which had never happened since she was brought here.

Cadfael forbore from eating that noon, and while the rest of the household, guests and all, were taking hasty refreshment, he went in and kneeled before her altar, as sometimes he did in silence, too full of remembering to pray, though there seemed, nevertheless, to be a dialogue in progress. If any kindly soul among the saints knew him through and through, it was Winifred, his young Welsh girl, who was not here at all, but safe and content away in her own Welsh earth at Gwytherin. No one knew it but the lady, her servant and devotee Cadfael, who had contrived her repose

47

there, and Hugh Beringar, who had been let into the secret late. Here in England, no one else; but in her own Wales, her own Gwytherin, it was no secret, but a central tenet of Welsh faith never needing mention. She was with them still; all was well.

So it was not her rest, not hers, that was threatened now, only the uneasy repose of an ambitious, unstable young man who had done murder in pursuit of his own misguided dreams, greed for the abbey of Shrewsbury, greed for his own advancement. His death had afforded Winifred peace to remain where her heart clove to the beloved soil. That, at least, might almost be counted alleviation against his sins. For she had not withdrawn her blessing, because a sinner lay in the coffin prepared for her, and was entreated in her name. Where he was, and she was not, she had done miracles of grace.

'*Geneth . . Cariad!*' said Cadfael silently. 'Girl, dear, has he been in purgatory long enough? Can you lift even him out of his mire?'

During the afternoon the gradual rise of the brook and the river seemed to slow and hold constant, though there was certainly no decline. They began to think that the peril would pass. Then in the late evening the main body of the upland water from Wales came swirling down in a riot of muddy foam, torn branches, and not a few carcasses of sheep caught and drowned on mounds too low to preserve them. Rolled and tumbled in the flood, trees lodged under the bridge and piled the turgid water even higher. Every soul in the enclave turned to in earnest, and helped to remove the precious furnishings to higher refuge, as brook and river and pond together advanced greedily into all the lower reaches of the court and cemetery, and gnawed at the steps of the west and south doors, turning the cloister garth into a shallow and muddy lake.

The vestments, furnishings, plate, crosses, all the treasury was carried up into the two rooms over the north porch, where Cynric the verger lived and Father Boniface robed. The reliquaries which held the smaller relics went out by the cemetery doors to the loft over the Horse Fair barn. A day which had never been fully light declined early into gloomy twilight, and there was a persistent, depressing drizzle that clung clammily to eyelids and lashes and lips, adding to the discomfort.

Two carters from Longner had brought down the promised load of wood for rebuilding, and begun to transfer it to the larger abbey wagon for the journey back to Ramsey. The coffer containing Shrewsbury's gifts for the cause still stood on the altar of the Lady Chapel, key in lock, ready to be handed over to the steward Nicol for safe transport on the morrow. That altar stood high enough to survive all but a flood of Biblical proportions. The Longner carters had brought with them a third willing helper, a shepherd from the neighbouring hamlet of Preston. But the three had barely begun transferring their load when they were haled away agitatedly by Brother Richard to help carry out from the church, or set at a safe height within, some of the abbey's threatened treasures. Brothers and guests were at the same somewhat confused task in near darkness.

Within an hour most of the necessary salvage had been done, and the guests began to withdraw to higher and dryer pastures, before the rising water should reach their knees. It grew quiet within the nave, only the light slapping of disturbed water against pillars as some stalwart splashed back thankfully to the upstairs comfort of the guesthall. Rémy's man Bénezet was the last

49

to go, booted to the knee, and well cloaked against the drizzle.

The Longner carters and their helper went back to stacking their timber; but a small brother, cowled and agitated, reached a hand to detain the last of them, the shepherd from Preston. 'Friend, there's one thing more here to go with the cart to Ramsey. Give me a hand with it.'

All but the altar lights had burned out by then. The shepherd let himself be led by the hand, and felt his way to one end of a long, slender burden well swathed in brychans. They lifted it between them, a weight easy for two. The single altar lamp cast yellowish light within the Benedictine cowl as they straightened up, stroked briefly over an earnest, smooth face, and guttered in the draught from the sacristy door. Together they carried their burden out between the graves of the abbots to where the abbey wagon stood drawn up outside the heavy double gates. The two men from Longner were up on their own cart, shifting logs along to the rear, to be the more easily lifted down between them for transfer to the larger wagon, and the dusk lay over all, thick with the beginning of a moist and clammy mist. The swathed burden was hoisted aboard, and aligned neatly alongside the cordwood already loaded. By the time the young brother had straightened his back, dusted his hands, and withdrawn briskly towards the open gate, the two carters had hefted another load of timber aboard, and were off to their cart again for the next. The last fold of the outer wrapping, a momentary glitter of gilt embroidery now frayed and threadbare, vanished under the gleanings of the Longner coppices.

Somewhere within the graveyard, and retreating into the darkness of the church, a light voice called thanks and blessings to them, and a hearty goodnight.

50

Chapter Three

N THE morning, immediately after High
Mass, the borrowed wagon set out for
Ramsey. The coffer from the altar was con-
fided to Nicol for safekeeping, and though
one of his companions from Ramsey was to travel on
with Herluin to Worcester, the addition to the party
for home of three craftsmen seeking work offered a
reassuringly stout guard for the valuables aboard. The
timber was well secured, the team of four horses had
spent the night comfortably in the stable at the Horse
Fair, above the flood level, and was ready for the road.

Their way lay eastward, out by Saint Giles, and once
clear of the watermeadows and over the bridge by
Atcham they would be moving away from the river's
coils, and out upon good roads, open and well used.
Nearer to their destination, considering how Geoffrey
de Mandeville's cut-throats must be scattering for cover
now, they might have occasion to be glad of three tough
Shropshire lads, all good men of their hands.

The cart rattled away along the Foregate. They

would be some days on the road, but at least in regions further removed from the mountains of Wales, which had launched such a weight of thaw-water down into the lowlands after the heavy winter snows.

An hour or so later Sub-Prior Herluin also set forth, attended by Tutilo and the third lay servant, to turn southeastward at Saint Giles. Possibly it had not yet dawned on Herluin that the floods he was thankfully leaving behind here might keep pace with him downstream and overtake him triumphantly at Worcester. The speed at which the flood-water travelled could be erratic in some winters; it might even be ahead of him when he reached the level meadows below the city.

Rémy of Pertuis made no move to depart. Even the lower living floor of the guesthall remained dry and snug enough, being raised upon a deep undercroft and approached by a flight of stone steps, so he was left to nurse his sore throat in comparative warmth and comfort. His best horse, his own riding horse, was still lame, according to his man Bénezet, who had the charge of the horses, and daily plashed impassively through the shallows of the court to tend them in the stable at the Horse Fair. The stable-yard within the enclave lay almost knee-deep in water, and might remain so for several days yet. Bénezet recommended a longer wait here, and his master, it seemed, thinking of possible inconveniences on the way north to Chester, what with the upstream Severn and the incalculable Dee to cope with, had no objection to make. He was dry and fed and safe where he was. And the rain seemed to be moving away. Westward the cloud was clearing, only a desultory shower or two punctuated the featureless calm of the day's routine.

The horarium proceeded stubbornly in spite of difficulties. The choir remained just above the level of the waters, and could be reached dryshod by the night stairs from the dortoir, and the floor of the chapter-house was barely covered on the first and second day, and on the third was seen to be retaining only the dark, moist lines between the flags. That was the first sign that the river had reasserted its powers, and was again carrying away its great weight of waters. Two more days passed before the change was perceptible by the fast flow of the brook, and the withdrawal of the over-flow into its bed, sinking gradually through the satu-rated grass and leaving a rim of debris to mark the decline. The mill pond sank slowly, clawing turf and leaves down from the lower reaches of the gardens it had invaded. Even along Severnside under the town walls the level sank day by day, relinquishing the fringe of little houses and fishermen's huts and boat-sheds stained by mud and littered with the jetsam of branches and bushes.

Within the week brook and river and pond were back in their confines, full but still gradually subsiding. The tide-mark left in the nave had after all reached no higher than the top of the second step of Saint Wini-fred's altar.

'We need never have moved her,' said Prior Robert, viewing the proof of it and shaking his head. 'We should have had more faith. Surely she is well able to take care of herself and her flock. She had but to command, and the waters would have abated.'

Nevertheless, an abode damp, clammy and cold, and filthy with mud and rubbish, was no fit place to bring a saint. They fell to work without complaint, sweeping and polishing and mopping up the puddles left in every irregularity in the floor tiles. They brought the cresset stones, all three, into the nave, filled all their cups with oil, and lit them to dry out the lingering dampness and warm the air. Floral essences added to the oil fought valiantly against the stink of the river. Undercrofts, storehouses, barns and stables would also need attention, but the church was the first priority. When it was again fit to receive and house them, all the treasures could be restored to their places here within the fold.

Abbot Radulfus marked the purification of the holy place with a celebratory Mass. Then they began to carry back from their higher sanctuaries the furnishings of the altars. the chests of vestments and plate, the candlesticks, newly polished, the frontals and hangings, the minor reliquaries. It was accepted without question that all must be restored and immaculate before the chief grace and adornment of the abbey of Saint Peter and Saint Paul was brought back with all due ceremony to her rightful place, newly swept and garnished to receive her.

'Now,' said Prior Robert, straightening joyfully to his full majestic height, 'let us bring back Saint Winifred to her altar. She was carried, as all here know, into the upper room over the north porch.' The little outer door there at the corner of the porch, and the spiral staircase within, very difficult for the transport of even a small coffin, had remained accessible until the highest point of the flood, and she had been well padded against any damage in transit. 'Let us go,' declaimed Robert, 'in devotion and joy, and bring her back to her mission and benediction among us.'

He had always, thought Cadfael, resignedly following through the narrow, retired door and up the tricky stair, this conviction that he owns the girl, because he believes – no, God be good to him, poor soul, he mistakenly but surely *knows*! – that he brought her here. God forbid he should ever find out the truth, that she is far away in her own chosen place. and her connivance

54

with his pride in her is only a kind-hearted girl's mercy to an idiot child.

Cynric, Father Boniface's parish verger, had surrendered his small dwelling above the porch to the housing of the church treasures while the flood lasted. He would be back in possession soon; a tall, gaunt, quiet man, lantern-faced, a figure of awe to ordinary mortals, but totally accepted by the innocents, for the children of the Foregate, and their inseparable camp-followers, the dogs, came confidently to his hand, and sat and meditated contentedly on the steps with him in summer weather. His narrow room was bare now of all but the last and most precious resident. The swathed and roped coffin was taken up with all reverence, and carefully manipulated down the tight confines of the spiral stair.

In the nave they had set up trestles on which to lay her, while they unwound the sheath of brychans they had used to keep her reliquary from injury. The wrappings unrolled one after another and were laid aside, and it seemed to Cadfael, watching, that with the removal of each one the swaddled shape, dwindling, assumed a form too rigid and rectangular to match with what he carried devoutly in his mind. But the final padding was thick enough to shroud the delicacies of fashioning he knew so well. Prior Robert reached a hand with ceremonious reverence to take hold of the last fold. and drew it back to uncover what lay within.

He uttered a muted shriek that emerged with startling effect from so august a throat, though it was not loud. He fell back a long, unsteady pace in shock, and then as abruptly started forward again and dragged the rug away, to expose to general view the inexplicable and offensive reality they had manipulated so carefully down from its place of safety. Not the silver-chased reliquary of Saint Winifred, but a log of wood, smaller and shorter than the coffin it had been used to represent, light enough, probably, for one man to handle; and not new, for it had dried and weathered to seasoned ripeness.

All that care and reverence had been wasted. Wherever Saint Winifred was, she was certainly not here.

After the stunned and idiot silence, babble and turmoil broke out on all sides, drawing to the spot others who had heard the strangled cry of dismay, and left their own tasks to come and stare and wonder. Prior Robert stood frozen into an outraged statue, the rug clutched in both hands, glaring at the offending log, and for once stricken dumb. It was his obsequious shadow who lifted the burden of protest for him.

'This is some terrible error,' blurted Brother Jerome, wringing his hands. 'In the confusion . . . and it grew dark before we were done . . . Someone mistook, someone moved her elsewhere. We shall find her, safe in one of the lofts . . .'

'And *this*?' demanded Prior Robert witheringly, pointing a damning finger at the offence before them. 'Thus shrouded, as carefully as ever we did for her? No error! No mistake made in innocence! Someone did this deliberately to deceive! *This* was laid in her place, to be handled and cherished in her stead. And where now . . . where is she?'

Some disturbance in the air, some wind of alarm, had caught the scent by then, and carried it through the great court, and minute by minute more open-mouthed onlookers were gathering, stray brothers summoned from scattered cleansing duties in the grange court and the stables, sharp-eared guests from their lodgings, a couple of round-eyed, inquisitive schoolboys who were chased away less indulgently than usual by Brother Paul.

'Who last handled her?' suggested Brother Cadfael reasonably. 'Someone . . more than one . . carried her up to Cynric's rooms. Any of you here?'

Brother Rhun came through the press of curious and frightened brothers, the youngest among them, the special protégé of his saint, and her most devoted servitor, as every man here knew.

'It was I, with Brother Urien, who wrapped her safely. But, to my grief, I was not here when she was moved from her place.'

A tall figure came looming over the heads of the nearest brothers, craning to see what was causing the stir. 'That was the load from the altar there?' asked Bénezet, and thrust his way through to look more closely. 'The reliquary, the saint's coffin? And now *this* . ? But I helped to carry it up to the verger's rooms. It was one of the last things we moved, late in the evening. I was here helping, and one of the brothers – Brother Matthew I've heard him named – called me to give him a hand. And so I did. We hefted her up the stairs and stowed her safely enough.' He looked round in search of confirmation, but Brother Matthew the cellarer was not there to speak for himself. 'He'll tell you,' said Bénezet confidently. 'And this – a log of wood? Is this what we took such care of?'

'Look at the brychan,' said Cadfael, reaching in haste to open it before the man's eyes and spread it wide. 'The outer wrapping, look at it closely. Did you see it clearly when you had the load in your hands? Is this the same?' By chance it was Welsh woollen cloth, patterned in a regular array of crude four-petalled flowers in a dim blue: many of its kind found their way into English homes through the market of Shrewsbury. It was worn thin in places, but had been of a solid, heavy weave, and bound at the edges with flax. Bénezet said without hesitation: 'The same.'

'You are certain? It was late in the evening, you say. The altar was still lighted?'

'I'm certain.' Bénezet's long lips delivered his certainty like an arrow launched. 'I saw the weave plainly. This is what we lifted and carried, that night, and who was to know what was inside the brychans?'

Brother Rhun uttered a small, grievous sound, more a sob than a cry, and came forward almost fearfully to touch and feel, afraid to trust his eyes, young and clear and honest though they might be.

'But it is *not* the same,' he said in a muted whisper, 'in which Brother Urien and I wrapped her, earlier that day, before noon. We left her ready on her altar, with a plain blanket bound round her, and an old, frayed altarcloth stretched over her. Brother Richard let us take it, as fitting her holiness. It was a beautiful one, great love went into the embroidery. That was her coverlet. This is no way the same. What this good man carried from here to the high place meant for Saint Winifred, was not that sweet lady, but this block, this mockery. Father Prior, where is our saint? What has become of Saint Winifred?'

Prior Robert swept one commanding glance round him, at the derisory object uncovered from its shroud, at the stricken brothers, and the boy bereaved and accusing, burning white as a candleflame. Rhun went whole, beautiful and lissome by Saint Winifred's gift, he would have no rest nor allow any to his superiors, while she was lost to him.

'Leave all here as it lies,' said Prior Robert with authority, 'and depart, all of you. No word be said,

58

nothing done, until we have taken this cause to Father Abbot, within whose writ it lies.'

'There is no possibility of mere error,' said Cadfael, in the abbot's parlour, that evening. 'Brother Matthew is as certain as this lad Bénezet of what they carried, or at least of the pattern of the brychan that was wound about it. And Brother Rhun and Brother Urien are just as certain of what they took to wrap and cover her. By all the signs, no one meddled with the wrappings. A new burden was substituted for the first one on the altar, and borne away to safety in good faith, no blame to those who aided.'

'None,' said Radulfus. 'The young man offered in all kindness. His merit is assured. But how did this come about? Who could wish it? Who perform, if he did wish it? Brother Cadfael, consider! There was flood, there was watchfulness but hope during the day, there was urgent need at night. Men prepare for a sudden and strange threat, but while it holds off they do not believe in it. And when it strikes, can everything be handled with calm and faith, as it should? In darkness, in confusion, mere feeble men do foolish things. Is there not still the possibility that this is all some error – even a stupid and malicious jest?'

'Never so stupid,' said Cadfael firmly, 'as to dress up a stock of wood to match the mass and weight of that reliquary. Here there was purpose. Purpose to humiliate this house, yes, perhaps, though I fail to see why, or who should harbour so vile a grudge. But purpose, surely.'

They were alone together, since Cadfael had returned to confirm Bénezet's testimony by the witness of Brother Matthew, who had carried the head end of the reliquary up the stairs, and tangled his fingers in the unravelling flaxen thread of the edging. Prior Robert had told his story with immense passion, and left the load, Cadfael suspected with considerable thankfulness, in his superior's hands.

'And this log itself,' said Radulfus, focusing sharply on details, 'was not from the Longner load?'

'Longner sent a proportion of seasoned wood, but not oak. The rest was coppice-wood. No, this has been cut a number of years. It is dried out so far that it could be used to balance, roughly at least, the weight of the reliquary. It is no mystery. In the southern end of the undercroft beneath the refectory, there is a small pile of timber that was left after the last building on the barns. I have looked,' said Cadfael. 'There is a place where such a log has been removed. The surfaces show the vacancy.'

'And the removal is recent?' asked Radulfus alertly.

'Father Abbot, it is.'

'So this was deliberate,' Radulfus said slowly. 'Planned and purposeful, as you said. Hard to believe. And yet I cannot see how it can have come about by chance, by whatever absurd combination of circumstances. You say that Urien and Rhun prepared her before noon. Late in the evening what lay on her altar, ready to be carried elsewhere, was this mere stock. During the time between, our saint was removed, and the other substituted. For what end, with what mischief in mind? Cadfael, consider! In these few days of flood scarcely anyone has gone in and out of our enclave, certainly no one can have taken out so noticeable a burden. Somewhere within our walls the reliquary must be hidden. At least, before we look beyond, every corner of this house and all its outer buildings must be searched.'

*

The hunt for Saint Winifred went on for two days, every moment between the Offices, and as if the honour of all within the walls was impugned in her loss, even the guests in the hall and the trusted regulars of the parish of Holy Cross trudged through the lingering mud to join in the search. Even Rémy of Pertuis, forgetting the tenderness of his throat, went with Bénezet to penetrate every corner of the Horse Fair stable and the loft over it, from which sanctuary the translated relics of Saint Elerius and certain minor treasures had already been reclaimed. It was not seemly for the girl Daalny to mingle with the brothers throughout the day, but she watched with tireless interest from the steps of the guesthall, as the hunters emerged from one doorway after another, from grange court to stable-yard, from the dortoir by the outer daystairs, into the cloister garth, out again by the scriptorium, across to the infirmary, and always empty-handed.

All those who had helped on the evening of the flood, when the need grew urgent, told what they knew, and the sum of what they knew covered the hurried movements of most of the church's treasury, and traced it back to its proper places, but shed no light on what had happened to Saint Winifred's swaddled reliquary between noon and evening of the day in question. At the end of the second day even Prior Robert, rigid with outrage, had to acknowledge defeat.

'She is not here,' he said. 'Not within these walls, not here in the Foregate. If anything was known of her there, they would have told us.'

'No blinking it,' agreed the abbot grimly, 'she is gone further. There is no possibility of mistake or confusion. An exchange was made, with intent to deceive. And yet what has left our gates during these days? Except for our brothers Herluin and Tutilo, and they certainly

61

took nothing with them but what they brought, the very least a man needs upon the road.'

'There was the cart,' said Cadfael, 'that set out for Ramsey.'

There fell a silence, while they looked at one another with misgiving, calculating uneasily the dangerous possibilities opening up before them.

'Is it possible?' ventured Brother Richard the sub-prior, almost hopefully. 'In the darkness and confusion? Some order misunderstood? Can it have been put on to the cart by mistake?'

'No,' said Cadfael, bluntly cutting off that consideration. 'If she was moved from her altar, then she was put somewhere else with deliberate intent. Nevertheless, yes, the cart departed next morning, and she may have gone with it. But not by chance, not in error.'

'Then this is sacrilegious theft!' declaimed Robert. 'Offence against the laws of God and of the realm, and must be pursued with all rigour.'

'We must not say so,' reproved Radulfus, lifting a restraining hand, 'until we have questioned every man who was present on that day and may have testimony to add to what we know. And that we have not yet done. Sub-Prior Herluin and Brother Tutilo were with us then, and as I know, Tutilo was helping with the removal of the altar furnishings until well into the evening. And were there not some others who came in to help? We should speak to every one who may have seen anything to the purpose, before we cry theft.'

'Eudo Blount's carters who came with the wood,' offered Richard, 'left the load and came in to help, until all was done, before they finished transferring the timber from the Longner cart. Should we not ask them? Dark as it was by then, they may have noticed something to the purpose.'

'We will neglect nothing,' said the abbot. 'Father Herluin and Brother Tutilo, I know, will be coming back here to return our horses, but that may be some days, and we should not delay. Robert, they will be in Worcester by now, will you ride after them and hear what account they can give of that day?'

'With very good will,' said Robert fervently. 'But, Father, if this becomes in all earnest a matter of theft, ought we not to confide it to the sheriff, and see if he thinks fit to have a man of his garrison go with me? In the end it may be as much for the king's justice as for ours, and as you say, time is precious.'

'You are right,' agreed Radulfus. 'I will speak with Hugh Beringar. And for the Longner men, we will send and hear what they have to say.'

'If you give me leave,' said Cadfael, 'I will undertake that.' He had no wish to see someone of Prior Robert's mind descending on Eudo Blount's decent household, probing in a manner suggestive of black suspicions of duplicity and theft.

'Do so, Cadfael, if you will. You know the people there better than any of us, they will speak freely to you. Find her,' said Abbot Radulfus grimly, 'we must and will. Tomorrow Hugh Beringar shall know what has happened, and pursue it as he sees fit.'

Hugh came from conference with the abbot half an hour after the end of Prime. 'Well,' he said, plumping himself down on the bench against the timber wall of Cadfael's workshop, 'I hear you've got yourself into a pretty awkward corner this time. How did you come to lose your seeming saint? And what will you do, my friend, if someone, somewhere, decides to take the lid off that very pretty coffin?'

'Why should they?' said Cadfael, but none too confidently.

'Given human curiosity, of which you should know more than I,' said Hugh, grinning, 'why should they not? Say the thing finds its way where no one knows what it is, or what it signifies, how better to find out what they have in their hands? You would be the first to break the seals.'

'I *was* the first,' said Cadfael, unguardedly since here a guard was useless, for Hugh knew exactly what was in Saint Winifred's reliquary. 'And also, I hope, the last. Hugh, I doubt if you are taking this with the gravity it deserves.'

'I find it difficult,' Hugh owned, 'not to be amused. But be sure I'll preserve your secrets if I can. I'm interested. All my local troublers of the peace seem to be frozen in until spring, I can afford to ride to Worcester. Even in Robert's company it may be entertaining. And I'll keep an eye open for your interests as well as I may. What do you think of this loss? Has someone conspired to rob you, or is it all a foolish tangle spawned out of the flood?'

'No,' said Cadfael positively, and turned from the board on which he was fashioning troches for queasy stomachs in the infirmary. 'No tangle. A clear mind shifted that reliquary from the altar, and swathed and planted a log of wood from the undercroft in its place. So that both could be moved away well out of sight and out of mind, possibly for several days, as indeed both were. The one to make a clear field for the other to be removed beyond recovery. At least beyond immediate recovery,' he amended firmly, 'for recover her we shall.'

Hugh was looking at him, across the glow of the brazier, with a twitch of the lips and an oblique tilt to

64

the brow that Cadfael remembered from of old, from the time of their first precarious acquaintance, when neither of them had been quite sure whether the other was friend or foe, and yet each had been drawn to the other in a half-grave, half-impish contest to find out.

'Do you know,' said Hugh softly, 'that you are speaking of that lost reliquary – some years now you have been speaking of it so – as if it truly contained the Welsh lady's bones. "She", you say, never "it", or even more truly, "him". And you know, none so well, that you left her to her rest there in Gwytherin. Can she be in two places at once?'

'Some essence of her certainly can,' said Cadfael, 'for she has done miracles here among us. She lay in that coffin three days, why should she not have conferred the power of her grace upon it? Is she to be limited by time and place? I tell you, Hugh, sometimes I wonder what would be found within there, if ever that lid was lifted. Though I own,' he added ruefully, 'I shall be praying devoutly that it never comes to the proof.'

'You had better,' Hugh agreed. 'Imagine the uproar, if someone somewhere breaks those seals you repaired so neatly, and prises off the lid, to find the body of a young man about twenty-four, instead of the bones of a virgin saint. And mother-naked, at that! Your goose would be finely cooked!' He rose, laughing, but even so a little wryly, for the possibility certainly existed, and might yet erupt into disaster. 'I must go and make ready. Prior Robert means to set out as soon as he has dined.' He embraced Cadfael briskly about the shoulders in passing, by way of encouragement, and shook him bracingly. 'Never fear, you are a favourite with her, and she'll look after her own – let alone that you've managed very well so far at looking after yourself.'

'The strange thing is, Hugh,' Cadfael said suddenly, as Hugh reached the door, 'that I'm concerned almost as anxiously for poor Columbanus.'

'Poor Columbanus?' Hugh echoed, turning to stare back at him in astonished amusement. 'Cadfael, you never cease to surprise me. Poor Columbanus, indeed! A murderer by stealth, and all for his own glory, not for Shrewsbury's, and certainly not for Winifred's.'

'I know! But he ended the loser. And dead! And now – flooded out of what rest was allowed him on a quiet altar here at home, taken away to some strange place where he knows no one, friend or enemy. And perhaps,' said Cadfael, shaking his head over the strayed sinner, 'having miracles expected of him, when he can do none. It would not be so hard to feel a little sorry for him.'

Cadfael went up to Longner as soon as the midday meal was over, and found the young lord of the manor in his smithy within the stockade, himself supervising the forging of a new iron tip for a ploughshare. Eudo Blount was a husbandman born, a big, candid, fair fellow, to all appearances better built for service in arms than his younger brother, but a man for whom soil, and crops and well kept livestock would always be fulfilment enough. He would raise sons in his own image, and the earth would be glad of them. Younger sons must carve out their own fortunes.

'Lost Saint Winifred?' said Eudo, gaping, when he heard the purport of Cadfael's errand. 'How the devil could you lose her? Not a thing to be palmed and slipped in a pouch when no one's looking. And you want speech with Gregory and Lambert? Surely you don't suppose they'd have any use for her, even if they did have a cart on the Horse Fair! There's no complaint of my men down there, is there?'

'None in the world!' said Cadfael heartily. 'But just by chance, they may have seen something the rest of us were blind enough to miss. They lent a hand when there was need of it, and we were heartily thankful. But no use looking further afield until we've looked close at home, and made sure no over-zealous idiot has put the lady away somewhere safely and mislaid her. We've asked of every soul within the walls, better consult these last two, or we might stop short of the simple answer.'

'Ask whatever you will,' said Eudo simply. 'You'll find them both across in the stable or the carthouse. And I wish you might get your easy answer, but I doubt it. They hauled the wood down there, and loaded it, and came home, and I recall Gregory did tell me what was going on in the church, and how high the water was come in the nave. But nothing besides. But try him!'

Secure among his own people, Eudo felt no need to watch or listen what might come to light, but went back practically to the bellows, and the ring of the smith's hammer resumed, and followed Cadfael across the yard to the wide-open door of the carthouse.

They were both within, wheeling the light cart by its shafts back into a corner, the warmth of the horse they had just unharnessed still hanging in the air about them. Square-built, muscular men both, and weather-beaten from outdoor living in all seasons, with a good twenty years between them, so that they might have been father and son. Most men of these local villages, tied to the soil by villeinage but also by inclination, and likely to marry within a very few miles' radius, tended to have a close clan resemblance and a strong clan loyalty. The Welsh strain kept them short, wiry and durable, and of independent mind.

They greeted him civilly, without surprise; in the past year or two he had been an occasional visitor, and grown into a welcome one. But when he had unfolded what was required from them, they shook their heads doubtfully, and sat down without haste on the shafts of the cart to consider.

'We brought the cart down before it darkened,' said the elder then, narrowing his eyes to look back through the week of labour and leisure between, 'but it was a black bitch of a day even at noon. We'd started shifting the load over to the abbey wagon, when the sub-prior comes out between the graves to the gate, and says, lads, lend us a hand to put the valuables inside high and dry, for it's rising fast.'

'Sub-Prior Richard?' said Cadfael. 'You're sure it was he?'

'Sure as can be, him I do know, and it was not so dark then. Lambert here will tell you the same. So in we went, and set to, bundling up the hangings and lifting out the chests as he told us, and putting them where we were directed, up in the loft over the barn there, and some over the porch in Cynric's place. It was dim inside there, and the brothers all darting about carrying coffers and candlesticks and crosses, and half the lamps ran out of oil, or got blown out with the doors open. As soon as the nave seemed to be clear we got out, and went back to loading the wood.'

'Aldhelm went back in,' said the young man Lambert, who had done no more than nod his head in endorsement until now.

'Aldhelm?' questioned Cadfael.

'He came down to help us out,' explained Gregory.

'He has a half-yardland by Preston, and works with the sheep at the manor of Upton.'

So there was one more yet before the job could be considered finished. And not today, thought Cadfael, calculating the hours left to him.

'This Aldhelm was in and out of the church like you? And went back in at the last moment?'

'One of the brothers caught him by the sleeve and haled him back to help move some last thing,' said Gregory indifferently. 'We were off to the cart and shifting logs by then, all I know is someone called him, and he turned back. It was not much more than a moment or two. When we got the next load between us to the abbey wagon and slung it aboard, he was there by the wheel to help us hoist it in and settle it. And the monk was off to the church again. He called back goodnight to us.'

'But he had come out to the road with your man?' persisted Cadfael.

'We were all breathing easier then, everything that mattered was high enough to lie snug and dry till the river went down. A civil soul, he came out to say thanks and leave us a blessing . . . why not?'

Why not, indeed, when honest men turned to for no reward besides? 'You did not,' asked Cadfael delicately, 'see whether between them they brought out anything to load into the wagon? Before he left you with his blessing?'

They looked at each other sombrely, and shook their heads. 'We were shifting logs to the back, to be easy to lift down. We heard them come. We had our arms full, hefting wood. When we got it to the wagon Aldhelm was reaching out to help us hoist it on, and the brother was away into the graveyard again. No, they never brought out anything that I saw.'

'Nor I,' said Lambert.

'And could you, either of you, put a name to this monk who called him back?'

'No,' said they both with one voice; and Gregory added kindly: 'Brother, by then it was well dark. And I know names for only a few, the ones every man knows.'

True, monks are brothers by name only to those within; willing to be brothers to all men, outside the pale they are nameless. In some ways, surely, a pity.

'So dark,' said Cadfael, reaching his last question, 'that you would not be able to recognize him, if you saw him again? Not by his face, or shape, or gait, or bearing? Nothing to mark him?'

'Brother,' said Gregory patiently, 'he was close-cowled against the rain, and black disappearing into darkness. And his face we never saw at all.'

Cadfael sighed and thanked them, and was gathering himself up to trudge back by the sodden fields when Lambert said, breaking his habitual and impervious silence: 'But Aldhelm may have seen it.'

The day was too far gone, if he was to get back for Vespers. The tiny hamlet of Preston was barely a mile out of his way, but if this Aldhelm worked with the sheep at Upton, at this hour he might be there, and not in his own cot on his own half-yardland of earth. Probing his memory would have to wait. Cadfael threaded the Longner woodlands and traversed the long slope of meadows above the subsiding river, making for home. The ford would be passable again by now, but abominably muddy and foul, the ferry was pleasanter and also quicker. The ferryman, a taciturn soul, put him ashore on the home bank with a little time in hand, so that he slackened his pace a little, to draw breath. There was a belt of close woodland on this side, too, before he could approach the first alleys and cots of the Foregate; open, heathy woodland over the ridge, then the trees drew in darkly, and the path narrowed. There would have to be some lopping done here, to clear it for horsemen. Even at this hour, not yet dusk but under heavy cloud, a man had all his work cut out to see his way clear and evade overgrown branches. A good place for ambush and secret violence, and all manner of skulduggery. It was the heavy cloud cover and the cheerless stillness of the day that gave him such thoughts, and even while they lingered with him he did not believe in them. Yet there was mischief abroad, for Saint Winifred was gone, or the token she had left with him and blessed for him was gone, and there was no longer any equilibrium in his world. Strange, since he knew where she was, and should have been able to send messages to her there, surely with greater assurance than to the coffin that did not contain her. But it was from that same coffin that he had always received his answers, and now the wind that should have brought him her voice from Gwytherin was mute.

Cadfael emerged into the Foregate at the Horse Fair somewhat angry with himself for allowing himself to be decoyed into imaginative glooms against his nature, and trudged doggedly along to the gatehouse in irritated haste to get back to a real world where he had solid work to do. Certainly he must hunt out Aldhelm of Preston, but between him and that task, and just as important, loomed a few sick old men, a number of confused and troubled young ones, and his plain duty of keeping the Rule he had chosen.

There were not many people abroad in the Foregate. The weather was still cold and the gloom of the day had sent people hurrying home, wasting no time once the day's work was done. Some yards ahead of him two figures walked together. one of them limping heavily Cadfael had a vague notion that he had seen those broad shoulders and that shaggy head before, and not so long ago, but the lame gait did not fit. The other was built more lightly, and younger. They went with heads thrust forward and shoulders down, like men tired after a long trudge and in dogged haste to reach their destination and be done with it. It was no great surprise when they turned in purposefully at the abbey gatehouse. tramping through thankfully into the great court with a recovered spring to their steps. Two more for the common guesthall, thought Cadfael, himself approaching the gate, and a place near the fire and a meal and a drink will come very welcome to them.

They were at the door of the porter's lodge when Cadfael entered the court, and the porter had just come out to them. The light was not yet so far gone that Cadfael failed to see, and marvel, how the porter's face, ready with its customary placid welcome and courteous enquiry, suddenly fell into a gaping stare of wonder and concern, and the words ready on his lips turned into a muted cry.

'Master James! How's this – you here? I thought – Man,' he said, dismayed, 'what's come to you on the road?'

Cadfael was brought up with a jolt, no more than ten paces towards Vespers. He turned back in haste to join this unexpected confrontation, and look more closely at the lame man.

'Master James of Betton? Herluin's master-carpenter?' No doubt of it, the same who had set out with the wagon-load of wood for Ramsey, more than a week ago, but limping and afoot now, and back where he had begun, and soiled and bruised not only from the road. And his companion, the elder of the two masons who had set off hopefully to find steady work at Ramsey, here beside him, with torn cotte and a clout bound about his head, and a cheekbone blackened from a blow.

'What's come to us on the road!' the master-carpenter repeated ruefully. 'Everything foul, short of murder. Robbery by cut-throats and outlaws. Wagon gone, timber gone, horses gone – stolen, every stick and every beast, and only by the grace of God not a man of us killed. For God's sake, let us in and sit down. Martin here has a broken head, but he would come back with me . . .'

'Come!' said Cadfael, with an arm about the man's shoulders. 'Come within to the warmth, and Brother Porter will get some wine into you, while I go and tell Father Abbot what's happened. I'll be with you again in no time, and see to the lad's head. Trouble for nothing now. Praise God you're safely back! All Herluin's alms couldn't buy your lives.'

Chapter Four

E DID well enough,' said Master James of Betton, in the abbot's panelled parlour an hour later, 'until we came into the forest there, beyond Eaton. It's thick woodland there south of Leicester, but well managed, as the roads go these days. And we had five good lads aboard, we never thought to run into any trouble we couldn't handle. A couple of wretches on the run, skulking in the bushes on the lookout for prey, would never have dared break cover and try their luck with us. No, these were very different gentry. Eleven or twelve of them, with daggers and bludgeons, and two wore swords. They must have been moving alongside us in cover, taking our measure, and they had two archers ahead, one either side the track. Someone whistled them out when we came to the narrowest place, bows strung and shafts fitted, shouting to us to halt. Roger from Ramsey was driving, and a good enough hand with horses and wagons, but what chance did he have with the pair of them drawing on him? He says he did think of whipping up and running them down, but it would have been useless, they could shoot far faster than we could drive at them. And then they came at us from both sides.'

'I thank God,' said Abbot Radulfus fervently, 'that you live to tell it. And all, you say, all your fellows are well alive? The loss is reparable, but your lives are greater worth.'

'Father,' said Master James, 'there's none of us but bears the marks of it. We did not let them put us down easily. There's Martin here was clubbed senseless and slung into the bushes. And Roger laid about him with his whip, and left the print of it on two of the rogues before they downed him and used the thong to bind him. But we were five against double as many, and armed villains very willing to kill. They wanted the horses most, we saw but three they already had with them, the rest forced to go afoot, and the wagon was welcome, too, they had one, I think, already wounded. They beat and drove us aside, and off with team and wagon at high speed into the forest by a track that turned southwards. All the load, clean gone. And when I ran after, and young Payne on my heels, they loosed a shaft at us that clipped my shoulder – you see the tear. We had no choice but to draw off, and go and pick up Martin and Roger. Nicol gave as good an account of himself as any of us, elder though he may be, and kept the key of the coffer safe, but they threw him off the cart, and coffer and all are gone, for it was there among the coppice-wood. What more could we have done? We never looked to encounter an armed company in the forest, and so close to Leicester.'

'You did all that could be expected of any man,' said the abbot firmly. 'I am only sorry you ever were put to it, and glad out of all measure that you came out of it without worse harm. Rest here a day or two and let your hurts be tended before you return to your homes. I marvel who these wretches could be, moving in such numbers, and so heavily armed. Of what appearance were they – beggarly and mean, or savage with less excuse for savagery?'

'Father,' said Master James earnestly, 'I never before saw poor devils living wild wearing good leather jerkins and solid boots, and daggers fit for a baron's guard.'

'And they made off southerly?' asked Cadfael, pondering this militant company so well found in everything but horses.

'Southwest,' amended the young man Martin. 'And in a mortal hurry by all the signs.'

'In a hurry to get out of the earl of Leicester's reach,' Cadfael hazarded. 'They'd get short shrift from him if he once laid hands on them. I wonder if these were not some of the horde Geoffrey de Mandeville collected about him, looking for safer pastures to settle in, now the king is master of the Fens again? They'll be scattering in all directions still, and hunted everywhere. In Leicester's lands they certainly would not want to linger.'

That raised a murmur of agreement from them all. No sane malefactor would want to settle and conduct his predatory business in territory controlled by so active and powerful a magnate as Robert Beaumont, earl of Leicester. He was the younger of the twin Beaumont brothers, sons of the elder Robert who had been one of the most reliable props of old King Henry's firm rule, and they in their turn had been as staunch in support of King Stephen. The father had died in possession of the earldom of Leicester in England, Beaumont, Brionne and Pontaudemer in Normandy, and the county of Meulan in France, and on his death the

76

elder twin Waleran inherited the Norman and French lands, the younger Robert the English title and honour.

'He is certainly not the man to tolerate thieves and bandits in his lands,' said the abbot. 'He may yet take these thieves before they can escape his writ. Something may yet be recovered. More to the purpose at this moment, what has become of your companions, Master James? You say all of them are living. Where are they now?'

'Why, my lord, when we were left alone – and I think if they had not been in such haste to move on they would not have left a man of us alive to tell the tale – we first tended the worst hurt, and took counsel, and decided we must take the news on to Ramsey, and also back here to Shrewsbury. And Nicol, knowing that by then Sub-Prior Herluin would be in Worcester, said that he would make his way there and tell him what had befallen us. Roger was to make his way home to Ramsey, and young Payne chose to go on there with him, as he had said he would. Martin here would have done as much, but that I was none too secure on my feet, and he would not let me undertake the journey home alone. And here at home I mean to stay, for I've lost my taste for travelling, after that mêlée, I can tell you.'

'No blame to you,' agreed the abbot wryly. 'So by this time this news of yours should also have reached both Ramsey and Worcester, if there have been no further ambushes on the way, as God forbid! And Hugh Beringar may already be in Worcester, and will know what has happened. If anything can be done to trace our cart and the hired horses, well! If not, at least the most precious lading, the lives of five men, come out of it safely, God be thanked!'

Thus far Cadfael had deferred his own news in favour

77

of the far more urgent word brought back by these battered survivors from the forests of Leicestershire. Now he thought fit to put in a word. 'Father Abbot, I'm back from Longner without much gained, for neither of the young men who brought down the timber has anything of note to tell. But still I feel that one more thing of immense value must have been taken away with that wagon. I see no other way by which Saint Winifred's reliquary can have left the enclave.'

The abbot gave him a long, penetrating look, and concluded at length: 'You are in solemn earnest. And indeed I see the force of what you say. You have spoken now with everyone who took part in that evening's work?'

'No, Father, there's yet one more to be seen, a young man from a neighbouring hamlet who came down to help the carters. But them I have seen, and they do say that this third man was called back into the church by one of the brothers, at the end of the evening, for some last purpose, after which the brother came out with him to thank them all, and bid them goodnight. They did not see anything being stowed on the wagon for Ramsey. But they were busy and not paying attention except to their own work. It's a vague enough notion, that something unauthorized was then loaded under cover of the dark. But I entertain it because I see no other.'

'And you will pursue it?' said the abbot.

'I will go again, and find this young man Aldhelm, if you approve.'

'We must,' said Radulfus. 'One of the brothers, you say, called back the young man, and came out afterwards with him. Could they name him?'

'No, nor would they be able to know him again. It was dark, he was cowled against the rain. And most

78

likely, wholly innocent. But I'll go the last step of the way, and ask the last man.'

'We must do what can be done,' said Radulfus heavily, 'to recover what has been lost. If we fail, we fail. But try we must.' And to the two returned travellers: 'Precisely where did this ambush take place?'

'Close by a village called Ullesthorpe, a few miles from Leicester,' said Master James of Betton.

The two of them were drooping by then, in reaction from their long and laborious walk home, and sleepy from the wine mulled for them with their supper. Radulfus knew when to close the conference.

'Go to your well-earned rest now, and leave all to God and the saints, who have not turned away their faces from us.'

If Hugh and Prior Robert had not been well mounted, and the elderly but resolute former steward of Ramsey forced to go afoot, they could not have arrived at the cathedral priory of Worcester within a day of each other. Nicol, since the disastrous encounter near Ullesthorpe, had had five days to make his way lamely across country to reach Sub-Prior Herluin and make his report. He was a stouthearted, even an obstinate man, not to be deterred by a few bruises, and not to surrender his charge without a struggle. If pursuit was possible, Nicol intended to demand it of whatever authority held the writ in these parts.

Hugh and Prior Robert had arrived at the priory late in the evening, paid their respects to the prior, attended Vespers to do reverence to the saints of the foundation, Saints Oswald and Wulstan, and taken Herluin and his attendants into their confidence about the loss, or at the very least the misplacement, of Saint Winifred's reliquary: with a sharp eye, at least on Hugh's part, for

79

the way the news was received. But he could find no fault with Herluin's reaction, which displayed natural dismay and concern, but not to excess. Too much exclaiming and protesting would have aroused a degree of doubt as to his sincerity, but Herluin clearly felt that here was nothing worse than some confused stupidity among too many helpers in too much panic and haste, and what was lost would be found as soon as everyone calmed down and halted the hunt for a while to take thought. It was impressive, too, that he instantly stated his intention of returning at once to Shrewsbury, to help to clarify the confusion, though he seemed to be relying on his natural authority and leadership to produce order out of chaos, rather than having anything practical in mind. He himself had nothing to contribute. He had taken no part in the hurried labours within the church, but had held himself aloof with dignity in the abbot's lodging, which was still high and dry. No, he knew nothing of who had salvaged Saint Winifred. His last sight of her reliquary had been at morning Mass.

Tutilo, awed and mute, shook his head, still in its aureole of unshorn curls, and opened his amber eyes wide at hearing the disturbing news. Given leave to speak, he said he had gone into the church to help, and had simply obeyed such orders as were given to him, and he knew nothing of where the saint's coffin might be at this moment.

'This must not go by default,' pronounced Herluin at his most majestic. 'Tomorrow we will ride back with you to Shrewsbury. She cannot be far. She must be found.'

'After Mass tomorrow,' said Prior Robert, firmly reasserting his own leadership as representing Shrewsbury, 'we will set out.'

And so they would have done, but for the coming of Nicol.

Their horses were saddled and waiting, their farewells to the prior and brothers already made, and Hugh just reaching for his bridle, when Nicol came trudging sturdily in at the gatehouse, soiled and bruised and hoisting himself along on a staff he had cut for himself in the forest. Herluin saw him, and uttered a wordless cry, rather of vexation than surprise or alarm, for by this time the steward should have been home in Ramsey, all his booty safely delivered. His unexpected appearance here, whatever its cause, boded no good.

'Nicol!' pronounced Herluin, suppressing his first exasperation, at this or any disruption of his plans. 'Man, what are you doing here? Why are you not back in Ramsey? I had thought I could have complete trust in you to get your charge safely home. What has happened? Where have you left the wagon? And your fellows, where are they?'

Nicol drew deep breath, and told him. 'Father, we were set upon in woodland, south of Leicester. Five of us, and a dozen of them, with cudgels and daggers, and two archers among them. Horses and wagon were what they wanted, and what they took, for all we could do to stop them. They were on the run, and in haste, or we should all be dead men. They had one at least of their number wounded, and they needed to move fast. They battered us into the bushes, and made off into the forest with the cart and the team and the load, and left us to limp away on foot wherever we would. And that's the whole tale,' he said, and shut his mouth with a snap, confronting Herluin with the stony stare of an elder provoked and ready to do battle.

The abbey's wagon gone, a team of horses gone, Longner's cartload of timber gone. worst of all,

Ramsey's little chest of treasure for the rebuilding, lost to a company of outlaws along the road! Prior Robert drew a hissing breath, Sub-Prior Herluin uttered a howl of bitter deprivation, and began to babble indignation into Nicol's set face.

'Could you do no better than that? All my work gone to waste! I thought I could rely on you, that Ramsey could rely on you '

Hugh laid a restraining hand on the sub-prior's heaving shoulder, and rode somewhat unceremoniously over his lament. 'Was any man of yours badly hurt?'

'None past making his way afoot. As I've made mine,' said Nicol sturdily, 'all these miles, to bring word as soon as I might.'

'And well done,' said Hugh. 'God be thanked there was no killing. And where have they headed, since they let you make for here alone?'

'Roger and the young mason are gone on together for Ramsey. And the master carpenter and the other lad turned back for Shrewsbury. They'll be there by this, if they had no more trouble along the way.'

'And where was this ambush? South of Leicester, you said? Could you lead us there? But no,' said Hugh decisively, looking the man over. An elder, well past fifty, and battered and tired from a dogged and laborious journey on foot. 'No, you need your rest. Name me some village close by, and we'll find the traces. Here are we, and ready for the road. As well for Leicester as for Shrewsbury.'

'It was in the forest, not far from Ullesthorpe,' said Nicol. 'But they'll be long gone. I told you, they needed the cart and the horses, for they were running from old pastures gone sour on them, and in the devil's own hurry.'

'If they needed the wagon and the team so sorely,'

said Hugh, 'one thing's certain, they'd want no great load of timber to slow them down. As soon as they were well clear of you, they'd surely get rid of that dead weight, they'd upend the cart and tip the load. If your little treasury was well buried among the coppice-wood, Father Herluin, we may recover it yet.' And if something else really was slipped aboard at the last moment, he thought, who knows but we may recover that, too!

Herluin had brightened and gathered his dignity about him wonderfully, at the very thought of regaining what had gone astray. So had Nicol perceptibly brightened, though rather with the hope of getting his revenge on the devils who had tumbled him from the wagon, and threatened his companions with steel and arrows.

'You mean to go back there after them?' he questioned, glittering. 'Then, my lord, gladly I'll come back with you. I'll know the place again, and take you there straight. Father Herluin came with three horses from Shrewsbury. Let his man make his way back there, and let me have the third horse and bring you the quickest way to Ullesthorpe. Give me a moment to wet my throat and take a bite, and I'm ready!'

'You'll fall by the wayside,' said Hugh, laughing at a vehemence he could well understand.

'Not I, my lord! Let me but get my hands on one of that grisly crew, and you'll put me in better fettle than all the rest in the world. I would not be left out! This was my charge, and I have a score to settle. I kept the key safe, Father Herluin, but never had time to toss the coffer into the bushes, before I was flung there myself, winded among the brambles, and scratches enough to show for it. You would not leave me behind now?'

'Not for the world!' said Hugh heartily. 'I can do with a man of spirit about me. Go, quickly then, get bread and ale. We'll leave the Ramsey lad and have you along for guide.'

The reeve of Ullesthorpe was a canny forty-five-year-old, wiry and spry, and adroit at defending not only himself and his position, but the interests of his village. Confronted with a party weighted in favour of the clerical, he nevertheless took a thoughtful look at Hugh Beringar, and addressed himself rather to the secular justice.

'True enough, my lord! We found the place some days past. We'd got word of these outlaws passing through the woods, though they never came near the villages, and then this master-carpenter and his fellow came back to us and told us what had befallen them, and we did what we could for them to set them on their way back to Shrewsbury. I reasoned like you, my lord, that they'd rid themselves of the load, it would only slow them down. I'll take you to the place. It's a couple of miles into the forest.'

He added nothing more until he had brought them deep into thick woodland, threaded by a single open ride, where deep wheel-ruts still showed here and there in the moist ground, even after so many days. The marauders had simply backed the wagon into a relatively open grove, and tipped the stack of wood headlong, raking out the last slim cordwood and dragging the cart away from under them. It did not surprise Hugh to see that the stack had been scattered abroad from the original untidy pile dumped thus, and most of the seasoned timber removed, leaving the flattened bushes plain to be seen. Thrifty villagers had sorted out the best for their own uses, present or future. Give them time, and the rest of the coppice-wood would also find a good home. The reeve, attendant at Hugh's elbow, eyed him sidelong, and said insinuatingly: 'You'll not think it ill of good husbandmen to take what God sends and be grateful for it?'

Herluin remarked, but with controlled resignation: 'This was the property of Ramsey Abbey, nevertheless.'

'Why, Father, there was but a few of us, those who talked with the lads from Shrewsbury, ever knew that. The first here were from an assart only cut from the woods a few years back, it was a godsend indeed to them. Why leave it to go to waste? They never saw the wagon or the men that brought it here. And the earl gives us the right to take fallen wood, and this was long felled.'

'As well mending a roof as lying here,' said Hugh, shrugging. 'Small blame to them.' The heap of logs, probed and hauled apart days since, had spread over the woodland ride and into the tangle of grass and undergrowth among the trees. They walked the circuit of it, sifting among the remains, and Nicol, who had strayed a little further afield, suddenly uttered a shout, and plunging among the bushes, caught up and brandished before their eyes the small coffer which had held Herluin's treasury. Broken apart by force, the lid splintered, the box shed a handful of stones and a drift of dead leaves as he turned it upside down and shook it ruefully.

'You see? You see? They never got the key from me, they never would have got it, but that was no hindrance. A dagger prising under the lid, close by the lock . . . And all that good alms and good will gone to rogues and vagabonds!'

'I expected no better,' said Herluin bitterly, and took the broken box in his hands to stare at the damage. 'Well, we have survived even worse, and shall survive

85

this loss also. There were times when I feared our house was lost for ever. This is but a stumble on the way, we shall make good what we have vowed, in spite of all.'

Small chance, however, reflected Hugh, of recovering these particular gifts. All Shrewsbury's giving, whether from the heart or the conscience, all Donata's surrendered vanities, relinquished without regret, all gone with the fugitive ruffians, how far distant already there was no guessing.

'So this is all,' said Prior Robert sadly.

'My lord . . . ' The reeve edged closer to Hugh's shoulder and leaned confidingly to his ear. 'My lord, there was something else found among the logs. Well hidden underneath it was, or either the rogues would have found it when they tipped the load, or else the first who came to carry off timber would have seen it. But it so chanced it was covered deep, and came to light only when I was here to see. I knew when we unwrapped it, it was not for us to meddle with.'

He had all their attention now, every eye was wide and bright upon him, Herluin and Robert irresistibly moved to hoping against hope, but very wary of disappointment, Nicol interested but bewildered, for nothing had been said to him of the loss of Saint Winifred's reliquary, or the possibility that he might have had it aboard his wagon, and had been robbed of it with all the rest. Tutilo hovered in the background, keeping himself modestly apart while his betters conferred. He had even suppressed, as he could do at will, the brightness of his amber eyes.

'And what was this thing you found?' asked Hugh cautiously.

'A coffin, my lord, by its shape. Not very large, if coffin it really is; whoever lies in it was fine-boned and

86

slender. Ornamented in silver, very chastely. I knew it was precious enough to be perilous. I took it in charge for safety.'

'And what,' pursued Prior Robert, beginning to glow with the promise of a triumph, 'did you do with this coffin?'

'I had it taken to my lord, since it was found in his territory. I was risking no man of my village or those round about being charged with stealing a thing of value. Earl Robert was and is in residence in his manor of Huncote,' said the reeve, 'a few miles nearer Leicester. We carried it to him there, and told him how we found it, and there in his hall it is yet. You may find it safe enough in his care.'

'Praise God, who has shown us marvellous mercies!' breathed Prior Robert in rapture. 'I do believe we have found the saint we mourned as lost.'

Hugh was visited by a momentary vision of Brother Cadfael's face, if he could have been present to appreciate the irony. Yet both virgin saint and unrepentant sinner must fall within the range of humanity. Maybe, after all, Cadfael had been right to speak so simply of 'poor Columbanus'. If only, thought Hugh, between amusement and anxiety, if only the lady has been gracious enough and considerate enough to keep the lid firmly on that reliquary of hers, we may yet come out of this without scandal. In any case, there was no escaping the next move.

'Very well so!' said Hugh philosophically. 'Then we'll go to Huncote, and have speech with the earl.'

Huncote was a trim and compact village. There was a thriving mill, and the fields of the demesne were wide and green, the ploughland well tended. It lay clear of the edge of the forest, closely grouped round the manor and its walled courtyard. The house was not large, but built of stone, with a squat tower as solid as a castle keep. Within the pale the strangers entering were observed immediately, and approached with an alertness and efficiency that probably stemmed from the fact that the earl himself was in residence. Grooms came at once, and briskly, to take the bridles, and a spruce page came bounding down the steps from the hall door to greet the newcomers and discover their business here, but he was waved away by an older steward who had emerged from the stables. The apparition of three Benedictines, two of them obviously venerable, and attended by two lay guests, one a servitor, the other with an authority equal to the monastic, but clearly secular, produced a welcome at once courteous and cool. Here every grace of hospitality would be offered to all who came, only warmth waited on further exchanges.

In a country still torn between two rivals for sovereignty, and plagued by numerous uncommitted lords more interested in carving out kingdoms of their own, wise men observed their hospitable duties and opened their houses to all, but waited to examine credentials before opening their minds.

'My lord, reverend sirs,' said the steward, 'you are very welcome. I am the steward of my lord Robert Beaumont's manor of Huncote. How may I serve the Benedictine Order and those who ride in their company? Have you business here within?'

'If Earl Robert is within, and will receive us,' said Hugh, 'we have indeed business. We come in the matter of something lost from the abbey of Shrewsbury, and found, as we have learned, here within the earl's woodlands. A little matter of a saint's reliquary. Your lord may even find it diverting, as well as enlightening, for he must have been wondering what had been laid on his doorstone.'

'I am the prior of Shrewsbury,' said Robert with ceremonious dignity, but was only briefly regarded. The steward was elderly, experienced and intelligent, and though he was custodian only of one of the minor properties in Leicester's huge and international honour, by the sharpening glint in his eye he was in his lord's confidence, and well acquainted with the mysterious and elaborate coffin so strangely jettisoned in the forest beyond Ullesthorpe.

'I am King Stephen's sheriff of Shropshire,' said Hugh, 'and in pursuit of that same errant saint. If your lord has her safe and sound, he is entitled to the prayers of all the brothers of Shrewsbury, and of half Wales into the bargain.'

'No man's the worse for an extra prayer or two,' said the steward, visibly thawing. 'Go within, brothers, and welcome. Robin here will show you. We'll see your beasts cared for.'

The boy, perhaps sixteen years old, pert and lively, had waited their pleasure with stretched ears and eyes bright with curiosity when their errand was mentioned. Some younger son from among Leicester's tenants, placed by a dutiful father where he could readily get advancement. And by his easy manner, Hugh judged, Leicester was no very hard master for such as met his standards. This lad bounded up the steps ahead of them, his chin on his shoulder, eyeing them brightly.

'My lord came down here from the town when he heard of these outlaws passing this way, but never a glimpse of them have we encountered since. They'll be well out of reach before this. He'll welcome diversion, if you have so curious a tale to tell. He left his countess behind in Leicester.'

89

'And the reliquary is here?' demanded Prior Robert, anxious to have his best hopes confirmed.

'If that is what it is, Father, yes, it's here.'

'And has suffered no damage?'

'I think not,' said the boy, willing to please. 'But I have not seen it close. I know the earl admired the silverwork.'

He left them in a panelled solar beyond the hall, and went to inform his master that he had unexpected guests; and no more than five minutes later the door of the room opened upon the lord of half Leicestershire, a good slice of Warwickshire and Northampton, and a large honour in Normandy brought to him by his marriage with the heiress of Breteuil.

It was the first time Hugh had seen him, and he came to the encounter with sharp and wary interest. Robert Beaumont, earl of Leicester like his father before him, was a man barely a year past forty, squarely built and no more than medium tall, dark of hair and darker of eyes, rich but sombre in his attire, and carrying the habit of command very lightly, not overstressed, for there was no need. He was cleanshaven, in the Norman manner, leaving open to view a face broad at brow and well provided with strong and shapely bone, a lean jaw, and a full, firm mouth, long-lipped and mobile, and quirking upward at the corners to match a certain incalculable spark in his eye. The symmetry of his body and the smoothness of his movements were thrown out of balance by the slight bulge that heaved one shoulder out of line with its fellow. Not a great flaw, but insistently it troubled the eyes of guests coming new to his acquaintance.

'My lord sheriff, reverend gentlemen,' said the earl, 'you come very aptly, if Robin has reported your errand rightly, for I confess I've been tempted to lift the lid on whatever it is they've brought me from Ulles-thorpe. It would have been a pity to break those very handsome seals, I'm glad I held my hand.'

And so am I, thought Hugh fervently, and so will Cadfael be. The earl's voice was low-pitched and full, pleasing to the ear, and the news he had communicated even more pleasing. Prior Robert melted and became at once gracious and voluble. In the presence of a Norman magnate of such power and dignity this other Norman, Robert, monastic though he was by choice, harked back to his own heredity, and blossomed as if preening before a mirror.

'My lord, if I may speak for Shrewsbury, both abbey and town, I must tell you how grateful we are that Saint Winifred fell into such noble hands as yours. Almost one might feel that she has herself directed matters in miraculous fashion, protecting herself and her devotees even among such perils.'

'Almost one might, indeed!' said Earl Robert, and the eloquent and sensitive lips curved into a gradual and thoughtful smile. 'If the saints can secure at will whatever their own wishes may be, it would seem the lady saw fit to turn to me. I am honoured beyond my deserts. Come, now, and see how I have lodged her, and that no harm or insult has been offered her. I'll show you the way. You must lodge here tonight at least, and as long as you may wish. Over supper you shall tell me the whole story, and we shall see what must be done now, to please her.'

His table was lavish, his welcome open and generous, they could hardly have fallen into richer pastures after all these vexations; and yet Hugh continued throughout the meal curiously alert, as though he expected something unforeseen to happen at any moment, and divert

91

events into some wild course at a tangent, just when Prior Robert, at least, was beginning to believe his troubles over. It was not so much a feeling of disquiet as of expectation, almost pleasurable anticipation. Tempting to speculate what could possibly complicate their mission now?

The earl had only a small household with him at Huncote, but even so they were ten at the high table, and all male, since the countess and her women were left behind in Leicester. Earl Robert kept the two monastic dignitaries one on either side of him, with Hugh at Herluin's other side. Nicol had betaken himself to his due place among the servants, and Tutilo, silent and self-effacing among such distinguished company, was down at the end among the clerks and chaplains, and wary of opening his mouth even there. There are times when it is better to be a listener, and a very attentive one, at that.

'A truly strange story,' said the earl, having listened with flattering concentration to Prior Robert's eloquent exposition of the whole history of Shrewsbury's tenure of Saint Winifred, from her triumphant translation from Gwytherin to an altar in the abbey, and her inexplicable disappearance during the flood. 'For it seems that she was removed from her own altar without human agency – or at least you have found none. And she has already been known, you tell me, to work miracles. Is it possible,' wondered the earl, appealing deferentially to Prior Robert's more profound instruction in things holy, 'that for some beneficent purpose of her own she may have transferred herself miraculously from the place where she was laid? Can she have seen fit to pursue some errand of blessing elsewhere? Or felt some disaffection to the place where she was?' He had the prior stiffly erect and somewhat pale in the face by this time, though the manner of the questioning was altogether reverent and grave, even deprecating. 'If I tread too presumptuously into sacred places, reprove me,' entreated the earl, with the submissive sweetness of a brand-new novice.

Precious little chance of that happening, thought Hugh, listening and observing with a pleasure that recalled to mind some of his earliest and most tentative exchanges with Brother Cadfael, dealing trick for trick and dart for dart, and feeling their way over small battlefields to a lasting friendship. The prior might possibly suspect that he was being teased, for he was no fool, but he would certainly not challenge or provoke a magnate of Robert Beaumont's stature. And in any case, the other austere Benedictine had taken the bait. Herluin's lean countenance had quickened into calculating if cautious eagerness.

'My lord,' he said, restraining what could easily have blossomed into a glow of triumph, 'even a layman may be inspired to speak prophecy. My brother prior has himself testified to her powers of grace, and says plainly that no man has been found to own that he carried the reliquary. Is it too much to suppose that Saint Winifred herself moved her relics to the wagon that was bound for Ramsey? Ramsey, so shamefully plundered and denuded by impious villains? Where could she be more needed and honoured? Where do more wonders for a house grossly misused? For it is now certain that she left Shrewsbury on the cart that was returning with gifts from the devout to our needy and afflicted abbey. If her intent was to come there with blessing, dare we contest her wishes?'

Oh, he had them locked antler to antler now, two proud stags with lowered heads and rolling eyes, gathering their sinews for the thrust that should send one of them backing out of the contest. But the earl insinuated a restraining hand, though without any indication that he had seen the impending clash.

'I do not presume to make any claim, who am I to read such riddles? For Shrewsbury certainly brought the lady from Wales, and in Shrewsbury she has done wonders, never renouncing their devotion to her. I seek guidance, never dare I offer it in such matters. I mentioned a possibility. If men had any hand in her movements, what I said falls to the ground, for then all is plain. But until we know . . .'

'We have every reason to believe,' said Prior Robert, awesome in his silvery indignation, 'that the saint has made her home with us. We have never failed in devotion. Her day has been celebrated most reverently every year, and the day of her translation has been particularly blessed. Our most dutiful and saintly brother was himself healed of his lameness by her, and has been ever since her particular squire and servant. I do not believe she would ever leave us of her own will.'

'Oh, never with any heart to deprive you,' protested Herluin, 'but in compassion for a monastic house brought to ruin might she not feel bound to exert herself to deliver? Trusting to your generosity to respect the need, and add to your alms already given the power and grace she could bestow? For certain it is that she did leave your enclave with my men, and with them took the road to Ramsey. Why so, if she had no wish to depart from you, and none to come and abide with us?'

'It is not yet proven,' declared Prior Robert, falling back upon the mere material facts of the case, 'that men – and sinful men, for if it happened so this was sacrilegious theft! – had no part in her removal from our care. In Shrewsbury our lord abbot has given orders to seek out all those who came to help us when the river rose into the church. We do not know what has been uncovered, what testimony given. There the truth may by now be known. Here it certainly is not.'

The earl had sat well back from between the bristling champions, absolving himself from all responsibility here except to keep the peace and harmony of his hall. His countenance was bland, sympathetic to both parties, concerned that both should have justice done to them, and be satisfied.

'Reverend Fathers,' he said mildly, 'as I hear, you intend in any case returning together to Shrewsbury. What hinders that you should put off all dispute until you are there, and hear all that has been discovered in your absence? Then all may be made plain. And if that fails, and there is still no hand of man apparent in the removal, then it will be time to consider a rational judgement. Not now! Not yet!'

With guarded relief but without enthusiasm they accepted that, at least as a means of postponing hostilities.

'True!' said Prior Robert, though still rather coldly. 'We cannot anticipate. They will have done all that can be done to unearth the truth. Let us wait until we know.'

'I did pray the saint's help for our plight,' Herluin persisted, 'while I was there with you. It is surely conceivable that she heard and had pity on us . . . But you are right, patience is required of us until we hear further on the matter.'

A little mischief in it, Hugh judged, content to be an onlooker and have the best view of the game, but no malice. He's amusing himself at a dull time of year, and being here without his womenfolk, but he's as adroit at calming the storm as he is at raising it. Now what more can he do to pass the evening pleasantly, and entertain his guests? One of them, at any rate, he admitted a shade guiltily, and reminded himself that he had still to get these two ambitious clerics back to Shrewsbury without bloodshed.

'There is yet a small matter that has escaped notice,' said the earl almost apologetically 'I should be loth to create more difficulties, but I cannot help following a line of thought to its logical end. If Saint Winifred did indeed conceive and decree her departure with the wagon for Ramsey, and if a saint's plans cannot be disrupted by man, then surely she must also have willed all that happened after   the ambush by outlaws, the theft of the cart and team, the abandonment of the load, and with it, her reliquary, to be found by my tenants, and brought to me here. All accomplished – does it not seem plain? – to bring her finally where she now rests. Had she meant to go to Ramsey, there would have been no ambush, there she would have gone without hindrance. But she came here to my care. Impossible to say of the first move, it was her will, and not to extend that to what followed, or reason is gone mad.'

Both his neighbours at table were staring at him in shocked alarm, knocked clean out of words, and that in itself was an achievement. The earl looked from one to the other with a disarming smile.

'You see my position. If the brothers in Shrewsbury have found the rogues or the fools who mislaid the saint in the first place, then there is no contention between any of us. But if they have not traced any such, then I have a logical claim. Gentlemen, I would not for the world be judge in a cause in which I am one party among three. I submit gladly to some more disinterested tribunal. If you are setting out for Shrewsbury tomorrow, so must Saint Winifred. And I will bear my part in escorting her, and ride with you.'

Chapter Five

ROTHER CADFAEL had made one journey to the hamlet of Preston in search of the young man Aldhelm, only to find that he was away in the riverside fields of the manor of Upton, busy with the lambing, for the season had been complicated by having to retrieve some of the ewes in haste from the rising water, and the shepherds were working all the hours of the day. On his second attempt, Cadfael made straight for Upton to enquire where their younger shepherd was to be found, and set out stoutly to tramp the further mile to a fold high and dry above the water-meadows.

Aldhelm got up from the turf on which a new and unsteady lamb was also trying to get to its feet, nuzzled by the quivering ewe. The shepherd was a loose-limbed fellow all elbows and knees, but quick and deft in movement for all that. He had a blunt, good natured face and a thick head of reddish hair. Haled in to help salvage the church's treasures, he had set to and done whatever was asked of him without curiosity, but there was nothing amiss with his sharp and assured memory, once he understood what was being asked of him.

'Yes, Brother, I was there. I went down to give Gregory and Lambert a hand with the timber, and Brother Richard called us in to help shift things within. There was another fellow running about there like us, someone from the guesthall, hefting things around off the altars. He seemed to know his way round, and what was needed. I just did what they asked of me.'

'And did any ask of you, towards the end of the evening, to help him hoist a long bundle on to the wagon with the wood?' asked Cadfael, directly but without much expectation, and shook to the simple answer.

'Yes, so he did. He said it was to go with the wagon to Ramsey, and we put it in among the logs, well wedged in. It was padded safely enough, it wouldn't come to any harm.'

It had come to harm enough, but he was not to know that. 'The two lads from Longner never noticed it,' said Cadfael. 'How could that be?'

'Why, it was well dark then, and raining, and they were busy shifting the logs in the Longner cart down to the tail, to be easy to heft out and carry across. They might well have missed noticing. I never thought to mention it again, it was what the brother wanted, just one more thing to move. I took it he knew what he was about, and it was no business of ours to be curious about the abbey's affairs.'

It was certainly true that the brother in question had known all too well what he was about, and there was small doubt left as to who he must be, but he could not be accused without witness.

'What was he like, this brother? Had you spoken with him before, in the church?'

'No. He came running out and took me by the sleeve in the darkness. It was raining, his cowl was drawn up close. A Benedictine brother for certain, is all I know. Not very tall, less than me. By his voice a young fellow. What else can I tell you? I could point him out to you, though, if I see him,' he said positively.

'Seen once in the dark, and cowled? And you could know him again?'

'So I could, no question. I went back in with him to hoist this load, and the altar lamp was still bright. I saw his face close, with the light on it. To picture a man in words, one's much like another,' said Aldhelm, 'but bring me to see him, I'll pick him out from a thousand.'

'I have found him,' said Cadfael, reporting the result of his quest in private to Abbot Radulfus, 'and he says he will know his man again.'

'He is certain?'

'He is certain. And I am persuaded. He is the only one who saw the monk's face, by the altar lamp as they lifted the reliquary. That means close and clear, the light falling directly into the cowl. The others were outside, in the darkness and the rain. Yes, I think he can speak with certainty.'

'And he will come?' asked Radulfus.

'He will come, but on his own terms. He has a master, and work to do, and they are still lambing. While one of his ewes is in trouble he will not budge. But when I send for him, by the evening, when his day's work is over, he'll come. It cannot be yet,' said Cadfael, 'not until they are back from Worcester. But the day I send for him, he will come.'

'Good!' said Radulfus, but none too happily. 'Since we have no choice but to pursue it.' No need to elaborate on why it would be useless to send for the witness yet, it was accepted between them without words. 'And, Cadfael, even when the day comes, we will not make it known at chapter. Let no one be forewarned, to go in fear or spread rumours. Let this be done as sensibly as possible, with the least harm to any, even the guilty.'

'If she comes back, unharmed, unchanged,' said Cadfael, 'this may yet pass without harm or disgrace to any. She is also to be reckoned with, I have no fears for her.' And it dawned upon him suddenly how right Hugh had been in saying that he, Cadfael, spoke by instinct of this hollow reliquary, as good as empty, as though it truly contained the wonder whose name it bore. And how sadly he had missed her, lacking the unworthy symbol she had deigned to make worthy.

Granted this authenticity even for the symbol, she came back the next day, nobly escorted.

Brother Cadfael was just emerging from the door of the infirmary in mid-morning, after replenishing Brother Edmund's stores in the medicine cupboard, when they rode in at the gatehouse before his eyes. Not simply Hugh, Prior Robert, and the two emissaries from Ramsey with their lay servant, who indeed seemed to be missing, but a company augmented by the addition of two attendant grooms or squires, whatever their exact status might be, and a compact personage in his prime, who rode unobtrusively at Hugh's side, behind the two priors, and yet dominated the procession without any effort or gesture on his part. His riding gear was rich but in dark colours, the horse under him was more ornamented in his harness than the rider in his dress, and a very handsome dark roan. And behind him, on a narrow wheeled carriage drawn by one horse, came Saint Winifred's reliquary, decently nested on embroidered draperies.

It was wonderful to see how the great court filled, as though the word of her return in triumph had been blown in on the wind. Brother Denis came out from the guesthall, Brother Paul from the schoolroom, with two of his boys peering out from behind his skirts, two novices and two grooms from the stable-yard, and half a dozen brothers from various scattered occupations, all appeared on the scene almost before the porter was out of his lodge in haste to greet Prior Robert, the sheriff and the guests.

Tutilo, riding modestly at the rear of the cortège, slipped down from the saddle and ran to hold Herluin's stirrup, like a courtly page, as his superior descended. The model novice, a little too assiduous, perhaps, to be quite easy in his mind. And if what Cadfael suspected was indeed true, he had now good reason to be on his best behaviour. The missing reliquary, it seemed, was back where it belonged, just as a witness had been found who could and would confirm exactly how it had been made to disappear. And though Tutilo did not yet know what lay in store for him, nevertheless he could not be quite sure this apparently joyous return would be the end of it. Hopeful but anxious, plaiting his fingers for luck, he would be wholly virtuous until the last peril was past, and himself still anonymous and invisible. He might even pray earnestly to Saint Winifred to protect him, he had the innocent effrontery for it.

Cadfael could not choose but feel some sympathy for one whose dubious but daring enterprise had come full circle, and now threatened him with disgrace and punishment; all the more as Cadfael himself had just been spared a possibly similar exposure. The lid of the reliquary, with its silver chasing exposed to view, no doubt to be instantly recognizable on entering the court, was still securely sealed down. No one had tampered with it, no one had viewed the body within. Cadfael at least could breathe again.

Prior Robert on his own ground had taken charge of all. The excited brothers raised the reliquary, and bore it away into the church, to its own altar, and Tutilo followed devotedly. The grooms and novices led away the horses, and wheeled away the light carriage into the grange court for housing. Robert, Herluin, Hugh and the stranger departed in the direction of the abbot's lodging, where Radulfus had already come out to greet them.

Stranger this new guest might be, certainly Cadfael had never seen him before, but it was no particular problem to work out who he must be, even if that left his presence here as a mystery. Not far from Leicester the ambush had taken place. Here was clearly a magnate of considerable power and status, why look further afield for his name? And Cadfael had not missed the heave of the misshapen shoulder, visible now in this rear view as a distinct hump, though not grave enough to disfigure an otherwise finely proportioned body. It was well known that the younger Beaumont twin was a marked man. Robert Bossu they called him, Robert the Hunchback, and reputedly he made no objection to the title.

So what was Robert Bossu doing here? They had all disappeared into the abbot's hall now, whatever chance had brought him visiting would soon be known. And what Hugh had to say to Abbot Radulfus would soon be talked over again with Brother Cadfael. He had only to wait until this conference of sacred and secular powers was over.

103

Meantime, he reminded himself, since the entire company was now assembled, he had better be about sending off Father Boniface's errand-boy to find Aldhelm at Upton among his sheep, and ask him to come down to the abbey when his work for the day was over, and pick out his shadowy Benedictine from among a number now complete.

There was a silence in Cadfael's workshop in the herb garden, once Hugh had told the full story of Saint Winifred's odyssey, and how, and in what mood, Robert Beaumont had entered the contest to possess her.

'Is he in earnest?' asked Cadfael then.

'Halfway. He is playing, passing the tedious time while there's virtually no fighting and very little man-oeuvring – and while he wants none, but is uneasy being still. Short of employment, barring a difficult business of protecting his brother's interests here, as Waleran is protecting Robert's over in Normandy, as well as he can, this one enjoys putting the fox among the fowls, especially two such spurred and hackled cockerels as your prior and Ramsey's Herluin. There's no malice in it,' said Hugh tolerantly. 'Should I grudge him his sport? I've done the like in my time.'

'But he'll hold to it he has a claim?'

'As long as it amuses him, and he has nothing better to do. Good God, they put the notion into his head themselves! One might almost think, says Robert – our Robert, must I call him? – that she has been directing affairs herself! Almost one might, says the other Robert, and I saw the seed fall on fertile ground, and there he's tended it ever since. But never fret about him, he'll never push it to the length of humiliating either of them, let alone Abbot Radulfus, whom he recognizes as his match.'

'It hardly shows,' said Cadfael thoughtfully, going off at a surprising tangent.

'What does?'

'The hump. Robert Bossu! I'd heard the name, who has not? Robert and Waleran of Beaumont seem to have parted company these last years, twins or no. The elder has been in Normandy for four years now, Stephen can hardly count him as the staunch supporter he used to be.'

'Nor does he,' agreed Hugh dryly. 'Stephen knows when he's lost a sound man. More than likely he fully understands the reason, and it can hardly be accounted any man's fault. The pair of them have lands both here in England and over in Normandy, and since Geoffrey of Anjou has made himself master of Normandy, on his son's behalf, every man in Stephen's backing fears for his lands over there, and must be tempted to change sides to keep Anjou's favour. The French and Norman lands matter most to Waleran, who can wonder that he's gone over there and made himself at least acceptable to Geoffrey, rather than risk being dispossessed. It's more than the lands. He got the French possessions, the heart of the honour, when their father died, he's count of Meulan, and his line is bound up in the title. Without Meulan he'd be nameless. Robert's inheritance was the English lands. Breteuil came only by marriage, this is where he belongs. So Waleran goes where his roots are, to keep them safe from being torn up, even if he must do homage to Anjou for the soil they've been firm in for generations. Where his heart is I am not sure. He owes allegiance to Geoffrey now, but does as little to aid him and as little to harm Stephen as possible, protecting both his own and his brother's interests there, while Robert does as much for him here. They both hold off from what action there is. Small wonder!' said Hugh. 'There is also a matter of sheer weariness. This chaos has gone on too long.'

'It is never easy,' said Cadfael sententiously, 'to serve two masters – even when there are two brothers to share the labour.'

'There are others with the same anxieties,' said Hugh.

'There will be more now, with one cause in the ascendant here and the other there. But we have a problem of our own here, Hugh, and even if the earl is only diverting himself, be sure Herluin is not. If I'd known,' said Cadfael dubiously, 'that you were going to bring her back safely, and no great harm done, I might not have been so busy about worrying out how she ever went astray.'

'I doubt if you'd have had any choice,' said Hugh with sympathy, 'and certainly you have none now.'

'None! I've sent for the lad from the Upton manor, as I told Radulfus I would, and before Compline he'll be here, and the truth will surely be out. Every man of us knows now how the reliquary was filched and borne away, it wants only this boy's testimony to give the thief a face and a name. A small figure and a young voice, says Aldhelm, who was tricked into helping him, and saw his face close. It hardly needs confirming,' admitted Cadfael, 'except that justice must be seen to proceed on absolute certainty. Herluin is neither small nor young. And why should any brother of Shrewsbury want to see our best patroness carted away to Ramsey? Once the method was out, as today it is, who could it be but Tutilo?'

'A bold lad!' remarked Hugh, unable to suppress an appreciative grin. 'He'll be wasted in a cowl. And do you know, I very much doubt whether Herluin would have raised any objection to a successful theft, but he'll have the youngster's hide now it's proved a failure.' He rose to leave, stretching limbs still a little stiff from the long ride. 'I'm away home. I'm not needed here until this Aldhelm has played his part and pointed the finger at your Tutilo, as I take it you're certain he will before the night's out. I'd as soon not be here. If there's a part for me, let it be left until tomorrow.'

Cadfael went out with him only into the herb garden, for he still had work to do here. Brother Winfrid, big and young and wholesome, was leaning on his spade at the edge of the vegetable patch beyond, and gazing after a diminutive figure that was just scuttling away round the corner of the box hedge towards the great court.

'What was Brother Jerome doing, lurking around your workshop?' asked Brother Winfrid, coming to put away his tools when the light began to fail.

'Was he?' said Cadfael abstractedly, pounding herbs in a mortar for a linctus. 'He never showed himself.'

'No, nor never intended to,' said Winfrid in his usual forthright fashion. 'Wanting to know what the sheriff had to say to you, I suppose. He was some minutes there outside the door, until he heard you stirring to come out, then he was off in a hurry. I doubt he heard any good of himself.'

'He can have heard nothing of himself at all,' said Cadfael contentedly. 'And nothing that can do him any good, either.'

Rémy of Pertuis had as good as made up his mind to leave that day, but the arrival of the earl of Leicester caused him to think again, and countermand his orders to Bénezet and Daalny to begin packing. The lame horse was fit and ready for action. But now might it not be wise to wait a few days, and examine the possibilities suggested by this magnate who had appeared so providentially? Rémy had no personal knowledge of Ranulf, earl of Chester, and could not be sure what kind of welcome he would get in the north. Whereas rumour led him to believe that Robert Beaumont was a cultivated man, likely to appreciate music. At least he was here, lodged in the same guesthall, dining at the same table. Why abandon an opportunity present and promising, to go after a distant and unproven one?

So Rémy set out to explore the situation, and laid himself out to please, and his gifts and graces, when he tried, were considerable. Bénezet had been in his service long enough to understand his own part in the operation in hand without having to be told. He made himself agreeable to the earl's squires in the stable-yard, and kept his ears open for any revealing mentions of Robert Bossu's tastes, temperament and interests, and what he garnered was encouraging. Such a patron would be a complete protection, a life of comparative luxury, and a very congenial employment. Bénezet was sauntering back to the guesthall with his gleanings, when he observed Brother Jerome rounding the box hedge from the garden, head down and in a hurry. Also, it seemed to Bénezet, in some excitement, and in haste to unburden himself to someone about whatever was on his mind. There was only one person to whom Jerome would be reporting with so much fervour; Bénezet, naturally curious about anything that might serve his turn or redound to his profit, was not averse to picking up a few crumbs of useful information by the way. He slowed his pace to observe where Jerome went, and followed him without haste into the cloister.

Prior Robert was replacing a book in the aumbry cupboard at the end of the scriptorium. Jerome made for him, heavy and urgent with news. Bénezet slipped into a carrel as near as he could approach unnoticed, and made himself invisible in the shadows. A convenient time, with the light fading, for all the brothers who were engaged in copying or reading had abandoned their books for the evening, leaving the prior to ensure that everything was decently replaced exactly where it should be. In the twilit quietness voices carried, and Jerome was excited, and Robert never one to subdue a voice he was fond of hearing. Crumbs of advantage, Bénezet had found, may be picked up in the most unexpected places.

'Father Prior,' said Brother Jerome, between outrage and satisfaction, 'something has come to my notice that you should know. It seems that there is one man who helped to carry Saint Winifred's reliquary to the cart for Ramsey, in all innocence, being asked by a habited brother of the Order. He has said he can recognize the man, and is coming here tonight to make the assay. Father, why has no word been said to us of this matter?'

'I do know of it,' said the prior, and closed the door of the aumbry upon the piety and wisdom within. 'The lord abbot told me. It was not made public because that would have been to give warning to the culprit.'

'But, Father, do you see what this means? It was the wickedness of men that removed her from our care. And I have heard a name given already to the impious thief who dared disturb her. I heard Brother Cadfael name him. The seeming innocent, the novice from Ramsey, Tutilo.'

'That was not said to me,' reflected Robert with slightly affronted dignity. 'No doubt because the abbot would not accuse a man until a witness gives proof positive of the felon's guilt. We have only to wait until tonight, and we shall have that proof.'

'But, Father, can one believe such wickedness of any man? What penance can possibly atone? Surely the lightning stroke of heaven should have fallen upon him and destroyed him in the very deed.'

'Retribution may be delayed,' said Prior Robert, and turned to lead the way out from the scriptorium, his agitated shadow at his heels. 'But it will be certain. A few hours only, and the illdoer will get his due penalty.'

Brother Jerome's vengeful and unsatisfied mutterings trailed away to the south door, and out into the chill of the evening. Bénezet let him go, and sat for some moments considering what he had heard, before he rose at leisure, and walked back thoughtfully to the guesthall. An easy evening awaited him; both he and Daalny were excused all service, for Rémy was to dine with the abbot and the earl, the first fruits of his campaign in search of place and status. No servant need attend him, and though there might well be music made before the evening ended, a girl singer could not fittingly be a part of the entertainment in the abbot's lodging. They were both free to do whatever they wished, for once.

'I have a thing to tell you,' he said, finding Daalny frowning over the tuning of a rebec under one of the torches in the hall. 'There's a hunt afoot tonight that I think your Tutilo would be well advised to avoid.' And he told her what was in the wind. 'Get the good word to him if you so please,' he said amiably, 'and let him make himself scarce. It might only postpone the day, but even one day is breathing space, and I fancy he's sharp enough to make up a plausible story, once he knows the odds, or to persuade this witness to a

110

different tale. Why should I wish the lad any worse harm than he's let himself in for already?'

'He is not my Tutilo,' said Daalny. But she laid down the rebec on her knees, and looked up at Bénezet with a fiercely thoughtful face. 'This is truth you're telling me?'

'What else? You've heard all the to-ing and fro-ing there's been, this is the latter end of it. And here you are free as a bird, for once, provided you come back to your cage in time. You do as you please, but I would let him know what's threatening. And as for me, I'm going to stretch my legs in the town, while I can. I'll say nothing, and know nothing.'

'He is not my Tutilo,' she repeated, almost absently, still pondering.

'By the way he avoids looking at you, he easily could be, if you wanted him,' said Bénezet, grinning. 'But leave him to stew, if that's your humour.'

It was not her humour, and he knew it very well. Tutilo would be warned of what was in store for him by the end of Vespers, if not before.

Sub-Prior Herluin, on his way to dine with Abbot Radulfus and the distinguished company at his lodging, and pleasantly gratified at the invitation, was confronted in mid-court with a meek petitioner in the shape of Tutilo, all duty and service, asking leave of absence to visit the Lady Donata at Longner.

'Father, the lady asks that I will go and play to her, as I have done before. Have I your permission to go?'

Herluin's mind was rather on his forthcoming dinner, and the marshalling of his arguments in the matter of Saint Winifred. Not a word had been said to him of any untoward suspicions, or of the threat of an eyewitness coming to judgement this very night. Tutilo got his permission with almost dismissive ease. He left by the gatehouse, openly, and took the road along the Foregate, in case anyone happened to notice and check that he set off in the appropriate direction. He was not going far, by no means as far as Longner, but far enough to be absent when the immediate danger threatened. He was not so simple as to believe that the danger would be over when Aldhelm went home frustrated, but what followed he would have to encounter and parry when it came. Sufficient unto the day was the evil thereof, and he had considerable confidence in his own ingenuity.

The news worked its way round by devious stages to the ears of Brother Jerome, that the bird he desired with all his narrow might to ensnare had taken flight to a safe distance. He was sick and sour with rage. Clearly there was no justice to be had, even from heaven. The devil was all too efficiently looking after his own.

He must have sickened on his own gall, for he disappeared for the rest of the evening. It cannot be said that he was missed. Prior Robert was conscious of his shadow only when he had an errand for him to run, or need of his obsequious presence to restore a balance when someone had managed to scar the priorial dignity. Most of the brothers were all too well aware of him, but in his absence relaxed, gave thanks and forgot him; and the novices and schoolboys evaded being in his proximity at all, so far as was possible. It was not until Compline that his non-appearance provoked wonder, comment and finally uneasiness, for he was unrelenting in observance, whatever else might be said of him. Sub-Prior Richard, a kindly soul even to those for whom he had no particular liking, grew anxious, and went to look for the stray, and found him on his bed in the dortoir, pallid and shivering, pleading sickness and looking pinched, grey and cold.

Since he was inclined to be dyspeptic at the best of times, no one was greatly surprised, unless perhaps at the severity of this attack. Brother Cadfael brought him a warming drink, and a draught to settle his stomach, and they left him to sleep it off.

That was the last mild sensation of the evening, for the final one, still to come, certainly could not be described as mild, and occurred somewhat after midnight. The halfhour after Compline seemed to be declining into total anticlimax. For the young man from the Upton manor, the anxiously awaited witness who was to uncover truth at last, did not come.

The abbot's guests had dispersed decorously. Rémy and Earl Robert in amicable company to the guesthall, where Bénezet was already returned from his evening in the town, in good time to attend his lord, as the earl's two squires stood ready and waiting for theirs. Daalny was shaking out and combing her long black hair in the women's rooms, and listening to the chatter of a merchant's widow from Wem, who had availed herself of a night's lodging here on her way to Wenlock for her daughter's lying-in Everything within the walls was preparing for sleep.

But Aldhelm did not come. And neither did Tutilo return from his visit to the lady of Longner.

The order of the day's observances being immutable, whoever fell ill and whoever defaulted, the bell for Matins sounded in the dortoir as it did every midnight, and the brothers arose and went sleepily down the night stairs into the church. Cadfael, who could sleep or wake virtually at will, always felt the particular solemnity of the night offices, and the charged vastness of the

113

darkened vault above, where the candlelight ebbed out and died into lofty distances that might or might not stretch into infinity. The silence, also, had an added dimension of cosmic silence in the midnight hours, and every smallest sound that disrupted the ordained sounds of worship seemed to jar the foundations of the earth. Such, he thought, in the pause for meditation and prayer between Matins and Lauds, as the faint, brief creak of the hinges of the south door from the cloister. His hearing was sharper than most, and as yet unmarred by the years; probably few of the others heard it. Yet someone had come in by that door, very softly, and was now motionless just within it, hesitating to advance into the choir and interrupt the second office of the day. And in a few moments a voice from that quarter, low and breathy, joined very softly in the responses.

When they left their stalls at the end of Lauds, and approached the night stairs to return to their beds, a slight, habited figure arose from its knees to confront them, stepping into what light there was very gingerly, but with resigned resolution, like one expecting a bleak welcome, but braced to endure and survive it. Tutilo's habit shimmered about the shoulders with the soft and soundless rain of spring, which had begun to fall in mid-evening, his curls were damp and ruffled, and the hand he passed across his forehead to brush them back left a dark smear behind. His eyes were wide and peering from within a blank shell of shock and his face, where his hand had not soiled it, was very pale.

At sight of him Herluin started forward from Prior Robert's side with a sharp explosive sound of exasperation, anger and bewilderment, but before he could recover his breath and pour out the fiery reproaches he undoubtedly intended to vent, Tutilo had found words, few and trenchant, to forestall all other utterance.

'Father, I grieve to come so late, but I had no choice. It was vital I should go first into the town, to the castle, where such news first belongs, and so I did. Father, on my way back, on the path from the ferry and through the wood, I found a dead man. Murdered . . . Father,' he said, showing the hand that had soiled his brow, 'I speak what I know, what was plain even in the pitch dark. I touched him . . . his head is pulp!'

Chapter Six

HEN HE saw his hands in the light he flinched, and held them away from him, to avoid letting them touch any other part of his person or habit, for the right was engrained with drying blood across the palm and between the fingers, and the fingers of the left were dabbled at the tips, as if they had felt at stained clothing. He would not or could not elaborate on his news until he had washed, twisting hand within hand as though he would scrub off his own defiled skin along with the blood. When at last he was private in the abbot's parlour with Radulfus, Prior Robert, Herluin, and Brother Cadfael, whose presence Tutilo himself had requested, he launched upon his story baldly enough.

'I was coming back by the path from the ferry, through the woodland, and where the trees are thickest I stumbled over him. He was lying with his legs across the path, and I fell on my knees beside him. It was pitch dark, but a man could follow the path by the pale line of sky between the branches. But on the ground nothing but blackness. I felt down beside me, and I knew the round of a knee, and cloth. I thought he was drunk, but he never made sound or move. I felt up from thigh to hip, and leaned close where I judged his face to be, but never a breath or a sign of life. God help me, I put my hand on the ruin of his head, and then I knew he was dead. And not by any accident! I felt the splintered bone.'

'Could you by any means guess who this man must be?' asked the abbot, his voice level and gentle.

'No, Father. It was too dark by far. There was no way of knowing, without torch or lantern. And I was knocked clean out of my right wits at first. But then I thought how this was the sheriff's business, and how the Church is held innocent and apart from all dealings in cases of blood. So I went on into the town, and told them at the castle, and the lord Beringar has set a guard on the place now until daylight. What I could tell I have told, and the rest must wait for the light. And, Father, he asked – the lord sheriff asked – that I should beg you to have Brother Cadfael informed also, and when the morning comes, if you permit, I am to lead him to the place, to meet the sheriff there. It is why I asked that he might attend here. And I will willingly show the place tomorrow, and if he has any question to ask me now, I will answer as well as I may. For he said – Hugh Beringar said – that Brother Cadfael understands wounds, having been many years a man-at-arms.'

He had run himself out of breath and almost out of effort by then, but heaved a great sigh at having got the load from his shoulders.

'If the place is guarded,' said Cadfael, meeting the abbot's questioning eye, 'whatever it has to tell us can safely be left until daylight. I think perhaps we should not speculate beforehand. It might be all too easy to take a wrong path. I would ask only, Tutilo, at what hour did you leave Longner?'

Tutilo started and shook himself, and took an unexpectedly long moment to think before he answered: 'It was late, past time for Compline when I started.'

'And you met no one on the walk back?'

'Not this side the ferry.'

'I think,' said Radulfus, 'we should wait, and let be until you have viewed the place by daylight, and the unfortunate soul is known. Enough now! Go to your bed, Tutilo, and God grant you sleep. When we rise for Prime, then will be the time to see and consider, before we try to interpret.'

But for all that, thought Cadfael, back in his own bed but with no will to sleep, how many of the five of us, one who spoke and four who listened, will close an eye again tonight? And of the three of us who knew there was to be a young man on his way down to us by that path during the evening, how many have already made the leap forward to give this nameless victim a name, and begin to see certain reasons why it might be expedient for some if he never reached us? Radulfus? He would not miss so plain a possibility, but he could and would refrain from entertaining and proceeding on it until more is known. Prior Robert? Well, give him his due, Prior Robert hardly said a word tonight, he will wait to have cause before he accuses any man, but he is intelligent enough to put all these small nothings together and make of them something. And I? It must have been for myself as much as any other that I issued that warning: It might be all too easy to take a wrong path! And heavens knows, once launched it's all too hard to turn back and look again for the missed trace.

So let us see what we have: Aldhelm – may he be home, forgetful and fast asleep at this moment! – was to come and pick out his man yesterday evening. The brothers had not been told, only Radulfus, Prior Robert, Hugh and I knew of it, leaving out of consideration Cynric's boy, who runs errands faithfully, but barely understands what he delivers, and forgets his embassage as soon as done and rewarded. Herluin was not told, and I am sure did not know. Neither, to the best of my knowledge, did Tutilo. Yet it is strange that the same evening Tutilo should be sent for to Longner. Was he so sent for? That can be confirmed or confuted, there's no problem there. Say he somehow got to know of Aldhelm's coming, even so by avoiding he could only delay recognition, not prevent it, he would have to reappear in the end. Yes, but say *he* reappeared, and Aldhelm never came. Not just that evening, but never.

Detail by detail built up into a formidable possibility, in which, nevertheless, he did not believe. Best to put off even thought until he had seen for himself the place where murder had been done, and the victim who had suffered it.

The early morning light, filtering grudgingly between the almost naked trees and the tangle of underbrush, reached the narrow thread of the path only dimly, a moist brown streak of rotted leaves and occasional outcrops of stone, striped with shadows like the rungs of a ladder where old coppicing had left the trunks spaced and slender. The sun was not yet clear of the eastward banks of cloud, and the light was colourless and amorphous from the evening's soft rain, but clear enough to show what had brought Tutilo to his knees in the darkness, and yet remained unseen.

The body lay diagonally across the path, as he had said, not quite flat on its face and breast, rather on the right shoulder, but with the right arm flung clear behind, and the left groping wide beside him, clear of the folds of the coarse hooded cloak he wore. The hood had slipped back from his head when he fell, by the way it lay bunched in his neck. He had fallen and lain with his right cheek pressed into the wet leaves. The exposed left side of his head was a dark, misshapen blot of dried blood, a crusted darkness, the ruin on which Tutilo had laid his hand in the night, and sickened with horror.

He looked composed enough now, standing a little apart in the fringe of bushes, staring steadily at what the night had hidden from him, with lids half-lowered over the dulled gold of his eyes, and his mouth shut too tightly, the only betrayal of the effort by which he maintained his stillness and calm. He had risen very early, from a bed probably sleepless, and led the way to this spot among the thickest of the woodland without a word beyond the whispered morning greeting, and obedient acknowledgement of any remarks directed at him. Small wonder, if his own account was truth, smaller still if today he was being forced back to a scene about which he had lied; lied to the law, lied to his superiors in the Order he had chosen of his own will and desire.

Down there, pressed into the earth, the face, or most of it, was intact. Cadfael kneeled close by the shattered head, and slid a hand gently under the right cheek, to turn the face a little upward to be seen.

'Can you name him?' asked Hugh, standing beside him. The question was directed at Tutilo, and could not be evaded; but there was no attempt at evasion. Tutilo said at once, in a still and careful voice:

'I do not know his name.'

Surprising, but almost certainly true; those few moments at the end of a chaotic evening had never called for names. He had been as anonymous to Aldhelm as Aldhelm had been to him.

'But you do know the man?'

'I have seen him,' said Tutilo. 'He helped us when the church was flooded.'

'His name is Aldhelm,' said Cadfael flatly, and rose from his knees, letting the soiled face sink back gently into the leafmould. 'He was on his way to us last night, but he never reached us.' If the boy had not known that before, let it be said now. He listened and gave no sign. He had shut himself within, and was not easily going to be drawn out again.

'Well, let us see what there is to be noted,' said Hugh shortly, and turned his back upon the slight, submissive figure standing so warily aside from the event he had himself reported. 'He was coming down this path from the ferry, and here he was struck down as he passed by. See how he fell! Back a yard or more – here where the covert is thick, someone struck him down from behind and to his left – here on the left side of the path, from ambush.'

'So it seems,' said Cadfael, and eyed the bushes that encroached halfway across the path. 'There would be rustling enough from his own passage to cover another man's sudden movement among the branches here. He fell just as he lies now. Do you see any sign, Hugh, that he ever moved again?' For the ground about him, with its padding of last year's thick leaf-fall sodden and trodden into soft pulp, showed no disturbance, but lay moist, dark and flat, unmarked by any convulsions of his feet or arms, or any trampling of an assailant round him.

'While he lay stunned,' said Hugh, 'the work was finished. No struggle, no defence.'

In a small, muted voice Tutilo ventured, out of the shadowy covert of his cowl: 'It was raining.'

'So it was,' said Cadfael. 'I had not forgotten. His hood would be up to cover his head. *This* – was done afterwards, as he lay.'

The boy stood motionless still, looking down at the body. Only the subtle curve of a cheekbone and the lowered eyelids and a lunette of brow showed within the shadows of the cowl. There were tears hanging on the long, girlish lashes.

'Brother, may I cover his face?'

'Not yet,' said Cadfael. 'I need to look more closely before we carry him back with us.' There were two of Hugh's sergeants waiting impassively along the path, with a litter on which to lay him for passage to castle or abbey, according as Hugh should direct. From their judicious distance they watched in silence, with detached interest. They had seen violent death before.

'Do whatever you need,' said Hugh. 'Whatever club or staff was used on him is surely gone with the man who used it, but if the poor wretch's corpse can tell us anything, let us discover it before we move him.'

Cadfael kneeled behind the dead man's shoulders, and looked closely at the indented wound, in which white points of bone showed in the centre of the encrusted blood. The skull was broken just above and behind the left temple, with what looked like a single blow, though of that he could not be sure. A staff with a heavy rounded handle might have done such damage, but the crater it had made was large indeed, and jagged, not regular. Cadfael took up carefully the edge of the hood, and rounded it out on his fist. It was seamed at the back, and running his fingertips the length of the seam he encountered a small patch half-way down that was sticky and stiffening, and withdrew

122

them smeared with drying blood. Very little blood, surely from the first blow that felled its victim through hood and all. And this was at the back of the head, only the central seam contaminated, and that only meagrely. He straightened the folds, and ran his fingers through the dead youth's thick thatch of reddish-brown hair, up from the nape to the rounding at the back of the head, where that seam had rested, and surely helped to break the force of the blow. He found a graze that had oozed a small crust of blood into the thick hair, almost dry now. There was no break there in the skull beneath the skin.

'It was no very fearful blow that felled him,' said Cadfael. 'It cannot have knocked him out of his wits for very long, had that been all. What was done after, was done quickly, before he could come to himself. He would never have died of this. And yet what followed was cold, deliberate and final. A drunken man in a squabble could have done this.'

'It did what was required of it,' said Hugh grimly. 'Laid him at his enemy's mercy. No haste! Time to judge and finish at leisure.'

Cadfael straightened out the coarse folds of the hood, and shook out a few pale feathery fragments from among them. He rubbed them in his palm, slivers of tindery, rotted wood. Plenty of that, no doubt, in this overgrown, untended woodland, even after it had been combed for firing by the urchins of the Foregate. But why here in Aldhelm's hood? He ran his hands over the shoulders of the cloak, and found no more such minute splinters. He lifted the edge of the hood, and laid it gently over the shattered head, hiding the face. Behind him he felt, rather than heard, Tutilo's deep intake of breath, and sensed the quiver that passed through him.

123

'Wait a few moments yet. Let's see if the murderer left any trace behind, if he stood here any length of time waiting for his man.' For here was certainly the closest cover on all that path from the ferry down into the Foregate. The track had, he recalled, two branches, separating as it dropped from the heathy ridge that looked down upon the river. One branch went down directly to the Horse Fair, the other, this one, cut through to emerge halfway along the Foregate, almost within sight of the abbey gatehouse. By this one Tutilo must have set out for Longner, and by this one he had returned, only to happen upon this grievous discovery along the way. If, of course, he had ever been nearer to Longner, that night, than this disastrous place.

Cadfael stepped back to measure again the angle at which the body lay, and the few paces back along the path where the assailant must have been hidden. Thick cover, bristling with dryish branches and twigs, dead wood among them; he looked for broken ends, and found them. 'Here!' He thrust through the screen of growth sidelong, into cramped space between trees, where a thin grass grew, mottled with dead leafage and glistening from the night's rain. Soft ground, trodden flat by uneasy, shifting feet not so many hours ago. Nothing else, except a thick dead branch lying tossed under the bushes, and just aside from it, the bleached shape in the grass where it had formerly lain. Cadfael stooped and picked it up, and the thicker end, broken and dangling, shed a fluttering debris of tindery flakes as he swung it in his hand. Thick enough and heavy enough, but brittle.

'Here he waited. Some time, by the way he's pounded the mould. And this, this was what he found to his hand. With this he struck the first blow, and broke it in striking.'

124

Hugh eyed the branch, and gnawed a thoughtful lip. 'But not the second blow, surely. Not with this! It would have shattered in flinders long before it did that damage.'

'No, this he threw back into the bushes when it snapped and turned in his hand. And looked quickly for something more deadly? For clearly, if ever he trusted to this in the first place, he had come without any weapon.' Perhaps even, thought Cadfael, prompted a step further, he came without even the intent to kill, since he did not come prepared. 'Wait! Let's see what offered.'

For he could not have had to look far for whatever it might be, there had been no time for that. A few minutes, and Aldhelm would have been stirring and hauling himself to his feet. Cadfael began to prowl uphill along the edge of the path, probing into the bushes, and then downhill again on the opposite side. Here and there the limestone that cropped out among the heather and rough grass on the ridge above broke through the grass and mould in stony patches, fretted away occasionally into small scattered boulders, bedded into the turf and moss. Cadfael turned downhill some yards. The assailant had hidden on the left of the track, he probed first on that side. A few paces below where the body lay, and a yard or so into the bushes, there was a patch of free stones, loosely overgrown with grass and lichen, and to all appearance undisturbed for a year or more; until something about the clear outlining of the upper stone made him look closer. It was not bonded to those below it by the neat filling of soil and small growth that bound all the rest, though it lay aligned precisely to fill the place it had surely filled for a year or more. Cadfael stooped and took it in both hands, and lifted it, and it parted from its setting without trailing a blade of grass or a torn edge of moss. Once already in the night it had been uprooted and replaced.

'No,' said Cadfael, low to himself, 'this I never expected. That we should find a mind of such devious ways.'

'This?' said Hugh, staring closely upon the stone. It was large and heavy, a weighty double handful, smoothed above by exposure, beneath its dappling of lichen and moss; but when Cadfael turned it over it showed rough and pale, with some jagged edges that were tipped with a dark crust, not yet dried out. 'That is blood,' said Hugh with certainty.

'That is blood,' said Cadfael. 'When the thing was done, there was no longer any haste. He had time to think, and reason. All cold, cold and deliberate. He put back the stone as he found it, carefully aligned. The small, severed roots that had held it he could not repair, but who was to notice them? Now we have done all we can do here, Hugh. What remains is to put all together and consider what manner of man this could be.'

'We may move the poor wretch?' said Hugh.

'May I have him home to the abbey? I would like to look yet again, and more carefully. I think he lived alone, without family. We shall confer with his own priest at Upton. And this stone . . . ' It was heavy for him, he was glad to set it down for a while. 'Bring this with him.'

And all this time the boy had stood close by, word-less himself, but listening to every word spoken around him. The brief dew on his lashes, that had caught the thin early rays of the risen sun, was dry enough now, his mouth was set in a rigid line. When Hugh's men had lifted Aldhelm's body on to the litter, and set off down the path with it towards the Foregate, Tutilo fell in behind the sorry little procession like a mourner, and went silently step for step with them, his eyes still upon the shrouded body.

'He'll not be leaving?' said Hugh in Cadfael's ear, as they followed.

'He'll not be leaving. I will see to that. He has a hard master to satisfy, and nowhere else to go.'

'And what do you make of him?'

'I would not presume to assay,' said Cadfael. 'He slips through my fingers. But time was when I would have said the same of you,' he added wryly, and took heart at hearing Hugh laugh, if only briefly and softly. 'I know! That was mutual. But see how it turned out in the end.'

'He came straight to me with the tale,' said Hugh, reckoning up in a low voice for Cadfael's ear alone. 'He showed very shaken and shocked, but clear of head. He had wasted no time, the body was almost warm as life, only no breath in him, so we let all alone until morning. This lad behaved every way as a man would who had happened unawares on murder. Only, perhaps, better than most would have managed.'

'Which may be the measure of his quality,' said Cadfael firmly, 'or of his cunning. As well the one as the other. And who's to tell?'

'It is not often,' said Hugh with a rueful smile, 'that I must listen to you as the devil's advocate, where a youngster in trouble is concerned. Well, keep him in your custody, and we'll take time over either condemning or absolving.'

In the mortuary chapel Aldhelm's body lay on its bier, limbs straightened, body composed, eyes closed, enshrined and indifferent, having told all Cadfael could induce it to tell. Not all the specks of pallor in the shattered brow had proved to be splinters of bone. There were enough fragments of limestone and specklings of dust to prove over again the use to which the stone had been put. A linen cloth was draped over the young man's face. Across his breast Cadfael and Tutilo confronted each other.

The boy was very pale, and drawn and grey with exhaustion. Cadfael had kept him with him of design, when Hugh departed to report to Abbot Radulfus what had been found and what had been done. Mutely Tutilo had fetched and carried, brought water and cloths, fetched candles and lit them, willingly sustaining the presence of death. Now there was no more to be done, and he was still.

'You do understand,' said Cadfael, meeting the tired eyes, dulled gold even in the candlelight, 'why this man was on his way here? You do know what he might – what he said he would – be able to tell, when he saw all the brothers of the Order, here in this house?'

Tutilo's lips moved, saying almost soundlessly: 'Yes, I do know.'

'You know in what manner Saint Winifred's reliquary was taken away from here. That is known now to all men. You know there was a brother of the Order who so contrived her departure and asked Aldhelm to help him. And that she was meant to reach Ramsey, not to be lost on the way. Do you think justice will look among the brothers of Shrewsbury, from whom she was stolen? Or rather at two from the house that stood to gain? And one in particular?'

Tutilo fronted him with unwavering eyes, but said nothing.

'And here lies Aldhelm, who could have given that brother a face and a name, beyond any question.

128

Except that he no longer has a voice with which to speak. And you were away, along the same road, the road to the ferry, to Preston from which he would be coming, to Longner, where you were bound, when he died.'

Tutilo neither affirmed nor denied.

'Son,' said Cadfael, 'you know, do you not, what will be said?'

'Yes,' said Tutilo, unlocking his lips at last, 'I do know.'

'It will be said and believed that you lay in wait for Aldhelm and killed him, so that he could never point the finger at you.'

Tutilo made no protest that he had been the one to cry murder, to invoke the law, to unloose the hunt after the murderer. He averted his eyes for a moment to Aldhelm's covered face, and raised them again to meet Cadfael's eyes squarely. 'Except,' he said at last, 'that it shall not be said. They shall not be able to say it. For I will go to the lord abbot and Father Herluin, and myself tell what I have done. There shall not need anyone but myself to point the finger at me. For what I have done I will answer, but not for murder which I have not done.'

'Child,' said Cadfael, after a long and thoughtful silence, 'do not deceive yourself that even that would still every tongue. There will not be wanting those who will say that you have weighed the odds, knowing yourself already suspect, and of two evils chosen the lesser. Who would not rather own to theft and deception within the Church's writ, rather than put his neck into the sheriff's noose for murder? Speak or keep silence, there will be no easy course for you.'

'No matter!' said Tutilo. 'If I deserve penance, let it fall on me. Whether I pay or go free, whatever the cost,

I will not let it be said I killed a decent man to keep him from accusing me. And if they twist things still to my disgrace in both counts, what more is there I can do? Brother Cadfael, help me to the lord abbot's presence! If you ask audience for me, he will hear me. Ask if Father Herluin may be present also, now, while the sheriff is there. It cannot wait until chapter tomorrow.'

He had made up his mind, and all at once was on fire to have it done: and for all Cadfael could see, it was his best course. The truth, if truth could be anticipated from this subtle creature, even in circumstances of desperation, might shed light in more than one direction.

'If that is truly what you want,' he said. 'But beware of defending yourself before you are accused. Tell what you have to tell, with no exclaiming, and Abbot Radulfus will listen, that I can promise you.'

He wished he could heartily have said as much for Sub-Prior Herluin. So, perhaps, Tutilo was wishing, too, for suddenly in the midst of his most solemn determination his set mouth twisted into a wry and apprehensive smile, gone in an instant. 'Come with me now,' he said.

In the abbot's parlour Tutilo had a larger audience than Cadfael had bargained for, but welcomed it, or so it seemed, perhaps as leavening further the bleak reception he could expect from Herluin. Hugh was still there, and it was natural enough that Earl Robert should be called into conference as a matter of courtesy where the law of the land and King Stephen's writ were concerned. Herluin was there at Tutilo's own request, since there was ultimately no help for it, and Prior Robert was not to be left out where Herluin was admitted. Better far to confront them all, and let them make of it what they would.

'Father Abbot . . . Father Herluin . . . my lords . . .'
He took his stand sturdily, folded his hands, and looked
round them all in turn, as at a panel of his judges. 'I
have that to tell you that I should have told before this,
since it has to do with the issue that is now in dispute
among all here. It is known that the reliquary of Saint
Winifred was taken away on the wagon that was loaded
with timber for Ramsey, but no one has shown how this
came about. This thing was my doing. I avow it. I
moved the reliquary from its altar, after it had been
swathed well for safety in moving it to a higher place. I
put a trimmed log in its place, to be taken up by the
stair. And at night I asked one of the young men who
was helping us, one who had come with the carters, to
help me load the saint on to the wagon, to go to
Ramsey to the aid and succour of our misused house.
This is all the truth. There was none had any part in it
but I. Enquire no further, for I stand here to declare
what I have done, and to defend it.'

Herluin had opened his mouth and drawn breath to
ride over his presumptuous novice with a torrent of
indignant words, but then held his breath even before
the abbot had cautioned him with a peremptory hand.
For to revile this troublesome boy at this moment was
to damage whatever claim Ramsey had to the stake for
which the bold wretch had made so perilous a bid.
What could not a miracle-working saint achieve for the
future glory of Ramsey? And the issue was still very
much alive, for here beside him, listening alertly and
with a dry little smile, was the earl of Leicester, who,
whether in earnest or in mischief, was urging a plea of
his own for the same prize. No, say nothing yet, not
until things become clearer. Leave the options open.
Bow gracefully to Abbot Radulfus's gesture of
restraint, and keep your mouth shut.

131

'You do right, at least, in confession,' said Radulfus mildly. 'As you yourself informed us last night, and the lord sheriff has since confirmed, to our endless regret, and surely to yours, the young man you so beguiled is now dead, here within our walls, and shall be at our charge for the rites due to him. It would have been better, would it not, if you had spoken earlier, and spared him the journey that was his death?'

Such colour as there was in Tutilo's weary face slowly drained away to leave him grey and mute. When he could wring the tight cords of his throat into speech he said in a throttled whisper: 'Father, it is my shame. But I could not know! Even now I do not understand!'

Cadfael considered, when he came to think it out afterwards, that that was the moment when he became certain that Tutilo had not killed, had not ever imagined that his deceit was putting another soul in danger of death.

'What is done, is done,' said the abbot neutrally. 'You speak of defending it. If you think it defensible, go on. We will hear you out.'

Tutilo swallowed, and rallied, straightening his shapely shoulders. 'Father, what I cannot sufficiently justify I can at least explain. I came here with Father Herluin, grieving for Ramsey's wrongs, and longing to do something great to benefit the restoration of our house. I heard of the miracles of Saint Winifred, and the many pilgrims and rich gifts she has brought to Shrewsbury, and I dreamed of finding such a patroness to give new life to Ramsey. I prayed that she would intercede for us, and show us her grace, and it came to me that she heard me, and that she willed to do us good. It seemed to me, Father, that she inclined to us, and willed to visit us. And I began to feel it heavy upon me, that I must do her will.'

132

Colour had come back into his cheeks, burning on the notable bones, a little hectic, a little fevered. Cadfael watched him and was in doubt. Had he convinced himself, or could he produce at will this rapture to convince others? Or, like any fallible human sinner, was he desperately constructing an armour of simplicity about his devious shiftings? Sin detected can contrive all manner of veils to cover its nakedness.

'I planned and did what I have already told you,' said Tutilo, suddenly brief and dry. 'I felt that I was doing no wrong. I believed I was instructed, and faithfully I obeyed. But bitterly I regret that I needed another man's hands to help me, and he in ignorance.'

'In innocence,' said the abbot, 'to his peril.'

'I acknowledge it,' said Tutilo, erect and wide-eyed. 'I regret it. God forgive me for it!'

'In due time,' said Radulfus with unremitting detachment, 'so he may. That is not for us to meddle with. As for us, we have your story, we have a saint who has made her way back to us by strange ways, and we have those who have been friends to her on that journey, and may well believe, as you believe, that the lady has been in control of her own destiny, and choosing her own friends and her own dependants. But before ever we come to that issue, we have here a murdered man. Neither God nor his saints will tolerate murder. This young man Aldhelm cries to us for justice. If there is anything you can tell us that may shed light on his death, speak now.'

'Father,' said Tutilo, burning into startling whiteness, 'I pledge you my faith I never did nor never would have done him any harm, nor do I know of any who might need to wish him ill. It is true he could have told you of me what now I have told you. It never was matter for such fear to me that I must have tried to

133

silence him. He helped me! He helped *her*! I would have said yes to him when he pointed at me. Granted I was a little afraid, I tried to be secret. But there are no secrets now.'

'Yet you are the only man,' insisted the abbot mercilessly, but without pressing the suggestion to an accusation, 'who is known to have had reason to fear his coming here with what he could tell. What you yourself have now chosen to tell us can neither undo that truth, nor absolve you from it. Until more is known concerning his death, I judge that you must be held in confinement within my custody. The only charge that can be made against you at this moment is of theft from our house, however that may be read hereafter. That leaves you within my writ. I think the lord sheriff may have somewhat to say to that disposition.'

'I have nothing to object to it,' said Hugh promptly. 'I trust him to your charge, Father Abbot.'

Herluin had said not a word for or against. He was nursing in silence the options left to him, and so far they did not appear to him totally unpromising. The silly boy might have made potentially disastrous mistakes, but he had preserved the basis of his claim. The saint had willed it! How does the incumbent house prove otherwise? She did set out, only the wickedness of men frustrated her journey.

'Ask Brother Vitalis to call the porters to take him away,' said the abbot. 'And, Brother Cadfael, see him into his cell, and if you will, come back to us.'

Chapter Seven

T WAS apparent to Cadfael, when he re-entered the abbot's parlour, that if battle had not actually been joined, war trumpets were certainly being tuned for the onset. Radulfus maintained his judicial calm, and the earl's broad brow was suave and benign, though there was no guessing what went on in the highly intelligent mind behind it; but Prior Robert and Sub-Prior Herluin sat very erect, stiff in the spine and with long, refined faces sharpened into steel, studiously not looking straight at each other, but maintaining each a bright gaze on distance, and the appearance of considering with magisterial detachment the situation that confronted them.

'Setting aside the issue of murder,' said Herluin, 'for which as yet we lack any kind of proof, surely his story is to be believed. This was a holy theft. He was doing what the saint willed.'

'I do not find it easy,' said Abbot Radulfus, with a distinct chill in his voice, 'to set aside the issue of murder. It takes precedence of any other matter.

Hugh, what can you say of this boy? He has told us now what he might well have feared the dead man could tell us. That leaves him with no cause to kill.'

'No,' said Hugh. 'He had cause, by his own admission, and we know of no other who had. It is possible that he did kill, but having killed, took thought to cover what he had done. Possible . . . I say no more than that. He came straight to us at the castle, and told us how he had found the body, and no question but he was greatly shaken and agitated, as well he might be, guilty or innocent. Today I must say he has behaved wholly in accordance with innocence, moved, pitying, patient in attendance. If all that was put on of design, to disguise guilt, then he is beyond his years bold, sharp-witted and devious. But,' he added wryly, 'I have it in mind that so he is, and may very well have had the hardihood to play it so.'

'But then,' said Radulfus, thoughtfully frowning, 'why come to me now, and confess the very thing of which the witness could have accused him?'

'Because he had not fully realized that suspicion would still follow him, and now it would be suspicion of murder. In such a case better to accept whatever penalties the Church might impose, however harsh, for theft and deceit, rather than fall into the hands of the secular law, *my* law,' said Hugh firmly, 'where murder is a hanging matter. If by submitting to the one guilt he could evade all suspicion upon the worse count . . . he is quite shrewd enough, I fancy, to make the choice and quite durable enough to abide it. Father Herluin should know him better than we.'

But Cadfael was certain by then that Herluin did not know his Tutilo at all, probably never had any clear idea what went on in the minds of any of his novices, because he paid no regard to them. Hugh's prompting, perhaps intentionally, had put him into a difficult position. He would want to distance himself and Ramsey in horror from any possibility of having harboured a murderer, but while the possibility still remained of profiting by a theft, holy or unholy, he would want to retain the appearance of valuing and believing in the thief.

'Brother Tutilo has not been in my especial care until this journey,' he said carefully, 'but I have always found him truly devoted to our house of Ramsey. He says that he had his directions in prayer and reverence from the saint, and I have every reason to believe him. Such saintly inspirations have been known. It would be presumptuous to flout them.'

'We are speaking of murder,' said Radulfus austerely. 'In all honesty, though I should be loth to say of any man that he is capable of killing, I dare not say of any man that he is wholly incapable of it. The boy was present on that path, by his own statement and actions, he had, however he might regret the act afterwards, cause to be rid of a man who could accuse him. That is as far as there is witness against him. For him it must be said that he went at once to report the death to authority, and then came back to us and again told the same story. Does it not seem to you that had the guilt been his, he could have come straight home and said never a word, and left it to some other to find the dead and sound the alarm?'

'We might well have wondered,' said Prior Robert flatly, 'at his state. The sheriff has said he was in great agitation. It is not easy to show calm and unshaken before others, after such a deed.'

'Or after the discovery of such a deed,' said Hugh fairly.

'Whatever the truth of it,' said the earl with

assurance, 'you have him safe in hold, you need only wait, and if he has indeed more and worse to tell, you may get it from the lad himself. I doubt if he is a hard enough case to brazen it out for long in confinement. If he adds nothing, after a few weeks, you may take it he has nothing to add.'

That might very well be wisdom, Cadfael thought, listening respectfully. What could be more debilitating to the young, what harder to bear with constancy, than being shut into a narrow stone cell, under lock and key, with only a narrow cot, a tiny reading desk and a crucifix on the wall for company, and the length of half a dozen stone flags for exercise? Though Tutilo had entered it, only half an hour ago, with evident relief and pleasure, and even heard the key turned in the lock without a tremor. The bed was gift enough. Narrow and hard it might be, but it was large enough for him, and blissfully welcome. But leave him there alone and snared for as long as ten days, and yes, if he had by then any secrets left, he would confide them all in exchange for the air of the great court, and the music of the Office.

'I have no time to spend here in waiting,' said Herluin. 'My mission is to take back to Ramsey such alms as I have been able to gain, at least by the goodwill of Worcester and Evesham. And unless some secular charge is made against Tutilo, I must take him back with me. If he has offended against Church law or the Rule of the Order, it is for Ramsey to discipline him. His own abbot must take that charge upon him. But by the leave of all here, I challenge your view, Father Abbot, that he has committed any offence touching the removal of Saint Winifred's reliquary. I repeat, this was a holy theft, undertaken in duty and reverence. The saint herself instructed him. If it were not so, she would never have allowed it to succeed.'

'I tremble at crossing swords with you,' said Robert Bossu in the sweetest and most reasonable of voices, his high shoulder leaned at ease against the panelled wall at his back, 'but I must observe that she did *not* allow it to succeed. The wagon that carried her was waylaid and stolen by vagabonds in the forests of my domain, and in my lands she came to rest.'

'That intervention was by the malice of evil men,' said Herluin, roused and fiery of eye.

'But you have acknowledged that the power of such a saint can and will frustrate the malice of evil men. If she did not see fit to prevent their actions, it must be because they served her purposes. She let pass her abduction from Shrewsbury, she let pass the onslaught of outlaws. In my woodland she came to rest, and to my house she was carried into sanctuary. By your own reasoning, Father, *all* this, if any, must have been achieved by her will.'

'I would remind you both,' said the abbot gently, 'that if she has been all this while consulting her own wishes, and imposing them upon us mortals, Saint Winifred is again on her own altar in our church. This, then, must be the end at which all this diversion was aiming. And she is where she desires to be.'

The earl smiled, a smile of extraordinary subtlety and charm. 'No, Father Abbot, for this last move was different. She is here again because I, with a claim of my own to advance, and having regard to yet another claim, with strict fairness, brought her back to Shrewsbury, from which she began her controversial odyssey, so that she herself might choose where she wished to rest. Never did she show any disposition to leave my chapel, where her repose was respected. Voluntarily I brought her with me. I do not therefore surrender my claim. She came to me. I welcomed her. If she so please, I will take her home with me, and provide her an altar as rich as yours.'

'My lord,' pronounced Prior Robert, stiff with resistance and outrage, 'your argument will not stand. As saints may make use even of creatures of illwill for their own purposes, so surely can they with more grace employ goodwill where they find it. That you brought her here, back to her chosen home, does not give you a better claim than ours, though it does you infinite credit. Saint Winifred has been happy here seven years and more, and to this house she has returned. She shall not leave it now.'

'Yet she made it known to Brother Tutilo,' retorted Herluin, burning up in his turn, 'that she has felt compassion towards afflicted Ramsey, and wishes to benefit us in our distress. You cannot ignore it, she wished to set out and she did set out to come to our aid.'

'We are all three resolved,' said the earl, with aggravating serenity and consideration. 'Should we not submit the decision to some neutral assessor and abide by his judgement?'

There was a sharp and charged silence. Then Radulfus said with composed authority: 'We already have an assessor. Let Saint Winifred herself declare her will openly. She was a lady of great scholarship in her later life. She expounded the Scriptures to her nuns, she will expound them now to her disciples. At the consecration of every bishop the prognosis for his ministry is taken by laying the Gospels upon his shoulders, and opening it to read the line decreed. We will take the *sortes Biblicae* upon the reliquary of the saint, and never doubt but she will make her judgement plain. Why delegate to any other the choice which is by right hers?'

140

Out of the longer silence while they all digested this fiat and readjusted to a suggestion so unexpected, the earl said with evident satisfaction – indeed, to Cadfael's ears bordering on glee: 'Agreed! There could be no fairer process. Father Abbot, grant us today and tomorrow to set our minds in order, examine our claims and take thought to pray only for what is due to us. And the third day let these *sortes* be taken. We will present our pleas to the lady herself, and accept whatever verdict she offers us.'

'Instruct me,' said Hugh an hour later, in Cadfael's workshop in the herb garden. 'I am not in the counsels of bishops and archbishops. Just how is the ordinance of heaven to be interpreted in these *sortes Biblicae* Radulfus has in mind? Oh, certainly I know the common practice of reading the future by opening the Evangel blindly, and laying a finger on the page, but what is this official use of it in consecrating a new bishop? Too late then, surely, to change him for a better if the word goes against him.'

Cadfael removed a simmering pot from the grid on the side of his brazier, set it aside on the earth floor to cool, and added a couple of turfs to damp down the glow, before straightening his back with some caution, and sitting down beside his friend.

'I have never been in attendance at such a consecration myself,' he said. 'The bishops keep it within the circle. I marvel how the results ever leak out, but they do. Or someone makes them up, of course. Too sharp to be true, I sometimes feel. But yes, they are taken just as Abbot Radulfus said, and very solemnly, so I'm told. The book of the Gospels is laid on the shoulders of the newly chosen bishop, and opened at random, and a finger laid on the page – '

'By whom?' demanded Hugh, laying his own finger on the fatal flaw.

'Now that I never thought to ask. Surely the archbishop or bishop who is officiating. Though, granted, he could be friend or enemy to the new man. I trust they play fair, but who knows? Bad or good, that line is the prognostic for the bishop's future ministry. Apt enough, sometimes. The good Bishop Wulstan of Worcester got: "Behold an Israelite indeed, in whom there is no guile." Some were not so lucky. Do you know, Hugh, what the *sortes* sent to Roger of Salisbury, who fell into Stephen's displeasure not so many years ago and died disgraced? "Bind his hands and feet, and cast him into outer darkness." '

'Hard to believe!' said Hugh, hoisting a sceptical eyebrow. 'Did not someone think of pinning that on him after his fall? I wonder what was heaven's response to Henry of Winchester when he achieved the bishopric? Even I can think of some lines that would come too near the knuckle for his liking.'

'I believe,' said Cadfael, 'it was something from Matthew, concerning the latter days when false prophets would multiply among us. Something to the effect that if any man should claim: Here is Christ! do not believe him. But much can be done with the interpretation.'

'That will be the sticking point this time,' Hugh said shrewdly, 'unless the Gospels speak all too plainly, and can't be misread. Why do you suppose the abbot ever suggested it? Doubtless it could be arranged to give the right answers. But not, I suspect, with Radulfus in charge. Is he so sure of heaven's justice?'

Cadfael had already been considering the same question, and could only conclude that the abbot had indeed total faith that the Gospels would justify Shrewsbury in

142

possession of its saint. He never ceased to wonder at the irony of expecting miracles from a reliquary in which her bones had once lain for only three days and nights, before being returned reverently to her native Welsh earth; and even more to be wondered at, the infinite mercy that had transmitted grace through all those miles between, forgiven the presence of a sorry human sinner in the coffin she had quitted, and let the radiance of miracle remain invisibly about her altar, unpredictable, accessible, a shade wanton in where it gave and where it denied, as the stuff of miracles is liable to be, at least to the human view. She was not here, had never been here, never in what remained of her fragile flesh; yet she had certainly consented to let her essence be brought here, and manifested her presence with startling mercies.

'Yes,' said Cadfael, 'I think he trusts Winifred to see right done. I think he knows that she never really left us, and never will.'

Cadfael came back to his workshop after supper, to make his final round for the night, damp down his brazier to burn slowly until morning, and make sure all his jars were covered and all his bottles and flasks stoppered securely. He was expecting no visitors at this hour, and swung about in surprise when the door behind him was opened softly, almost stealthily, and the girl Daalny came in. The yellow glow from his little oil lamp showed her in unusual array, her black hair braided in a red ribbon, with curls artfully breaking free around her temples, her gown deepest and brightest blue like her eyes, and a girdle of gold braid round her hips. She was very quick; she caught the glance that swept over her from head to foot, and laughed.

'My finery for when he entertains. I have been

singing for his lordship of Leicester. Now they are talking intimate possibilities, so I slipped away. I shall not be missed now. I think Rémy will be riding back to Leicester with Robert Bossu, if he plays his cards cleverly. And I told you, he is a good musician. Leicester would not be cheated.'

'Is he in need of my medicines again?' asked Cadfael practically.

'No. Nor am I.' She was restless, moving uneasily about the hut as once before, curious but preoccupied, and slow to come to what had brought her on this errand. 'Bénezet is saying that Tutilo is taken for murder. He says Tutilo killed the man he tricked into helping him to steal away your saint. That cannot be true,' she said with assured authority. 'There is no harm and no violence in Tutilo. He dreams. He does not *do*.'

'He did more than dream when he purloined our saint,' Cadfael pointed out reasonably.

'He dreamed that before he did it. Oh, yes, he might thieve, that's a different matter. He longed to give his monastery a wonderful gift, to fulfil his visions and be valued and praised. I doubt if he would steal for himself, but for Ramsey, yes, surely he would. He was even beginning to dream of freeing me from my slavery,' she said tolerantly, and smiled with the resigned amusement of one experienced beyond young Tutilo's innocent understanding. 'But now you have him somewhere under lock and key, and with nothing good to look forward to, whatever follows. If your saint is to remain here now, then even if Tutilo escapes the sheriff's law, if Herluin takes him back to Ramsey they'll make him pay through his skin for what he attempted and failed to bring to success. They'll starve and flay him. And if it goes the other way, and he's called guilty of murder, then, worse, he'll hang.' She had arrived, finally, at

144

what she really wanted to know: 'Where have you put him? I know he's a prisoner.'

'He is in the first penitentiary cell, close to the passage to the infirmary,' said Cadfael. 'There are but two, we have few offenders in the general way of things. At least the locked door designed to keep him in also keeps his enemies out, if he can be said to have any enemies. I looked in on him not half an hour ago, and he is fast asleep, and by the look of him he'll sleep until past Prime tomorrow.'

'Because he has nothing on his conscience,' Daalny snapped triumphantly, 'just as I said.'

'I would not say he has always told us all the truth,' said Cadfael mildly, 'if that's a matter for his conscience. But I don't grudge him his rest, poor imp, he needs it.'

She shrugged that off lightly, pouting long lips. 'Of course he is a very good liar, that's part of his fantasies. You would have to be very sure of him and of yourself to know when he's lying, and when he's telling the truth. One knows another!' she agreed defiantly, meeting Cadfael's quizzical look. 'I've had to be a good liar myself to keep my head above water all this time. So has he. But do murder? No, that's far out of his scope.'

And still she did not go, but hovered, touching with long fingers along his shelves of vessels, reaching up to rustle the hanging bunches of herbs overhead, keeping only her profile towards him. There was more she wanted to know, but hesitated how to ask, or better, how to find out what she needed without asking.

'They will feed him, will they not? You cannot starve a man. Who will look after him? Is it you?'

'No,' said Cadfael patiently. 'The porters will take him his food. But I can visit him. Can, and will. Girl, if you wish him well, leave him where he is.'

'Small choice I have!' said Daalny bitterly. Not, however, quite bitterly enough, Cadfael thought. Rather to present the appearance of resignation than to accept it. She was beginning to have dreams of her own and hers would proceed to action. She had only to watch the porter's moves next day to learn the times when he visited his charge, and espy where the two keys of the penal cells hung side by side in the gatehouse. And Wales was not far, and in any princely llys in that country, great or small, such a voice as Tutilo's, such a deft hand on strings, would easily find shelter. But to go with the slur of murder still upon him, and always the threat of pursuit and capture? No, better far sit it out here and shame the devil. For Cadfael was certain that Tutilo had never done violence to any man, and must not be marked with that obloquy for life.

Still Daalny lingered, as if minded to say or ask something more, her thin oval face sharply alert and her eyes half-veiled but very bright within the long dark lashes. Then she turned and departed very quietly. From the threshold she said: 'Goodnight, Brother!' without turning her head, and closed the door behind her.

He gave little thought to it then, reasoning that she was not in such grave earnest that she would actually attempt to turn her indignant dream into action. But he did reconsider next day, when he saw her watching the passage of the porter from the refectory before noon, and following him with her eyes as he turned in between infirmary and schoolroom, where the two small stony cells were built into the angle of the wall, close to the wicket that led through to the mill and the pond. When he was out of sight she crossed the great court to the gatehouse, passed by the open door

146

apparently without a glance, and stood for some minutes in the gateway, looking along the Foregate, before turning back towards the guesthouse. The board that held the keys in the porter's charge hung just within the doorway, and she had sharp enough eyes to pick out the nail that was empty, and the fellow to the absent key close beside it. Alike in size and general appearance, but not in the guards that operated them.

And even this unobtrusive surveillance might be only a part of her fantasy. She might never try to turn it into reality. All the same, Cadfael had a word with the porter before evening. She would not move until dusk or even darkness; no need to observe the passage of Tutilo's supper, she knew now which key she needed. All that was necessary was for the porter to replace it on the wrong nail before going to Compline, and leave her its ineffective twin.

He did not keep a watch on her; there was no necessity, and in his own mind he was almost convinced that nothing would happen. Her own position was so vulnerable that she would not venture. So the day passed normally, with the usual ritual of work and reading, study and prayer punctuated by the regular round of the hours. Cadfael went about his work all the more assiduously because a part of his mind was elsewhere, and he felt its absence as guilt, even though his concern was with a serious matter of justice, guilt and innocence. Tutilo must somehow be extricated from such opprobrium as he had not earned, no matter what penalties he might deserve for his real offences. Here in the enclave, imprisonment was also safety from any secular threat; the Church would look after its own, even its delinquents. Once outside, unless cleared of all suspicion, he would be a fugitive, liable to all the rigours of the law, and the very act of flight would be evidence against him. No, here he must remain until he could come forth vindicated.

It was almost time for Compline when Cadfael came from the gardens after his last round of the evening, and saw horsemen riding in at the gate. Sulien Blount, on a piebald gelding, leading a brown cob on a rein, saddled ready for riding, and after him two grooms in attendance. At this hour, in twilight, an unexpected invasion. Cadfael went to meet them as Sulien lighted down to speak hurriedly to the porter. Only some matter of great urgency could have brought messengers from Longner so late.

'Sulien, what is it? What brings you here at this hour?'

Sulien swung round to him gratefully. 'Cadfael, I have a request to make of the abbot. Or we may need the good word of this sub-prior from Ramsey, no less . . . My mother asks for that young musician of his, Tutilo, the one who has played and sung to her before, and helped her to sleep. She took kindly to him, and he to her. This time it will be a long sleep, Cadfael. She can't last the night through. And there's something she wants and needs to do . . . I have not questioned. Neither would you, if you could see her . . .'

'The lad you want is under lock and key,' said Cadfael, dismayed. 'He's under suspicion of felonies since the lady sent for him, two nights ago. Is she so near her end? The abbot can scarcely let him out to her except with guarantees for his return.'

'I know it,' said Sulien. 'Hugh Beringar has been with us, I know how things stand. But under escort . . . You see we'll keep good hold of him, and bring him back to you bound, if need be. At least ask! Tell Radulfus it is her last request of him. Death's mercy has held

148

off all too long, but now I swear to you this is ending. He knows all her story, he'll listen!'

'Wait,' said Cadfael, 'and I will go and ask.'

'But, Cadfael . . . two nights ago? No, we never sent for him two nights ago.'

Well, there was no great surprise there. The possibility had been at the back of Cadfael's mind for some time. No, it had been too apt, too opportune. He had found out what awaited him, and removed himself from the scene long enough, he had hoped, to escape the judgement. It made no difference now. 'No, no matter, that's understood,' he said. 'Wait here for me!'

Abbot Radulfus was alone in his panelled parlour. He listened to this late embassage with drawn brows, and eyes looking inward. And having heard, he said sombrely: 'It is high time for her. How can she be denied? You say they have guards enough to keep him safe? Yes, let him go.'

'And Father Herluin? Should I ask his leave also?'

'No. Tutilo is within my walls and in my charge. I give him leave. Go yourself, Cadfael, and release him to them. If time is so short for her, waste none of it.'

Cadfael returned in haste to the gatehouse. 'He will come. We have the abbot's leave. Wait, and I'll bring the boy.'

It scarcely surprised him to find, when he plucked the key from its nail in the gatehouse, that the nail beside it was also vacant. Everything was happening now with a distant, dreamlike certainty. Daalny had acted, after all; she must have taken the second key during Vespers, from the nail where at noon she had watched the porter hang the first one, but she had had to wait for near-darkness before using it. Now would be her favoured time, now when the brothers would be gathering in the church for Compline. Cadfael left the messengers from Longner waiting uneasily within the gate, and went hurrying round the corner of the school-room to the penitential cells beyond, where deeper shadows were already filling the narrow passage to the wicket in the enclave wall, and the mill and the pool beyond.

And she was there. He was aware of her at once, though she was only a slender additional shadow pressed close within the deep doorway of the cell. He heard the key grating ineffectively in the wards of the lock it did not fit, and her vexed, angry breathing as she wrestled to make it enter where it would not go. He heard her stamp her foot in frustrated rage, and grit her teeth, too intent to become aware of his approach until he reached an arm to put her aside, quite gently.

'No use, child!' he said. 'Let me!'

She uttered a muted cry of despair, and plucked her-self furiously backward out of his grasp. There was no sound from within the cell, though the prisoner's little lamp was lighted, its faint glow showed at the high, barred window.

'Wait, now, wait!' said Cadfael. 'You have a message to deliver here, and so have I. Let's be about it.' He stooped to pick up the wrong key, which had been jerked out of the lock and out of her hand when she started away. 'Come, and I'll let you in.'

The right key turned sweetly in the heavy lock, and Cadfael opened the door. Tutilo was standing fronting them, erect and rigid, his face a narrow, pale flame, his amber eyes wide and wild. He had known nothing of her plans, he did not know now what to expect, why this confining door should ever have been opened now, at this end of the day, after all permitted visits were over.

'Say what you came to say to him,' said Cadfael. 'But

briefly. Waste no time, for I have none to waste, and neither has he.'

Daalny stood tense and at a loss for one moment, before she flung herself bodily into the open doorway, as though she feared the door might be slammed again before she could prevent, though Cadfael made no move. Tutilo stood staring in bewilderment from one of them to the other, without understanding, almost without recognition.

'Tutilo,' she said, low-voiced and urgent, 'come away now. Through the wicket here, and you're free. No one will see you, once outside the walls. They're all at Compline. Go, quickly, while there's time. Go west into Wales. Don't wait here to be made a scapegoat, go, now . . . quickly!'

Tutilo came to life with a shudder and a start, golden flames kindling in his eyes. 'Free? What have you done? Daalny, they'll only turn on *you* . . . ' He turned to stare at Cadfael, braced and quivering, unsure whether this was friend or enemy facing him. 'I do not understand!'

'That is what she came to say to you,' said Cadfael. 'I have a message for you, too. Sulien Blount is here with a horse for you, and begs that you will come to his mother, now, at once, for the Lady Donata is dying, and is asking to see you again, and hear you, before she dies.'

Tutilo stiffened into marble stillness. The yellow flames darkened and softened into the pure glow of a steady fire. His lips moved, saying her name silently: 'Donata?'

'Go, now!' Daalny ordered, past anger now that the contest was joined and could not be evaded. 'I have dared this for you, how dare you now cast it in my face?

151

Go, while there's time. He is one and we are two. He cannot prevent!'

'I would not prevent,' said Cadfael. 'The choice is his to make.'

'Dying?' said Tutilo, finding a voice clear, quiet and grieving. 'Truly, she is dying?'

'And asking for you,' said Cadfael. 'As you said she did two nights ago. But tonight it is true, and tonight will be the last time.'

'You have heard,' said Daalny, smouldering but still. 'The door is open. He says he will not prevent. Choose, then! I have done.'

Tutilo did not seem to hear her. 'I used her!' he said, lamentably shaken. And to Cadfael he said doubtfully: 'And Herluin lets me go?'

'Not Herluin, but the abbot lets you go. On your honour to return, and under escort.'

Tutilo took Daalny suddenly between his hands, with grieving gentleness, and moved her aside from the doorway. He raised a hand with abrupt, convulsive passion and stroked her cheek, long fingers smoothing eloquently from temple to chin in a gesture of helpless apology.

'She wants me,' he said softly. 'I must go to her.'

Chapter Eight

AALNY HAD discarded at once her anger and her pleading as soon as the choice was made, and made in such a fashion that she knew it could not be changed. She followed to the corner of the schoolroom, and there stood watching in silence as Tutilo mounted, and the little cavalcade filed out at the gate and turned along the Foregate. The broader track from the Horse Fair was better for riding; he would not have to pass by on the narrow path where he had stumbled over Aldhelm's body.

The bell for Compline rang, the time she had set herself for hounding him out at the wicket, into a world he was, perhaps, already beginning to regret surrendering, but which he might have found none too hospitable to a run-away Benedictine novice. Better, at all costs, however, or so she had reasoned, to put twenty miles and a border between him and a hanging. Now she stood thoughtful, with the chime of the bell in her ears, and wondered. And when Cadfael came slowly back to her across the empty court, she stood in his way great-eyed, fronting him gravely as if she would penetrate into the most remote recesses of his mind.

'You do not believe it of him, either,' she said with certainty. 'You know he never harmed this poor shepherd lad. Would you really have stood by and let him go free?'

'If he had so chosen,' said Cadfael, 'yes. But I knew he would not. The choice was his. He made it. And now I am going to Compline.'

'I'll wait in your workshop,' said Daalny. 'I must talk to you. Now that I'm sure, now I will tell you everything I know. Even if none of it is proof of anything, yet you may see something there that I have not seen. He has need of more wits than mine, and two who will stand by him is better than one.'

'I wonder, now,' said Cadfael, studying her thin, bright, resolute face, 'whether you would be wanting that young man for yourself, or is this pure disinterested kindness?' She looked at him, and slowly smiled. 'Well, I'll come,' he said. 'I need a second wit, too. If it's cold within, you may use the bellows on my brazier. I have turfs enough there to damp it down again before we leave it.'

In the close, timber-scented air of the hut, with the herbs rustling overhead in the rising warmth from the brazier, she sat leaning forward to the glow, the light gilding her high cheekbones and the broad sweep of brow beneath the curling black hair.

'You know now,' she said, 'that he was not sent for to Longner that night. It was a tale that could be believed, but what he wanted was to have a reason to be somewhere else, not to be here when the shepherd came. That would not have been the end of it, but it would

154

have put off the worst, and Tutilo seldom looks beyond the day. If he could have evaded meeting the poor man for even a few days, this squabble over the saint's bones would have been settled, one way or another, and Herluin would have been off on his travels, and taken Tutilo with him. Not that that promises him much of a life,' she added, jutting a doubtful lip, 'now he's getting over his saintliness. If the biblical fates go against him, Herluin will take all the vexation and shame out on Tutilo, with usury. You know it as well as I do. These monastics, they are what they are born, only with a vengeance. If they come into the world hard and cold, they end harder and colder, if they come generous and sweet, they grow ever sweeter and more generous. All one or all the other. And just when Tutilo is beginning to wake up to where he belongs, and what he has it in him to be,' she said vehemently. 'Well, so it was. He lied about Longner to be out of here all the evening long. Now he owes her a debt, and goes to pay it.'

'There is more than a debt in it,' said Cadfael. 'That lady tamed him the first time he set eyes on her. He would have gone to her no matter what lure you could have put in the other scale. And what you are telling me is that he knew very well Aldhelm was to come here that night. How did he know? It never was made known to the brothers. Only the abbot and I knew, though he may have felt that he must tell Prior Robert.'

'He knew,' she said simply, 'because I told him.'

'And how did you know?'

She looked up sharply, stung into alert attention. 'Yes, it's true, few people knew. It was quite by chance. Bénezet overheard Prior Robert and Brother Jerome talking about it, and he came and told me. He knew I should warn Tutilo, I think he meant me to. He knew,' said Daalny, 'that I liked Tutilo.'

The simplest and most temperate words are the best to express complex and intemperate feelings. She had said more than she knew.

'And he?' said Cadfael with careful detachment.

But she was not so simple. Women never are, and she was a woman who had experienced more of life than her years would contain. 'He hardly knows what he feels,' she said, 'for me or for anything. The wind blows him. He sees a splendid dream, and runs headlong. He even persuades himself of the splendour. The monastic dream is fading now. I know it *has* splendour, but not for him. And he is not the man to go with it for the peace and the quiet bliss.'

'Tell me, then,' said Cadfael mildly, 'what happened that night, after he asked and got leave to go to Longner.'

'I would have told it at once,' she said ruefully, 'but that it would not have helped him. For past all doubt he was on that path, he did find the poor soul dead, he did run to the castle, like an honest man, and tell the sheriff what he had found. What I can tell does not change that. But if you can find a grain of good wheat in it, for God's sake pick it out and show it to me, for I have overlooked it.'

'Tell me,' said Cadfael.

'We made it up between us,' she said, 'and it was the first time ever we two met outside these walls. He went out and took the path that leads up over the ridge to the ferry. I slipped out through the double gates of the burial ground to the Horse Fair, and we crept into the loft over the stable there. The wicket in the main doors was still unlocked then, after they brought the horses back after the flood. It was more than a week before the stable-yard here had dried out. And that is where we stayed together, until we heard the Compline bell.

156

By that time, we thought, he must have been and gone again. So late, and the night dark.'

'And raining,' Cadfael reminded her.

'That, too. Not a night to linger on the road. We thought he would be off home, and none too keen to make another wasted journey.'

'And what did you do all that time?' asked Cadfael.

She smiled ruefully. 'We talked. We sat together in the hay to keep warm, and talked. Of his vocation freely entered into, and my being born into slavery with no choice at all, and how the two came to be much alike in the end,' she said hardly. 'I was born into the trap, he walked into it in avoiding another kind of servitude, with his eyes open, but not looking where he was going. And now with his own hands and feet tied he has great notions of delivering me.'

'As you offered him his freedom tonight. Well, and then? You heard the Compline bell, and thought it safe to return. Then how came he alone on the path from the ferry?'

'We dared not come back together. He might be seen returning, and it was needful he should come by the way he would have taken to Longner. I slipped in by the cemetery gate, as I left, and he went up through the trees to the path by which he had made his way to join me. It would not have done to come together. He has forsworn women,' she said with a bitter smile, 'and I must have no dealings with men.'

'He has not yet taken final vows,' said Cadfael. 'A pity he went alone, however. If two together had happened upon a dead man, they could have spoken for each other.'

'Us two?' she said, staring, and laughed briefly. 'They would not have believed us . . . a bondwoman and a novice near his final vows out in the night and

157

fresh from a romp in the hay? They would have said we compounded together to kill the man. And now, I suppose,' she said, cooling from bitterness into a composed sadness, 'I have told you everything, and told you nothing. But it is the whole truth. A good liar and a bold thief he may be, but on most counts Tutilo is as innocent as a babe. We even said the night prayers together when the bell rang. Who's to believe that?'

Cadfael believed it, but could imagine Herluin's face if ever the claim had been made to him. 'You have told me, at least,' he said, musing, 'that there were more people knew Aldhelm would be coming down that path than just the few of us, as it began. If Bénezet heard Jerome baying his knowledge abroad, how many more, I wonder, learned of it before night? Prior Robert can be discreet, but Jerome? . . . I doubt it. And might not Bénezet have passed on all his gleanings to Rémy, as he did to you? Whatever the bodyservant picks up may be grist to his master's mill. And what Rémy hears may very well be talked of with the patron he's courting. Oh, no, I would not say this hour had been altogether wasted. It means I have much thinking to do. Go to your bed now, child, and leave troubling for this while.'

'And if Tutilo never comes back from Longner?' she asked, wavering between hope and dread.

'Never give a thought to that,' said Cadfael. 'He will come back.'

They brought Tutilo back well before Prime, in the pearly light of a clear, still dawn. March had come in more lamb than lion, there were windflowers in the woods, and the first primroses, unburned by frost, undashed and unmired by further rain, were just opening. The two Longner men who rode one on either side their borrowed minstrel brought him as far as the

158

gatehouse, waiting in silence as he dismounted. The farewells they made to him, as they took his pony's rein and made to turn back for home, were quiet and constrained, but clearly friendly. The elder of the two leaned down from the saddle to clap him amiably on the shoulder, and said a word or two in his ear, before they trotted away along the Foregate towards the Horse Fair.

Cadfael had been awake and afield more than an hour by then, for want of a quiet mind, and had filled in the time by ranging along the bushy edges of his pease-fields and the shore of the mill pond to gather the white blossoms of the blackthorn, just out of the bud and at their best for infusing, to make a gentle purge for the old men in the infirmary, who could no longer take the strenuous exercise that had formerly kept their bodies in good trim. A very fine plant, the blackthorn, good for almost anything that ailed a man's insides, providing bud and flower and bitter black fruit were all taken at their best. Good in the hedges, too, for keeping cattle and sheep out of planted places.

From time to time he broke off his labours to return to the great court to look out for Tutilo returning. He had a full scrip of the small white flowers when he made the journey for the seventh time, and saw the three riders pace in at the gatehouse, and stood unobserved to watch Tutilo dismount, part amicably from his guards, and come wearily towards the gatehouse door, as if he would himself take the key and deliver himself dutifully back to his captivity.

He walked a little unsteadily, and with his fair crest drooping over something he cradled in his arms. Once he stumbled on the cobbles. The light, clearing and brightening to the pure pale gold of primroses where its slanting rays could reach, still left the gatehouse and the court within the gates in shadow, and Tutilo kept his eyes on the cobbles and trod carefully, as though he could not see his way clearly. Cadfael went to meet him, and the porter, who had heard the stir of arrival and come out into the doorway of his lodge, halted on the threshold, and left it to Cadfael as an elder of the house to take charge of the returned prisoner.

Tutilo did not look up until they were very close, and then blinked and peered as though he had difficulty in recognizing even a well known face. His eyes were red-rimmed, their gilded brightness dulled from a sleepless night, and perhaps also from weeping. The burden he carried with such curious tenderness was a drawstring bag of soft leather, with some rigid shape within it, that filled his arms and was held jealously to his heart, the anchoring strings around one wrist for safety, as though he went in dread of loss. He stared over his treasure at Cadfael, and small, wary sparks kindled in his eyes, and flared into anxiety and pain in an instant. In a flat, chill voice he said: 'She is dead. Never a quiver or a moan. I thought I had sung her to sleep. I went on . . . silence might have disturbed her rest . . .'

'You did well,' said Cadfael. 'She has waited a long time for rest. Now nothing can disturb it.'

'I started back as soon afterwards as seemed right. I did not want to leave her without saying goodbye fairly. She was kind to me.' He did not mean as mistress to servant or patroness to protégé. There had been another manner of kindness between them, beneficent to both. 'I was afraid you might think I was not coming back. But the priest said she could not live till morning, so I could not leave her.'

'There was no haste,' said Cadfael. 'I knew you would come. Are you hungry? Come within the lodge, and sit a while, and we'll find you food and drink.'

'No . . . They have fed me. They would have found me a bed, but it was not in the bargain that I should linger after I was no longer needed. I kept to terms.' He was racked by a sudden jaw-splitting bout of yawning that brought water to his eyes. 'I need my bed now,' he owned, shivering.

The only bed he could claim at this point was in his penitential cell, but he went to it eagerly, glad to have a locked door between himself and the world. Cadfael took the key from the porter, who hovered with slightly anxious sympathy, and was relieved to see a delinquent for whom he might be held responsible returning docilely to his prison. Cadfael shepherded his charge within, and watched him subside gratefully on to the narrow cot, and sit there mute for a moment, laying his burden down beside him with a kind of caressing gentleness.

'Stay a little while,' said the boy at length. 'You knew her well. I came late. How was it she had heart even to look at me, as tormented as she was?' He wanted no answer, and in any case there could be none. But why should not one dying too soon for her years and too late by far for her comfort take pleasure in the sudden visitation of youth and freshness and beauty, however flawed, and all the more for its vulnerability and help-lessness in a world none too kind to the weak.

'You gave her intense pleasure. What she has known most intimately these last years has been intense pain. I think she saw you very clearly, better than some who live side by side with you and might as well be blind. Better, perhaps, than you see yourself.'

'My sight is as sharp as it need be,' said Tutilo. 'I know what I am. No one need be an angel to sing like one. There's no virtue in it. They had brought the harp into her bedchamber for me, all freshly strung. I

161

thought it might be loud for her, there between close walls, but it was her wish. Did you know her, Cadfael, when she was younger, and hale, and beautiful? I played for a while, and then I stole up to look at her, because she was so still I thought she had fallen asleep, but her eyes were wide open, and there was colour, all rosy, high on her cheeks. She did not look so gaunt and old, and her lips were red and full, and curved, like a smile but not quite a smile. I knew she knew me, though she never spoke word, never, night-long. I sang to her, some of the hymns to the Virgin, and then, I don't know why, but there was no one to tell me do, or don't, and it was the way I felt her taking me, all still as she was, and growing younger because there was no pain left . . . I sang love songs. And she was glad. I had only to look at her, and I knew she was glad. And sometimes the young lord's wife stole in and sat to listen, and brought me to drink, and sometimes the lady the younger brother is to marry. Their priest had already shriven her clean. In the small hours, around three o'clock, she must have died, but I didn't know . . . I thought she had truly fallen asleep, until the young one stole up and told me.'

'Truly she had fallen asleep,' said Cadfael. 'And if your singing went with her through the dark, she had a good passage. There's nothing here for grieving. She has waited patiently for this ending.'

'It was not that broke me,' said Tutilo simply. 'But see what followed. See what I brought away with me.'

He drew open the neck of the leather bag that lay beside him, and reached inside to withdraw with loving care that same psaltery he had once played in Donata's bedchamber, polished sounding-board and stretched strings shining like new. A broken key had been replaced by one newly cut, and it was triple-strung with

162

new gut strings. He laid it beside him, and stroked across the strings, conjuring forth a shimmer of silvery sound.

'She gave it to me. After she was dead, after we had said the prayers for her, her son, the young one, brought it to me, all newly furbished like this, and said it was her wish that I should have it, for a musician without an instrument is a warrior without weapon or armour. He told me all that she had to say when she left it in trust for me. She said a troubadour needs only three things, an instrument, a horse, and a lady love, and the first she desired to give me, and the other two I must find for myself. She had even had new quills cut for me, and some to spare.'

His voice had grown hushed and childish with wonder and his eyes filled, looking back to record this playful divination which might yet predict a future far removed from the cloister, which in any case was already losing its visionary charm for him. She might well be right. She had warmed to him not as a spiritual being, but as vigorous young flesh and blood, full of untested potentialities. And dying men, and perhaps even more, dying women, had been formidable oracles at times.

Distantly from the dortoir, across the court, the bell sounded for Prime. Cadfael picked up the psaltery with due respect, and laid it safely aside on the little prayer-desk.

'I must go. And you, if you'll take advice, will sleep, and put everything else clean out of mind, while we go try the *sortes Biblicae*. You've done well by the lady, and she has done well by you. With her grace, and a few prayers the rest of us may find for you, you can hardly go unblessed.'

'Oh, yes,' said Tutilo, his tired eyes dilating. 'That is

today, is it not? I had forgotten.' The momentary shadow touched but could not intimidate him; he had gone somewhat beyond fear for himself.

'And now you can forget it again,' said Cadfael firmly. 'You of all people should have faith in the saint you set such store by. Lie down and sleep through all, and believe in Saint Winifred. Do you not think she must be up in arms by this time, at being treated like a bone between three dogs? And if she could tell you her mind privately some while ago, do you suppose she cannot make it very plain to us in public today? Sleep the morning through, and let her dispose of all of us.'

In the halfhour between chapter and High Mass, when Cadfael was busy sorting his harvest of blackthorn blossoms in his workshop, discarding occasional spines and fragments of wiry dark twigs, Hugh came in to share the gleanings of his own labours. They were meagre enough, but at least the ferryman had been able to supply one scrap of information that might yet be useful.

'He never went near Longner that night. He never crossed the river. You know that, I think? No, but the other poor wretch did, and the ferryman remembers when. It seems the parish priest at Upton has a servant who visits his brother's family in Preston once a week, and that night this fellow walked the road from Upton to Preston along with Aldhelm, who works at the demesne, and lives in the neighbouring village. A shepherd can never be sure at what hour he'll be done for the day, but the priest's man leaves Upton as soon as Vespers is over, and so he did this time. He says it must have been a little before the sixth hour when Aldhelm parted from him at Preston to go on to the ferry. From there, the crossing and the distance he had

164

covered on that path, to the place where he was found, would take him no more than half an hour – less, if he was a brisk walker, and it was raining, he'd be no longer than he need out in it. It seems to me that he was waylaid and killed round about a quarter or half of the hour past six. Hardly later. Now if your lad could tell us just where he was, while he was supposed to be at Longner, and better still, bring us a witness to confirm it, that would go far to get him out of the mire.'

Cadfael turned to give him a long, thoughtful look, and a few white petals that had floated and lodged in the rough cloth of his sleeve caught the stirring of air from the door, and floated free again, riding the draught into the pale, bright sunlight. 'Hugh, if what you say is true, then I hope something good may come of it. For though I doubt if *he's* ready to own to it yet, I know of another who can and will testify that the two of them were together until the bell sounded for Compline, which would be the better part of an hour later than you have in mind, and a quarter of an hour's walk from the place, into the bargain. But since it suits ill with his vocation, and perhaps bodes no good to – the other one – neither of them may be anxious to say it openly for all to hear. In your ear, with a little persuasion, they might both whisper it.'

'Where is the boy now?' asked Hugh, considering. 'Fast in his penitentiary?'

'And fast asleep, I trust. You were not at Longner last night, Hugh? No, or he would have said so. Then probably you have not heard that he was sent for last night just before Compline, to go to Donata, at her express wish. And Radulfus gave him leave, under escort. She died, Hugh. God and the saints remembered her at last.'

'No,' said Hugh, 'that I did not know.' He sat silent

for a long moment, recollecting how the past few years had dealt with Donata Blount and her family. Nothing there for grieving, no, rather for gratitude and thanksgiving. 'No doubt the news will be waiting for me around the garrison by now,' he said. 'And she asked for Tutilo?'

'You find that strange?' Cadfael asked mildly.

'It disappoints me when human creatures fail to provide something strange. No, all that's strange about this is that those two ever came to touch hands at any point. A man would have said that two such were never likely in this world to come within sight, let alone touch, of each other. Once met, yes, all things were possible. And she is dead. In his presence?'

'He thought he had sung her to sleep,' said Cadfael. 'So he had. He had grown fond, and so had she. Where there's nothing at stake there's no barrier, either. Nothing to join, so nothing to divide them. And he has come home this morning worn out with experience, all grief and all wonder, because she gave him the psaltery on which he played to her, and sent him a message straight out of the jongleurs' romances. He went back to his cell gladly, and I hope he'll sleep until all this business we have in hand after Mass is finished and done. And God and Saint Winifred send us a good ending!'

'Ah, that!' said Hugh, and smiled somewhat cryptically. 'Is not this *sortes* a rather dangerous way of deciding an issue? It seems to me it would not be at all difficult to cheat. There was a time, by your own account, when *you* cheated – in a good cause, of course!'

'I cheated to prevent a theft, not to achieve one,' said Cadfael. 'I never cheated Saint Winifred, nor will she suffer cheating now. She won't charge me with more

166

than my due, nor will she let that lad pay for a death I'm sure he does not owe. She knows what we need and what we deserve. She'll see wrongs righted and quarrels reconciled, in her own good time.'

'And without any aid from me,' Hugh concluded, and rose, laughing. 'I'll be off and leave you to it, I'd as lief be elsewhere while your monastics fight it out. But afterwards, when he wakes – poor rogue, I wouldn't disturb him! – we must have words with your songbird.'

Cadfael went into the church before High Mass, uneasy for all his declarations of faith, and guiltily penitent over his uneasiness, a double contortion of the mind. In any case there was no time left to make his infusion before the assay: he left his blackthorn blossoms, cleansed of all thorns and husks, waiting in a clean vessel for his return, and covered from any floating particles of dust by a linen cloth. A few petals still clung about his sleeves, caught in the rough weave. He had others in his grizzled russet tonsure, dropped from the higher branches as the wind stirred them. Distantly this springtime snow stirred his memory of other springs, and later blossom, like but unlike this, when the hawthorns came into heady, drunken sweetness, drowning the senses. Four or five weeks more, and that greater snow would blanch the hedgerows. The smell of growth and greenness was already in the air, elusive but constant, like the secret rippling of water, the whispering water of February, now almost hushed into silence.

By instinct rather than design he found himself at Saint Winifred's altar, and kneeled to approach her, his creaky knees settling gingerly on the lowest step of her elevated place. He offered no words, though he thought words within, in the Welsh tongue, which had been native to her as it was to him. Where she belonged and wished to be, she would direct. What he asked was guidance in the matter of a young man's death, a clean young man who handled lambs with gentleness and care, as lambs of God, and never deserved to be done to death suddenly before his time, however the love of God might have set a secure hand under him as he fell, and lifted him into light. And another young man suspect of a thing far out of his scope, who must not die a similarly unjust death.

What he never doubted was that she was listening. She would not turn her back on an appellant. But in what mood she would be listening was not so certain, considering everything that had happened. Cadfael hoped and thought his prayers towards her in resigned humility, but always in good north Welsh, the Welsh of Gwynedd. She might be indignant: she would still be just.

When he rose from his knees, helping himself up by the rim of her altar, newly draped in celebration of her return, and expectation of her continued residence, he did not at once leave her. The quiet here was at once grateful and ominous, like the hush before battle. And the Gospels, not the great illuminated book, but a smaller and stouter one, calculated to resist too crafty fingers by its less use and lighter pages, already lay on the silver-chased reliquary, centrally placed with accurate and reverent precision. He let his hand rest on it, and summed up all his prayers for guidance and enlightenment into the touch of his fingers, and suddenly he was resolved to open it. Girl, now show me my way, for I have a child to care for. A liar and a thief and a rogue, but what this world has made him, and sweet as he can be false. And not a murderer, whatever else you may know him to be. I doubt he ever harmed a soul in his

168

twenty or so years. Say me a word, one enlightening word, to let him out of this cage.

The book of the fates was already there before him. Almost without conscious thought he laid both hands upon it, raised it, and opened it. He closed his eyes as he set it down on its place, flattening it open under his left hand. and laid the index finger of his right hand upon the exposed page.

Aware abruptly of what he had done, he held very still, not shifting a finger, above all not that index finger, as he opened his eyes. and looked where it pointed.

He was in the Apostle Matthew, Chapter 10, and the fervent finger, pressing so hard it dimpled the leaf, rested on Verse 21.

Cadfael had learned his Latin late, but this was simple enough:

'   and the brother shall deliver up the brother to death.'

He stood gazing at the words, and at first they made no sense to him, apart from the ominous mention of death, and death of intent, not the quiet closing of a life like Donata's passing. The brother shall deliver up the brother to death   It was a part of the prophecy of disintegration and chaos to be expected in the latter days; within that context it was but one detail in a large picture, but here it was all, it was an answer. To one long years a member of a brotherhood the wording was significant. Not a stranger, not an enemy, but a brother betraying a brother.

And suddenly he was visited by a brief vision of a young man hurrying down a narrow woodland path on a dark night, in drizzling rain, a dun-coloured cloak on him. its hood drawn close over his head. The shape passed by. and was no more than a shape, dimly descried under the faint tempering of the darkness the thread of sky made between the trees: but the shape was familiar, a hooded man shrouded in voluminous cloth. Or a cowled man in a black habit? In such conditions, where would the difference be?

It was as if a door had opened before him into a dim but positive light. A brother delivered to death . . . How if that were true, how if another victim had been intended, not Aldhelm? No one but Tutilo had had known cause to fear Aldhelm's witness, and Tutilo, though abroad from the enclave that night, firmly denied any attack upon the young man, and small points were emerging to bear out his testimony. And Tutilo was indeed a brother, and at large that night, and expected to be upon that path. And in build, and in age, yes, striding along to get out of the rain the sooner, he might well be close enough to the shape Aldhelm would present, to an assassin waiting.

A brother delivered up to death indeed, if another man had not taken that road before him. But what of the other, that one who had planned the death? If the meaning of this oracle was as it seemed, the word 'brother' had surely a double monastic significance. A brother of this house, or at least of the Benedictine Order. Cadfael knew of none besides Tutilo who had been out of the enclave that night, but a man intending such a deed would hardly publish his intent or let anyone know of his absence. Someone within the Order who hated Tutilo enough to attempt his murder? Prior Robert might not have been very greatly grieved if Tutilo had been made to pay for his outrageous offence with his skin, but Prior Robert had been at dinner with the abbot and several other witnesses that night, and in any case could hardly be imagined as lurking in wet woods to strike down the delinquent with his own elegant hands. Herluin might hold it against the boy that he had disgraced Ramsey not so much by attempting theft, but by making a botch of it, but Herluin had also been of the abbot's party. And yet the oracle had lodged in Cadfael's mind like a thorn from the blackthorn bushes, and would not be dislodged.

He went to his stall with the words echoing and re-echoing in his inward ear: 'and the brother shall deliver up the brother to death'. It took all his willpower and concentration to banish the sound of it, and fix heart and soul on the celebration of the Mass.

Chapter Nine

T THE end of Mass, when the children had been dismissed to their schooling with Brother Paul, and only the choir monks were left as awed witnesses, Abbot Radulfus offered a brief and practical prayer for divine guidance, and approached Saint Winifred's altar.

'With respect,' said Earl Robert, standing courteously aloof, and in the mildest and most reasonable of voices, 'how should we determine who should be first to try the fates? Is there some rule we ought to follow?'

'We are here to ask,' said the abbot simply. 'Let us ask from beginning to end, from contention to resolution, and advance no plea or reservation of our own. We agreed. Keep to that. Of the order of procedure I will ask, and beyond that I leave Shrewsbury's cause to Prior Robert, who made the journey to Wales to find Saint Winifred, and brought her relics here. If any one of you has anything to object, name whom you will. Father Boniface would not refuse to do us this service, if you require it.'

No one had any observation to make, until Robert Bossu took it upon himself, very amiably, to give voice to a consent otherwise expressed in silence. 'Father Abbot, do you proceed, and we are all content.'

Radulfus mounted the three shallow steps, and with both hands opened the Gospels, his eyes fixed above, upon the cross, so that he might not calculate where, on the exposed page, his finger should rest.

'Come close,' he said, 'and confirm for yourselves that there is no deceit. See the words, that what I read aloud to you is what the *sortes* have sent me.'

Herluin without hesitation came hungrily to peer. Earl Robert stood tranquilly where he was, and bowed away the necessity for any such confirmation.

Abbot Radulfus looked down to where his index finger rested, and reported without emotion: 'I am in the Gospel of Saint Matthew, the twentieth chapter. And the line reads: "The last shall be first, and the first last." '

No arguing with that, thought Cadfael, looking on with some anxiety from his retired place. If anything, it was rather suspicious that the first assay should produce an answer so apt; the prognostics of bishops were often known to be ambiguous in the extreme. Had this been anyone but Radulfus testing the waters, Radulfus in his inflexible uprightness, a man might almost have suspected . . . But that was to limit or doubt the range of the saint's power. She who could call a lame youth to her and support him with her invisible grace while he laid down his crutches on the steps of her altar, why doubt that she could turn the leaves of a Gospel, and guide a faithful finger to the words her will required?

'It would seem,' said Earl Robert, after a moment of courteous silence in deference to any other who might wish to speak, 'that as the last comer, this verdict sends me first into the lists. Is that your reading, Father?'

'The meaning seems plain enough,' said Radulfus; carefully he closed the Gospels, aligned the book scrupulously central upon the reliquary, and descended the steps to stand well aside. 'Proceed, my lord.'

'God and Saint Winifred dispose!' said the earl, and mounted without haste, to stand for a moment motionless, before turning the book, with slow, hieratic gestures that could be clearly seen by all, upon its spine between his long, muscular hands, thumbs meeting to part the pages. Opening it fully, he flattened both palms for a moment upon the chosen pages, and then let his finger hover a moment again before touching. He had neither glanced down nor passed a fingertip over the edges of the leaves, to determine how far advanced in the book his page might be. There are ways of trying to manipulate even the *sortes Biblicae*, but he had meticulously and demonstratively avoided them. He never was in earnest, Cadfael reflected with certainty, and it would spoil his sport to use contrivance. His interest is in pricking Prior Robert and Sub-Prior Herluin into bristling at each other with wattles glowing scarlet and throats gobbling rage.

The earl read aloud, translating into the vernacular as fluently as any cleric: ' "Ye shall seek me, and shall not find me; and where I am, thither ye cannot come." ' He looked up, musing. 'It is John, the seventh chapter and the fifty-fourth verse. Father Abbot, here is a strange saying, for she came to me when I was not seeking her at all, when I knew nothing of her. It was she found me. And here surely is a hard riddle to read, that where she is I cannot come, for here indeed she is, and here am I beside her. How do you decypher this?'

Cadfael could have told him, but kept his mouth very

174

firmly closed, though it would have been interesting to answer the query, and hear how this subtle man would respond. It was even tempting, for here was a man who would have appreciated every irony. Robert Bossu had pursued the dispute here to Shrewsbury in search of diversion in a time of frustration and inaction, a pity he must be denied the best of the joke that was so much more than merely a joke. That would still have to be shared only with Hugh, who knew the best and the worst of his friend Cadfael. No, there was one more who knew everything. Surely Saint Winifred sometimes remembered and smiled, in her tranquil sleep in Gwytherin, even laughed when she roused to extend the sunrays of her grace to lift up a lame boy here in Shrewsbury.

And in a way this answer, like the first, was astonishingly appropriate, brandishing a secret truth and a paradox before a man who would have appreciated it to the full, but could not be let into the secret. If his will was to tantalize and bewilder, why should not she take her own gentle revenge?

'I am in the same case as you,' said the abbot, and smiled. 'I listen and labour to understand. It may be that we must wait until all has been answered before hoping for enlightenment. Shall we proceed, and wait for revelation?'

'Willingly!' said the earl, and turned to descend the three steps, the skirts of his crimson surcoat swirling around him. From this angle, stepping down with the altar candles behind him, his high shoulder and the bulge behind it scarcely broke the symmetry of a body beautifully compact and admirably handled. He withdrew at once to a gracious distance, not to disturb in any way the privacy and composure of the next contender, and his two young squires, well trained to be

175

equally unobtrusive in attendance, drew in silently at either shoulder.

If he plays games to while away the tedious time, thought Cadfael, he plays them by noble rules, even those he makes up as he goes. Hugh liked him from the first; and so do I like him, I like him very well. And it entered his mind uninvited to wonder about the strangeness of human relationships. What has such a man as this, he marvelled, to do with our loud, head-long, candid Stephen, who charges at events like a stamping bull? For that matter, now that I see them for this moment so clearly, what has Hugh to do with the king, either? Must not all such thinking souls be grow-ing hideously weary with this long contention that makes no progress, that wastes men and harvests and the very wellbeing of the land? Weary not only with Stephen, but also, perhaps even more, with this lady who sinks her teeth into empire and will not let go. Somewhere there must be an inheritor of more prom-ise, a hint before sunrise of a sun fit to disperse doubts like morning mists, and dazzle out of our vision both king and empress, with all the confusion, chaos and waste they have visited upon this land.

'Father Herluin,' said Radulfus, 'will you assay?'

Herluin advanced upon the altar very slowly, as though these few paces, and the climbing of the three steps, must be utilized to the full for prayer, and pas-sionate concentration on this single effort which would make or break for him a dear ambition. In his long, pale lantern face his eyes burned darkly, like half-consumed embers. For all his eagerness, when he came to the testing time he hesitated to touch, and two or three times poised his hands over the book, only to withdraw them again from contact. An interesting study, this, of the varying techniques with which different men approached the moment of truth. Robert Bossu had stood the book briskly on edge between his flattened palms, parted the leaves with both thumbs, opened them fully, and poised a finger wherever chance guided it. Herluin, when finally he did touch, touched as if the vellum might burn him, timidly and convulsively, and even when he had the book open, for better or worse, agonized a few moments over where to choose on the page, shifting from recto to verso and back again before settling. Once committed, he drew breath hard, and stooped nearsightedly to see what fate had granted him. And swallowed, and was silent.

'Read!' Radulfus prompted him delicately.

There was no help for it. His voice grated, but he spoke out clearly, perhaps even a little louder than was natural because it cost him such an effort to get it out at all. 'It is the thirteenth chapter of Luke, the twenty-seventh verse. "I tell you, I know you not, whence you came. Depart from me, ye workers of iniquity . . ." ' He lifted his head, his face grey with outrage, and firmly closed the book before he looked round at all the carefully respectful countenances ringing him round like the pales of a fence, a barrier through which he found the only dignified way, at someone else's expense. 'I have been shamefully beguiled and deceived. She shows me my fault, that ever I trusted a liar and thief. It was not with her will, not at her command, that Brother Tutilo – dare I even call him Brother still? – stole her away, and worse, in the blackness of his offence brought another innocent soul into sin, if not to his death. His crime is blasphemy no less than theft, for from the beginning he lied impiously, saying he had his revelation from the saint, and he has covered his offence ever since with lie after lie. Now she has clearly given me to know his villainy, and

177

shown that all this wandering since her abduction she has indeed herself devised, to return to this place from which she was taken. Father Abbot, I withdraw with grief and humility. Such pity as she well may have felt for Ramsey in its distress, he has traduced and despoiled, and here we have no rights. I acknowledge it with tears, and pray her pardon!'

For himself! Certainly not for that hapless lad sleeping in a narrow stone cell at this moment. Small pardon there would be for him if Herluin had his way. Every pang of this humiliation would be visited upon Tutilo, as every particle of guilt was being visited upon him now, the more successfully to extricate Herluin, innocent and devout, only wickedly deceived, with nothing to repent but his too profound faith.

'Wait!' said Abbot Radulfus. 'Make no judgements yet. It is possible to deceive oneself, no less than others. In the first anger no man should be condemned. And the saint has not yet spoken to us of Shrewsbury.'

Only too true, reflected Cadfael, for she may well have some strictures to level at us, no less than at Ramsey. How if she chooses this moment and this audience to make it known that she visits us only out of pure charity, that what lies in her handsome reliquary is in reality the body of the young man who committed murder to secure her for Shrewsbury, and himself died by accident, in circumstances that made it vital he should vanish? A worse offence than Tutilo committed in a similar cause, to win her for Ramsey. In laying her reverently back in the grave from which he had taken her, and sealing the murderer in her abandoned coffin, Cadfael had been and still was convinced that he did her will, and restored her to the resting-place she desired. But was it not possible that Tutilo had believed just as sincerely?

The one venture the saint had just condemned. Now to put the other to the test! Lucky for Prior Robert that this moment at least he approached in absolute innocence. But I, thought Cadfael, on thorns, may be about to pay in full for all my sins.

Well, it was fair!

Prior Robert may have had some qualms concerning his own worthiness, though that was a weakness to which he seldom succumbed. He ascended the steps of the altar very solemnly, and joined his hands before his face for a final convulsive moment of prayer, his eyes closed. Indeed, he kept them closed as he opened the Gospels, and planted his long index finger blindly upon the page. By the length of the pause that followed, before he opened his eyes and looked dazedly down to see what fate had granted him, he went in some devout fear of his deserving. Who would ever have expected the pillar of the house to shake?

The balance was instantly restored. Robert erected his impressive silvery head, and a wave of triumphant colour swept up from his long throat and flushed his cheeks. In a voice hesitant between exultation and awe he read out: 'Saint John, the fifteenth chapter and the sixteenth verse: "Ye have not chosen me, but I have chosen you." '

All round the assembly of brothers waiting and watching with held breath, the great shudder and sigh passed like a gust of wind, or the surging of a wave up the shore, and then, like the shattering of the wave in spray, disintegrated into a whispering, stirring murmur as they shifted, nudged one another, shook with relief and a suggestion of hysterical emotion between laughter and tears. Abbot Radulfus stiffened instantly into rigid authority, and lifted a sobering hand to still the incipient storm.

'Silence! Respect this holy place, and abide all fates with composure, as mankind should. Father Prior, come down to us now. All that was needful has been done.'

Prior Robert was still so blind that he almost stumbled on the steps, but recovered himself with aristocratic dignity and by the time he reached the tiles of the floor was his complacent official self again. Whether the experience of religious dread had left any permanent effect would have to be left to the test of time. Cadfael thought, probably not. It had left at any rate a forcible temporary effect upon his own more cautious but equally human complacency. For a while he would be treading very softly, for awe of this little Welsh saint's indignation and forbearance.

'Father,' said Prior Robert, his voice again all measured and mellifluous resonance, 'I have delivered faithfully the lot committed to me. Now these fates can be interpreted.'

Oh, yes, he was himself again, he would be trailing this glory after him for as long as it still shed lustre. But at least for those few moments he had shown as human, like other men. No one who had seen would quite forget it.

'Father Abbot,' said the earl handsomely, 'I withdraw all claim. I surrender even the question as to how I can be standing here in her virgin company, and still be told that where she is I may never come. Though I confess there is probably a story there that I should very much like to hear.' Yes, he was very quick, as Cadfael had realized, paradox was pleasure to him. 'The field is yours, out and out,' said Robert Bossu heartily. 'Clearly this blessed lady has brought herself home again without aid from me or anyone. I give you joy of her! And I would not for the world meddle with

180

her plans, though I am proud that she has consented on the way to visit me for a while. With your leave, I will make an offering by way of acknowledgement.'

'I think,' said Radulfus, 'that Saint Winifred might be pleased if you think fit to make your offering, in her honour, to the abbey of Ramsey. We are all brothers of one Order. And even if she has been put out by human errors and offences, I am sure she will not hold that against a brother-house in distress.'

They were both of them talking in these high and ceremonious terms, Cadfael suspected, in order to smooth away the first sore moments, and give Sub-Prior Herluin time to master his chagrin, and achieve a graceful retreat. He had swallowed the worst of his gall, although with a gulp that almost choked him. He was capable of acknowledging defeat with decent civility. But nothing, nothing would soften his mind now against that hapless youngster held safely under lock and key to await his penance.

'I feel shame,' said Herluin tightly, 'for myself and for my abbey, that we have nourished and sheltered and trusted in a very false aspirant to brotherhood. My abbey I dare excuse. Myself I cannot. Surely I should have been better armed against the deceits of the devil. Blind and foolish I confess myself, but I never willed evil against this house, and I abase myself in acknowledgement of the wrong done, and ask forgiveness. His lordship of Leicester has spoken also for me. The field is yours, Father Abbot. Receive all its honour and all its spoils.'

There are ways of abasing oneself – though Prior Robert would perhaps have managed them with better grace had things gone otherwise! – as a means of exalting oneself. Those two were well matched, though Robert, being somewhat more nobly born, had the more complete mastery, and perhaps rather less burning malice when bested.

'If all are content,' said Radulfus, finding these exchanges growing not merely burdensome, but long-winded, 'I would desire to close this assembly with prayer, and so disperse.'

They were still on their knees after the last Amen, when a sudden gust of wind arose, blowing past the nave altar and into the choir, as though from the south door, though there had been no sound of the latch lifting or the door creaking. Everyone felt it, and the air being still pregnant with prophecy and contention, everyone started and pricked attentive ears, and several opened their eyes to look round towards the source of this abrupt wind from the outer world. Brother Rhun, Saint Winifred's devoted cavalier, turned his beautiful head instantly to look towards her altar, his first jealous care being always for her service and worship. High and clear through the silence he cried aloud: 'Father, look to the altar! The pages of the Gospels are turning!'

Prior Robert, descending from his high place still blinded, with his triumph swirling about him in clouds of glory, had left the Gospels open where his victory had been written, Saint John, the last of the evangelists, far on in the volume. All eyes opened now to stare, and indeed the pages of the book were turning back, slowly, hesitantly, lingering erect only to slide onward, sometimes a single leaf, sometimes a stronger breath riffling several over together, almost as though fingers lifted and guided them, even fluttered them past in haste. The Gospels were turning back, out of John into Luke, out of Luke into Mark . . . and beyond . They were all watching in fascination, hardly noticing, hardly understanding, that the abrupt wind from the south door had fallen into total stillness, and still, leaf by leaf now and slowly and deliberately, the leaves kept turning. They rose, they hung almost still, and gradually they declined and were flattened into the bulk of the later books of the Evangel.

For by now they must be in Matthew. And now the pace slowed, leaf by leaf rose, quivered erect, and slowly descended. The last to turn settled lightly, not quite flat to its fellows, but then lay still, not a breath left of the wind that had fluttered the pages.

For some moments no one stirred. Then Abbot Radulfus rose and went to the altar. What spontaneous air had written must be of more than natural significance. He did not touch, but stood looking down at the page.

'Come, some of you. Let there be witnesses more than myself.'

Prior Robert was at the foot of the steps in a moment, tall enough to see and read without mounting. Cadfael came close on the other side. Herluin held off, too deeply sunk in his own turmoil of mind to be much concerned about further wonders, but the earl drew close in candid curiosity, craning to see the spread pages. On the left side the leaf rose a little, gently swaying from its own tensions, for there was now no breath of wind. The righthand page lay still, and in the spine a few white petals lay, and a single hard bud of blackthorn, the white blossom just breaking out of the dark husk.

'I have not touched,' said Radulfus, 'for this is no asking of mine or any here. I take the omen as grace. And I accept this bud as the finger of truth thus manifested. It points me to the verse numbered twenty-one, and the line is: "And the brother shall deliver up the brother to death." '

*

There was a long, awed silence. Prior Robert put out a reverent hand to touch the tiny drift of loose petals, and the one bursting bud that had lodged in the spine.

'Father Abbot, you were not with us in Gwytherin, or you would recognize this wonder. When the blessed saint visited us in the church there, as before in vision, she came with showers of may-blossom. The season is not yet ripe for the hawthorn flowers, but these these she sends in their place, again the whiteness of her purity. It is a direct sign from Saint Winifred. What she confides to us we are bound by our office to heed.'

A stir and a murmur passed round the watching brothers, and softly they drew in more closely about the wonder. Somewhere among them someone drew breath sharp and painful as a sob, hurriedly suppressed.

'It is a matter of interpretation,' said Radulfus gravely. 'How are we to understand such an oracle?'

'It speaks of death,' said the earl practically. 'And there has been a death. The threat of it, as I understand, hangs over a young man of your Order. The shadow over all. This oracle speaks of a brother as the instrument of death, which fits with the case as it is yet known. But it speaks also of a brother as the victim. The victim was not a brother. How is this to be understood?'

'If she has indeed pointed the way,' said the abbot firmly, 'we cannot but follow it. "Brother" she says, and if we believe her word, a brother it was whose death was planned by a brother. The meaning that word has within these walls the saint knows as well as we. If any man among you has a thought to share upon this most urgent matter, speak now.'

Into the uneasy silence, while brother looked most earnestly at brother, and wondered, and sought or evaded the eyes of his neighbours, Brother Cadfael said: 'Brother Abbot, I have thoughts to share that never visited me until this morning, but are become very relevant now. The night of this murder was dark, not only as to the hour, but also the weather, for cloud was low, and there was a drizzling rain. The place where Aldhelm's body was found is within close woodland, untended, on a narrow path, where the only light would come from the open sky above the track. Enough to show a shape, an outline, to a man waiting, and with eyes accustomed to the dark. And the shape Aldhelm would present was that of a man young by his step and pace, in a dun-coloured cloak wrapped about him against the rain, and with the pointed hood drawn up over his head. Father, how is that to be distinguished, in such conditions, from a Benedictine brother in dark habit and cowl, if he be young and stepping out briskly to get out of the rain?'

'If I read you rightly,' said Radulfus, having searched Cadfael's face, and found it in very grave earnest, 'you are saying that the young man was attacked in mistake for a Benedictine brother.'

'It accords with what is written here in the fates,' said Cadfael.

'And with the night's obscurity, I grant you. Are you further suggesting that the intended quarry was Brother Tutilo? That he was not the hunter, but the hunted?'

'Father, that thought is in my mind. In build and years the two matched well enough. And as all men know, he was out of the enclave that night, with leave, though leave he got by deceit. It was known on what path he would be returning – or at least, according to what he had led us all to believe. And, Father, be it admitted, he had done much to raise up enemies to himself in this house.'

'Brother turning upon brother . . .' said the abbot

heavily. 'Well, we are fallible men like the rest of mankind, and hatred and evil are not out of our scope. But, then, how to account for this second and deadly brother? There was no other out of the enclave upon any errand that night.'

'None that we know of. But it is not difficult,' said Cadfael, 'to become unnoticed for a while. There are ways in and out for any who are determined to pass.'

The abbot met his eyes without a smile; he was always in command of his countenance. For all that, there was not much that went on in this household that Radulfus did not know. There had been times when Cadfael had both departed and returned by night, without passing the gatehouse, on urgent matters in which he found justification for absence. Of the instruments of good works listed in the Rule of Saint Benedict, second only to the love of God came the love of mankind, and Cadfael reverenced the Rule above the detailed and meticulous rules.

'No doubt you speak out of long experience,' said the abbot. 'Certainly that is true. However, we know of no such defector on that night. Unless you have knowledge that I have not?'

'No, Father, I have none.'

'If I may venture,' said Earl Robert deprecatingly, 'why should not the oracle that has spoken of two brothers be asked to send us a further sign? We are surely required to follow this trail as best we can. A name might be too much to ask, but there are other ways, as this blessed lady has shown us, of making all things plain.'

Gradually, almost stealthily, all the brothers had crept out of their stalls, and gathered in a circle about this altar and the group debating at its foot. They did not draw too close, but hovered within earshot of all that was said. And somewhere among them, not readily to be located, there was a centre of desperate but controlled unease, a disquiet that caused the air within the choir to quake, with a rapid vibration of disquiet and dread, like a heartbeat driven into the fluttering panic of a bird's wings. Cadfael felt it, but thought it no more than the tension of the *sortes*. And that was enough. He himself was beginning to ache as though stretched on the rack, with the worst still to come. It was high time to end this, and release all these overcharged souls into the moist, chilly, healing air of early March.

'If in some sort the brothers all stand accused by this present word,' said Earl Robert helpfully, 'it is they, the humbler children of the household, who have the best right to ask for a name. If you see fit, Father Abbot, let one of them appeal for a judgement. How else can all the rest be vindicated? Justice is surely due to the innocent, by even stronger right than retribution to the guilty.'

If he was still amusing himself, thought Cadfael, he was doing it with the eloquent dignity of archbishops and all the king's judges. In jest or earnest, such a man would not wish to leave this human and more than human mystery unresolved. He would thrust and persuade it as far as he could towards an ending. And he had a willing listener in Prior Robert, his namesake. Now that the prior was assured of retaining his saint, together with all the lustre accruing to him as her discoverer and translator, he wanted everything tidied up and ended, and these troublesome visitors from Ramsey off his premises, before they contrived some further mischief.

'Father,' he said insinuatingly, 'that is fair and just. May we do so?'

'Very well,' said Radulfus. 'In your hands!'

187

The prior turned to cast a sweeping glance over the silent array of monks, watching him wide-eyed in anticipation and awe. The name he called was the inevitable name. He even frowned at having to look for his acolyte.

'Brother Jerome, I bid you undertake this testing on behalf of all. Come forth and make this assay.'

And indeed, where was Brother Jerome, and why had no word been heard from him and nothing seen of him all this time? When, until now, had he ever been far from the skirts of Prior Robert's habit, attendant with ready flattery and obsequious assent to every word that fell from his patron's lips. Now that Cadfael came to think of it, less than usual had been seen and heard of Jerome for the past few days, ever since the evening when he had been discovered on his bed, quaking and sick with belly-aches and headaches, and been soothed to sleep by Cadfael's stomachics and syrups.

A furtive swirl of movement troubled the rear ranks of the assembled household, and cast up Brother Jerome from his unaccustomed retirement, emerging through the ranks without eagerness, almost reluctantly. He shuffled forward with bent head and arms folded tightly about his body as if he felt a mortal chill enclosing him. His face was greyish and pinched, his eyes, when he raised them, inflamed. He looked ill and wizened. I should have made a point of following up his sickness, thought Cadfael, touched, but I thought he, of all people, would make good sure he got all the treatment he needed.

That was all that he had in mind, as Prior Robert, bewildered and displeased by what seemed to him very grudging acceptance of a duty that should have conveyed honour upon the recipient, waved Jerome imperiously to the altar.

188

'Come, we are waiting. Open prayerfully.'

The abbot had gently brushed the petals of black-thorn from the spine, and closed the Gospels. He stood aside to make way for Jerome to mount.

Jerome crept to the foot of the steps, and there halted, baulked, rather, like a startled horse, drew hard breath and assayed to mount, and then suddenly threw up his arms to cover his face, fell on his knees with a lamentable, choking cry, and bowed himself against the stone of the steps. From under the hunched shoulders and clutching arms a broken voice emerged in a stammering howl a stray dog might have launched into the night after company in its loneliness.

'I dare not . . . I dare not . . . She would strike me dead if I dared . . . No need, I submit myself, I own my terrible sin! I went out after the thief, I waited for him to return, and God pity me, I killed that innocent man!'

Chapter Ten

N THE horrified hush that followed, Prior Robert, guiding hand still uplifted and stricken motionless, was momentarily turned to stone, his face a mask of utter incredulity. That a creature of his should fall into mortal sin, and that of a violent kind, was astonishment enough, but that this pliable mortal should ever undertake personal action of any kind came as an even greater shock. And so it did to Brother Cadfael, though for him it was equally a shock of enlightenment. This poor soul, pallid and puffy on his bed after desperate vomiting, sick and quiet and unregarded ever since, spent and ulcered mind and spirit by what he had so mistakenly undertaken, Jerome was for the first time wholly pitiful.

Brother Rhun, youngest and freshest and the flower of the flock, went after his nature, asking no leave, and kneeled beside Jerome, circling his quaking shoulders with an embracing arm, and lifting the hapless penitent closer into his hold before he looked up confidently into the abbot's face.

'Father, whatever else, he is ill. Suffer me to stay!'

'Do after your kind,' said Radulfus, looking down at the pair with a face almost as blanched as the prior's, 'and so must I. Jerome,' he said, with absolute and steely authority, 'look up and face me.'

Too late now to withdraw this confession into privacy, even had that been the abbot's inclination, for it had been spoken out before all the brothers, and as members of a body they had the right to share in the cure of all that here was curable. They stood their ground, mute and attentive, though they came no nearer. The half-circle had spread almost into a circle.

Jerome had listened, and was a little calmed by the tone. The voice of command roused him to make an effort. He had shed the first and worst load, and as soon as he lifted his head and made to rise on his knees, Rhun's arm lifted and sustained him. A distorted face appeared, and gradually congealed into human lineaments. 'Father, I obey,' said Jerome. 'I want confession. I want penance. I have sinned most grievously.'

'Penance in confession,' said the abbot, 'is the beginning of wisdom. Whatever grace can do, it cannot follow denial. Tell us what it is you did, and how it befell.'

The lame recital went on for some time, while Jerome, piteously small and shrunken and wretched, knelt in Rhun's supple, generous arm, with that radiant, silent face beside him, to point searing differences. The scope of humanity is terrifyingly wide.

'Father, when it became known that Saint Winifred's relics had been loaded with the timber for Ramsey, when there was no longer any doubt of how it came there – for we knew, every man of us, that there was none, for who else could it have been? – then I was burning with anger against the thief who had dared such sacrilege against her, and such a gross offence against our house. And when I heard that he had asked and been given leave to go forth to Longner that night, I feared he meant to escape us, either by absence, or even by flight, having seen justice might overtake him yet. I could not bear it that he should go free. I confess it, I hated him! But, Father, I never meant to kill, when I slipped out alone, and went to wait for him on the path by which I knew he must return. I never intended violence. I hardly know what I meant to do – confront him, accuse him, bring it home to him that hellfire awaited him at the reckoning if he did not confess his sin and pay the price of it now.'

He paused to draw painful breath, and the abbot asked: 'You went empty-handed?' A pertinent question, though Jerome in his throes failed to understand it.

'Surely, Father! What should I want to take with me?'

'No matter! Go on.'

'Father, what more can there be? I thought, when I heard him coming down through the bushes, it could be no one but Tutilo. I never knew by what road the other man would come; for all I knew he had already been, and gone again, and all in vain, as the thief intended. And this one – So jauntily he came, striding along in the dark, whistling profane songs. Offence piled upon offence, so lightly to take everything mortal   I could not endure it. I picked up a fallen branch, and as he passed I struck him on the head. I struck him down,' moaned Jerome, 'and he fell across the path, and the cowl fell back from his head. He never moved hand again! I went close, I knelt, and I saw his face then.

192

Even in the dark I saw enough. This was not my enemy, not the saint's enemy, not the thief! And I had killed him! I fled him then . . . Sick and shaking, I fled him and hid myself, but every moment since he has pursued me. I confess my grievous sin, I repent it bitterly, I lament the day and the hour ever I raised hand against an innocent man. But I am his murderer!'

He bowed himself forward into his arms and hid his face. Muted sounds emerged between his tearing sobs, but no more articulate words. And Cadfael, who had opened his mouth to continue the story where this miserable avenger had left it, as quickly closed his lips again upon silence. Jerome had surely told all he knew, and if the burden he was carrying was even more than his due, yet he could be left to carry it a while longer. 'Brother shall deliver up brother to death' could be said to be true of Jerome, for if he had not killed he had indeed delivered Aldhelm to his death. But if what had followed was also the work of a brother, then the murderer might be present here. Let well alone! Let him go away content, satisfied that this solution offered in terrible good faith by Jerome had been accepted without question by all, and that he himself was quite secure. Men who believe themselves out of all danger may grow careless, and make some foolish move that can betray them. In private, yes, for the abbot's ear alone, truth must be told. Jerome had done foully, but not so foully as he himself and all here believed. Let him pay his dues in full, but not for someone else's colder, viler crime.

'This is a very sombre and terrible avowal,' said Abbot Radulfus, slowly and heavily, 'not easily to be understood or assessed, impossible, alas, to remedy. I require, and surely so do all here, time for much prayer and most earnest thought, before I can begin to do right

193

or justice as due. Moreover, this is a matter outside my writ, for it is murder, and the king's justice has the right to knowledge, if not immediately to possession, of the person of a confessed murderer.'

Jerome was past all resistance, whatever might have been urged or practised against him. Emptied and drained, he submitted to all. The disquiet and consternation he had set up among the brothers would go on echoing and re-echoing for some time, while he who had caused it had recoiled into numbness and exhaustion.

'Father,' he said meekly, 'I welcome whatever penance may be laid upon me. I want no light absolution. My will is to pay in full for all my sins.'

Of his extreme misery at this moment there could be no doubt. When Rhun in his kindness lent an arm to raise him from his knees, he hung heavily still, clinging to his desperate humility.

'Father, let me go from here. Let me be desolate and hidden from men's eyes . . .'

'Solitude you shall have,' said the abbot, 'but I forbid despair. It is too soon for counsel or judgement, but never too soon or too late for prayer, if penitence is truly felt.' And to the prior he said, without taking his eyes from the broken creature on the tiles of the floor, like a crushed and crumpled bird: 'Take him in charge. See him lodged. And now go, all of you, take comfort and pursue your duties. At all times, in all circumstances, our vows are still binding.'

Prior Robert, still stonily silent and shocked out of his normal studied dignity, led away his shattered clerk to the second of the two penitentiary cells; and it was the first time, as far as Cadfael could recall, that the two had ever been occupied at the same time. Sub-Prior

Richard, decent, comfortable, placid man, marshalled the other ranks out to their ordinary labours, and to the refectory shortly afterwards for dinner, and by his own mildly stupid calm had calmed his flock into a perfectly normal appetite by the time they went to wash their hands before the meal.

Herluin had sensibly refrained from playing any part in the affair, once it turned towards the partial restoration of Ramsey's credit and the grievous embarrassment of Shrewsbury. He would welcome the earl's promised offering gladly, and withdraw in good order to his own monastery, though what he would visit on Tutilo when he got him safely back there might be dreadful to think of. He was not a man to forget and forgive.

As for the withdrawal from the battlefield of Robert Bossu, that restless, conscientious, subtle and efficient man, it was a model of consideration and tact, as always, with a quiet word to Abbot Radulfus, and a sharp glance at his two squires, who understood him at the lift of an eyebrow or the flash of a smile. He knew when to make use of his status, and when and how to temper its brilliance and make himself unobtrusive among a multitude.

Brother Cadfael waited his opportunity to draw close to the abbot's shoulder as he left the choir.

'Father, a word! There is more to be added to this story, though not publicly, perhaps, not yet.'

'He has not lied, as well as murdered?' said the abbot, without turning his head. His voice was grim, but pitched no further than Cadfael's ear.

'Neither the one nor the other, Father, if what I believe is true. He has told all he knows, and all he thinks he knows, and I am sure he has kept nothing back. But there are things he does not know, and the knowledge will somewhat better a case which even so is still black enough. Give me audience alone, and then judge what should be done.'

Radulfus had halted in mid-stride, though still not looking round. He watched the last of the brothers slip away still awed and silent through the cloister, and followed with a glance the swirl of Robert Bossu's crimson skirts as he crossed the court with his two attendants at his heels.

'You say we have as yet only heard the half – and the worse half of all that is to be told? The young man is coffined decently, his own priest takes him hence today to Upton, for burial among his people. I would not wish to delay his departure.'

'There is no need,' said Cadfael. 'He has told me all he had to tell. I would not for the world keep him from his rest. But what I have to add, though I had the proofs of it from his body, and from the place where he was found, I have but now understood clearly. All that I saw was seen also by Hugh Beringar, but after what has come to light this morning these details fall into place.'

'In that case,' said Radulfus, after some thought, 'before we go further, I think Hugh should join us. I need his counsel, as he may need yours and mine both. The thing happened beyond our walls, and is not within my jurisdiction, though the offender may be. Church and State must respect and assist each other, even in these fractured and sorry times. For if we are two, justice should be one. Cadfael, will you go into the town, and ask Hugh to come into conference here this afternoon? Then we will hear all that you may have to tell.'

'Very willingly I will go,' said Cadfael.

*

'And how,' demanded Hugh over his midday table, 'are we to take this chapter of wonders you've been unfolding this morning? Am I to believe in it, that every response should come so neatly, as if you had been through the Gospels and marked all the places to trap each enquirer? Are you sure you did not?'

Cadfael shook his head decisively. 'I do not meddle with my saint. I played fair, and so, I swear, did they all, for there was no mark, no leaf notched for a guide, when I handled the book before any other came near. I opened it, and I got my answer, and it set me thinking afresh and seeing clearly where I had formerly been blind. And how to account for it I do not know, unless indeed it was she who spoke.'

'And all the oracles that followed? Ramsey not only rejected but denounced . . . That came a little hard on Herluin, surely! And with Earl Robert the saint condescended to tease him with a paradox! Well, I won't say but that was fair enough, a pity he has not the key he needs to read it, it would give him pleasure. And then, to Shrewsbury – "Ye have not chosen me, but I have chosen you." I take that as a warning rather than an acknowledgement. She chose you, and she can as well abandon you if she chooses, and you had better be on your guard in future, for she won't put up with another such turmoil upsetting her established rule. Meant especially for Prior Robert, I should hazard, who indeed thinks he chose her and ranks as her proprietor. I hope he took the allusion?'

'I doubt it,' said Cadfael. 'He wore it like a halo.'

'And then finally, Cadfael, for the leaves to turn of themselves, and open again at that same place. Too many miracles for one morning!'

'Miracles,' said Cadfael somewhat sententiously, 'may be simply divine manipulation of ordinary circumstances. Why not? For as to the last oracle, the Gospels had been left open, and there was a wind blew through from the south doorway and ruffled the pages over, turning back from John to Matthew. It's true that no one came in, but I think someone must have lifted the latch and set the door ajar, and then after all drawn back and closed it again, hearing the voices within and not wanting to interrupt. No mistake about the wind, everyone felt it. And then, you see, it halted where it did because there were some petals and fragments from the blackthorn I had been handling fallen into the spine there, shaken out of my sleeve or my hair when I closed the book. Such a slight obstruction was not enough to affect the taking of the *sortes*, when they were opening the book with ceremony, both hands parting the leaves and a finger pointing the line. But when the wind turned the leaves, the blackthorn flowers were enough to arrest the movement at that place. Yet even so, dare we call that chance? And now that I come to think back,' said Cadfael, shaking his head between doubt and conviction, 'that wind that blew in was gone before ever the page settled. I watched the last one turn, slowly, halting before it was smoothed down. The air above the altar was quite still. The candles were stark erect, never a tremor.'

Aline had sat throughout this colloquy listening attentively to every word, but contributing none of her own. There was about her something distant and mysterious, Cadfael thought, as if a part of her being was charmed away into some private and pleasant place, even while her blue eyes dwelt upon her husband and his friend with sharp intelligence, following the argument back and forth with a kind of indulgent and amused affection, appropriate to a matriarch watching her children.

'My lady,' said Hugh, catching her eye and breaking into a resigned grin, 'my lady, as usual, is making fun of both of us.'

'No,' said Aline, suddenly serious, 'it is only that the step from perfectly ordinary things into the miraculous seems to me so small, almost accidental, that I wonder why it astonishes you at all, or why you trouble to reason about it. If it were reasonable it could not be miraculous, could it?'

In the abbot's parlour they found not only Radulfus, but Robert of Leicester waiting for them. As soon as the civil greetings were over the earl with his nicely judged courtesy made to withdraw.

'You have business here which is out of my writ and competence, and I would not wish to complicate the affair for you. The lord abbot here has been good enough to admit me to his confidence so far as is appropriate, since I was a witness of what happened this morning, but now you have cause to enquire further, as I understand. I have lost my small claim to the saint,' said Robert Bossu, with a flashing smile and a shrug of his high shoulder, 'and should be about taking my leave here.'

'My lord,' said Hugh heartily, 'the king's peace, such as it is and as we manage to maintain it, is very much your business, and your experience in it is longer than mine. If the lord abbot agrees, I hope you will stay and give us the benefit of your judgement. There's matter to assess concerning murder. Every man's business, having a life to keep or lose.'

'Stay with us!' said Radulfus. 'Hugh is right, we need all the good counsel we can get.'

'And I have as much human curiosity in me as the next man,' owned the earl, and willingly sat down again. 'The abbot tells me there is more to add to what we witnessed here this morning. I take it, sir, you have been informed, as far as the tale yet carries us?'

'Cadfael has told me,' said Hugh, 'how the *sortes* went, and of Brother Jerome's confession. He assures me we both, from what he and I saw on the spot, can go beyond what Jerome himself knows.'

Cadfael settled himself beside Hugh on the cushioned bench against the abbot's dark panelling. Outside the window the light was still full and clear, for the days were drawing out. Spring was not far away when the spiny mounds of blackthorn along the headlands of the fields turned from black to white, like drifts of snow.

'Brother Jerome has told truth, the whole truth as he knows it, but it is not the whole. You saw him, he was in no case and no mind to hold anything back, nor has he done so. Recall, Father, what he said, how he stood and waited. So he did, we found the place, just withdrawn into the bushes by the path, where he had trampled uneasily and flattened the grass. How he snatched up a fallen branch, when the young man came down the path, and struck him with it, and he fell senseless, and the hood fell back from his head. All true, we found – Hugh will bear me out – the branch lying where he had cast it aside. It was partly rotten, and had broken when he struck with it, but it was sound enough and heavy enough to stun. And the body lay as Jerome described, across the path, the hood fallen from his head and face. And Jerome says that on realizing what he had done, and believing that what he had done was murder, he fled, back here into hiding. So he did, and sick indeed he was, for Brother Richard found him grey and shaking on his bed, when he failed to attend at Compline. But he never said word but that he was ill, as plainly he was, and I gave him medicine. In confession now he has spoken of but one blow, and I am convinced he struck but once.'

'Certainly,' said Radulfus, thoughtfully frowning, 'he said no word of any further assault. I do not think he was holding anything back.'

'No, Father, neither do I. He has gone creeping about us like a very sick man since that night, in horror of his own act. Now that one blow is borne out by the examination I made of Aldhelm's head. At the back it was stained with a little blood, and in the rough texture of the wool I found fragments of tinder from the broken branch. The blow to the back of his head might lay him senseless a short while, but certainly had not broken his skull, and could not have killed him. Hugh, what do you say?'

'I say his head would have ached fiercely after it,' said Hugh at once, 'but nothing worse. More, it would not have left him out of his wits above a quarter of an hour at the longest. The worst Jerome could do, perhaps, but not enough to do his quarry much harm.'

'So I say also. And he says he struck, looked close and knew his error, and fled the place. And I believe him.'

'I doubt he had the hardihood left to lie,' said the earl. 'No very bold villain at the best of times, I should judge, and greatly in awe of the Gospel verdict today. Yet he was sure he had killed.'

'He fled in that terror,' said Cadfael, 'and the next he heard was that Tutilo had found the man dead, and so reported him. What else should Jerome think?'

'And in spite of doubts,' the abbot reminded them wryly, 'should not we still be thinking the same? He who had begun so terrible an undertaking, how can we be sure he did not, after all, stay and finish it?'

'We cannot be sure. Not absolutely sure. Not until we are sure of everything, and every detail is in the open. But I think he has told us truly, so far as he knows truth. For what followed was very different. Hugh will remember, and bear out all I have to tell.'

'I remember all too well,' said Hugh.

'A few paces lower down the path we found a pile of stones, long grown in there with mosses and lichens. There is limestone cropping out on the ridge above, and in places it breaks through the thin ground cover even among the trees below. In this heap the upper stone, though it was fitted carefully back into its bed, showed the sealing growths of moss disturbed and broken. Heavy, a double handful when I raised it. On the rough underside there was blood. Quite hidden when the stone was in place, but present. We brought the stone back with us to examine more closely. It was certainly the instrument of death. As Aldhelm's blood was blackening on the stone, so fragments of lichen and stone-dust were embedded in Aldhelm's wounds. His head was crushed, and the stone coldly fitted back into its mound. Unless a man looked close, it appeared undisturbed. In a week or so weather and growth would have sealed up again all the raw edges that betrayed its use. I ask myself, is this something of which Jerome could be capable? To wrench up a heavy stone, batter in the head of a man lying senseless, and then fit the stone coolly back into its former place? I marvel he ever steeled himself to hit hard enough to stun, and to break the branch in the blow, even though it was partly rotted. Remember that he says he then, in his fright at what he had done, went to peer at his victim, and found that he had struck down the wrong man. With Aldhelm he had no quarrel. And recollect, too, that no one had seen him, no one then knew he had ever left the

202

enclave. He did what any timorous man in a panic would do, ran away and hid himself within the community, where he was known and respected, and no one would ever guess he had attempted such a deed.'

'So you are saying plainly,' said Earl Robert, attentive and still, 'that there were two murderers, at least in intent, and this wretched brother, once he knew he had struck down the wrong man, had no reason in the world to wish him further harm.'

'That is what I believe,' said Cadfael.

'And you, my lord sheriff?'

'By all I know of Jerome,' said Hugh, 'that is how I read it.'

'Then, by the same token,' said the earl, 'you are saying that the man who finished the work was one who *did* have cause to want Aldhelm removed from the world, before he ever reached the abbey gatehouse. Not Tutilo, but Aldhelm. This one *did* know his man, and made sure he should never arrive. For the shepherd's hood fell back when he fell. This time there was no mistake made, he was known, and killed not for another, but for himself.'

There was a brief, deep silence, while they looked at one another and weighed possibilities. Then Abbot Radulfus said slowly: 'It is logical. The face was then exposed to view, though Jerome had to kneel and look closely, for the night was dark. But if he could distinguish and recognize, so could the other.'

'There is another point,' said Hugh. 'I doubt if Aldhelm would have lain helpless for more than a quarter of an hour from that blow on the head. Whoever killed him, killed him within that time, for he had not stirred. There was no sign of movement. If his body jerked when he was struck again, and fatally, it was no more than an instant's convulsion. The murderer must have been close. Perhaps he witnessed the first assault. Certainly he was on the spot within a very short time.' And he asked sharply: 'Father, have you released Tutilo?'

'Not yet,' said Radulfus, unsurprised. Hugh's meaning was plain enough. 'Perhaps there should be no haste. You are right to remind us. Tutilo came down that same path and found the dead man. Unless – unless at that time he was still living. Yes, it could still have been Tutilo who finished what Jerome had begun.'

'He told me,' said Hugh, 'as I think he told you, that he did not know in the darkness who the dead man might be. If the murderer had been before him, that would be truth. Even by daylight we could not tell who he was until Cadfael turned up the whole side of his face to the light. He told you, Father Abbot, how he put his hand upon the shattered left side of the dead man's head. All that, everything about him, his bearing, his voice, the cold of horror that was on him, for he shook as he spoke of it, all rang true to me. And yet it may still be true that he came within minutes of Jerome's flight, found the man only stunned, stooped close and knew him, for then knowing was possible, and killed him, and only then took thought how to escape suspicion, and came running into the town, to me.'

'Neither of the pair of them looks a likely case,' said the earl consideringly, 'to crush another man's head with a stone, though there's no saying what any man may do in extremes. But then to have the wit and the cold blood to fit the stone back and cover the traces – that could be out of reach of most of us. Well, you have them both under guard, there's no haste.'

'There is a matter of timing,' said Cadfael. 'You told me, Hugh, what the priest's man of Upton said, how he parted from Aldhelm at Preston, while Aldhelm went on to the ferry.'

'At about six they separated,' Hugh confirmed positively. 'From there, ferry and all, to the place where he was ambushed, would take him at the most half an hour. The ferryman speaks to the same effect. By half past six at the latest he reached the place where he died. If you can show me plainly where Tutilo was until past that hour, we may strike him from the roll and forget him.'

Chapter Eleven

I HAVE not so far had the opportunity,' said Robert Bossu, 'of cultivating your acquaintance. But I must tell you – if you do not already know it, for I think you miss very little, and can see as far through a forest by moonlight as the next man – that the name of Hugh Beringar has not gone unnoted by men of sense. How could it, when the exchequer is in chaos most of the time, and the chancery clerks out of touch with much of the land? How many shires, how many sheriffs, do you suppose, pay their annual farms regularly and on time? Yours is known never to be in default, and your county enjoys at least a kind of peace, a man can hope to travel to the Abbey fair here safely, and your courts manage to keep the roads relatively free of what we modestly call evil customs. Moreover, you contrive to be on amicable terms with Owain Gwynedd, as I know, even if Powys boils over now and again.'

'I study and practise to keep my place,' said Hugh with a grin.

'You study and practise to keep your shire function-
ing as quietly as may be,' said the earl. 'So do all men of
sense, but against the odds.'

They were sitting in the earl's apartment in the guesthall, facing each other across a small table, with wine
passing amiably between them, and a curtained door
closed and shrouded against the world. Robert Bossu
was well served. His squires were prompt to his call,
and soft-footed and neat-handed with flask and glass,
and seemed to go in no awe of him, but rather to take
pride in matching his poise and serenity; but for all
that, he dismissed them before he opened his confidence to one almost a stranger, and Hugh had no doubt
that they kept his rules and betook themselves well out
of earshot of his conversation, though close enough to
jump to respond if he called.

'I like order,' said Hugh, 'and I have a preference for
keeping my people alive and whole where possible,
though you have seen it cannot always be done. I hate
waste. Waste of lives, waste of time that could be
profitable, waste of the earth that could be fruitful.
There's been more than enough of all three. If I try to
keep it out of my bailiwick, at least, is that matter for
wonder?'

'Your opinion,' said the earl with deliberation, 'I
should value. What you say here, I have said before
you. Now, do you see any ending? How many more
years of this to-ing and fro-ing that always fetches up in
stalemate? You are Stephen's man. So am I. Men every
bit as honourable follow the empress. We entangle ourselves like this with little thought, but I tell you, Hugh,
the time is coming when men will be forced to think,
upon both sides, before waste has wasted all, and no
man can lift a lance any more.'

'And you and I are conserving what we can for that

day?' Hugh enquired, with raised brows and a rueful mouth.

'Oh, not for a few years yet, but it will come. It must. There was some vestige of sense in it when we began, when Stephen had Normandy as well as England, and victory was in view. But four years and more ago that was all changed, when Geoffrey of Anjou wormed and bludgeoned his way into Normandy and made it his past doubt, even if it was in his wife's right and his son's name.'

'Yes,' agreed Hugh flatly, 'the year the Count of Meulan left us, to protect his right in Normandy by coming to terms with Geoffrey as overlord in Stephen's place.'

'What else,' asked Robert, undisturbed and unindignant, even wryly smiling, 'could my brother do? His right and title rest there. He is Waleran, Count of Meulan; however dear his titles in England may be, his line and identity is there. Not even Normandy, though the greater part of his inheritance is in Normandy. But the name, the name is in France itself, he owes homage to the king of France for that, and now for the larger heritage to Geoffrey of Anjou. Whatever else he jettisons, the root and blood of his name he cannot live without. I am the luckier of the two, Hugh. I came into my father's English lands and titles, I can dig my heels in here, and sit it out. True, my wife brought me Breteuil, but that is the lesser part of my heart, as my brother's title of Worcester is the lesser part of his. So he is there, and written off as a turncoat in Maud's favour as I am here, and credited as a loyal man to Stephen. And what difference, Hugh, do you see between us two? Twin brothers, the closest blood-kin there can be?'

'None,' said Hugh, and was silent a moment,

weighing and discarding the cautious selection of words. 'I understand very well,' he said then, 'that with Normandy gone, this followed. For others, besides the Beaumont brothers. There's not a man among us would not make some concessions to protect his rooted right and his sons' inheritance. We may reckon your brother as Anjou's man now, yet he will do Stephen as little harm as he can, and give Geoffrey as little active support. And you, left here still Stephen's man, you will keep your loyalty, but keep it as quietly as may be, avoiding action against the brood of Anjou as Waleran avoids action against Stephen. And there he will gloze over your continued allegiance and protect your lands and interests, as you are doing here for him. The division between you is no division at all. It is a drawing together that will draw together the interests of many others like you. Not in Stephen's cause, not in the cause of the empress and her son.'

'In the cause of sanity,' said the earl flatly, and studied Hugh with alert and critical interest, and smiled. 'You have felt it, too. This has become a war which cannot be won or lost. Victory and defeat have become alike impossible. Unfortunately it may take several years yet before most men begin to understand. We who are trying to ride two horses know it already.'

'If there is no winning and no losing,' said Hugh, 'there has to be another way. No land can continue for ever in a chaotic stalemate between two exhausted forces, without governance, while two groups of bewildered old men squat on their meagre gains and stare helplessly at each other, unable to lift a hand for the *coup de grâce*.'

Robert Bossu contemplated that summing up and his own fine finger-ends with a considering gravity, and then looked up sharply, his eyes, which had sparks of burning purple in their blackness, meeting Hugh's unmoving stare with appreciative attention. 'I like your diagnosis. It has gone on too long, and it will go on some years yet, make no mistake. But there is no ending that way, except by the death of all the old men, and not from wounds, from stagnation and old age and disgust. I would rather not wait to make one of them.'

'Nor I!' said Hugh heartily. 'And therefore,' he asked, with an eyebrow cocked expectantly to meet the bright imperial stare, 'what does a sane man do while he's enduring such waiting as he can endure?'

'Tills his own ground, shepherds his own flock, mends his own fences, and sharpens his own sword,' said Robert Bossu.

'Collects his own revenues?' suggested Hugh. 'And pays his own dues?'

'Both. To the last penny. And keeps, Hugh . . . keeps his own counsel. Even while terms like traitor and turncoat are being bandied about like arrows finding random marks. You will know better. I loved Stephen. I still do. But I do not love this ruinous nothing he and his cousin have made between them.'

The afternoon was drawing on towards the first hint of dusk. Soon it would be time for the Vesper bell. Hugh drained his cup and set it down on the board. 'Well, I had better be about shepherding my own flock, if I can count the abbot's two prisoners as any charge of mine. This is still a murder we have on our hands. And you, my lord? I take it you will be away now to your own country? These are no times to turn one's back for longer than a few days.'

'I'm loth to go without knowing the ending,' the earl admitted, warming into slightly self-deprecating laughter. 'I know murder is no jest, but these two prisoners of yours . . . Can you believe either of them capable of killing? Oh, I know there's no reading in the face what the mind can conceive, you handle them as you best can. As for me, yes, in a day or so I must make ready and take my leave. I am glad,' he said, rising as Hugh rose, 'that I have got to know you. Oh, and I have made other gains, for Rémy and his servants will be coming with me. There's room in my household for so good a poet and maker of songs. My luck, that I happened on him before he made off to the north, to Chester. His luck, too, for he'd have wasted his eloquence there. Ranulf has things on his mind graver than music, even if he has a note of music in him, which I doubt.'

Hugh took his leave, and was not pressed to remain, though the earl came a few formal steps towards the hall door with him. He had said what no doubt he was choosing to say to all such men holding authority, however limited, once he had measured them and liked and respected what he found. He had seed to sow, and was selecting the ground where it might root and flourish. When Hugh had reached the top of the steps the voice behind him said with mild but impressive emphasis: 'Hugh! Bear it in mind!'

Hugh and Cadfael came together from Tutilo's cell, and refuged in the herb garden in the twilight after Vespers, to consider what little they had got from him; and it was little enough, but sturdily consistent with what he had affirmed from the beginning. The boy was puffy-eyed and drunken with sleep, and if he felt any great anxiety about his fate he was too dulled still to be capable of appreciating the many pitfalls that lay in wait for him every way. Not a word of Daalny; for her he was fiercely on guard. He sat on his narrow pallet languidly composed, close to resignation, answered questions without any suspect pauses, and listened with dropped jaw and startled eyes when Cadfael told him how the Gospels had decisively restored Saint Winifred to Shrewsbury, and how Brother Jerome had babbled out his astonishing confession rather than wait to be accused by heaven.

'Me?' blurted Tutilo, incredulous. 'He meant it for *me*?' And for one instant he laughed aloud at the absurdity of the idea of Jerome as assassin, and himself as victim, and then in revulsion was stricken aghast at himself, and clapped both hands to his face as if to crush out the very lines of laughter. 'And the poor soul helpless, and someone . . . Oh, God, how could any man . . . ' And then, suddenly comprehending what was inferred, and instantly springing to refute it: 'Oh, no, not that! Not Jerome, that's impossible.' Quite certain, quite firmly stating his certainty, he who had found the wreckage of a man. 'No, of course you can't and don't believe that.' Not protesting, not exclaiming, but stating another certainty. He was fully awake and alive by then, his golden eyes wide and confident upon his questioners, both monastic and secular. As sound, sensible men both, they could not possibly credit that Jerome, narrow, meagre, malicious little soul though he might be, could have battered a senseless man's head to pulp with a heavy stone.

'Since you were not at Longner,' said Hugh, 'where did you take yourself off that night, to be coming back by that same path?'

'Anywhere to be out of sight and mind,' said Tutilo fervently. 'I lay up in the loft above the Horse Fair stable until I heard the bell for Compline, and then went up almost to the ferry, to be seen to come back by the Longner path if anyone noticed me.'

'Alone?' said Hugh.

'Of course alone.' He lied cheerfully and firmly. No use lying at all unless you can do it with conviction.

And that was all that was to be got out of him. No, he had met no one, going or returning, who would be able to vouch for his movements. He had told all the worst of what he had done, and did not seem greatly concerned about the rest. They locked the door upon him again, restored the key to its place in the gatehouse, and withdrew to the privacy of the herbarium to blow the brazier into a comfortable glow, and shut out the encroaching darkness of the night.

'And now,' said Cadfael, 'I think I shall be forgiven if I tell you the rest of what he did that night, the part he was not willing to tell.'

Hugh leaned back against the timber wall and said equally: 'I might have known you would have right of entry where no one else was let in. What is it he has not told me?'

'He has not told me, either. It was from someone else I got it, and with no licence to pass it on, even to you, but I think she'll hold me justified. The girl Daalny – you'll have seen her about, but she keeps discreetly apart within these walls . . .'

'Rémy's singing girl,' said Hugh, 'the little thing from Provence.'

'From Ireland, properly speaking. But yes, that's the one. Her mother was put up for sale in Bristol, a prize from oversea. This one was born into servitude. The trade still goes on, and Bishop Wulstan's sermons haven't made it illegal, only frowned upon. I fancy our holy thief is between enthusiasms just now, unsure whether he wants to be a saint or a knight errant. He has dreams now of delivering the only slave he's likely to encounter in these parts, though I doubt if he's fully

213

realized yet that she's a girl, and a fine one, and has already taken his measure.'

'Are you telling me,' demanded Hugh, beginning to sparkle with amusement, 'that he was with her that night?'

'He was, and won't say so because her master sets a high value on her voice, and goes in fear that she may slip through his fingers somehow. What happened was that the manservant who travels with them overheard somewhere about Aldhelm being on his way here to identify the brother who cozened him, and told Daalny, knowing very well that she had an eye to the lad herself. She warned him, he made up the tale that he was summoned to Longner, and got his permission from Herluin, who knew nothing about Aldhelm being expected here. Tutilo went out by the gate, like an honest fellow, and took the path from the Foregate towards the ferry, but turned aside to the Horse Fair and hid in the loft over our stable, just as he says. And she slid out by the broad gate from the cemetery, and joined him there. They waited there until they heard the bell for Compline, and then parted to return by the same ways they had come. So she says, and so he won't say, in case it rebounds on her.'

'So all that evening they were cosily employed in the hayloft, like many a lad and lass before them,' said Hugh, and laughed.

'So they were, in a manner of speaking, but not like every such pair. Not quite. For she says they talked. Nothing more. And those two had much to talk about, and little chance until then. The first time they ever were together outside these walls. Even then I doubt if they got to the real meat of what they should have been saying. For believe me, Hugh, she has already set her mark on him, and he, though he may not know it yet, is in thrall to her fathoms deep. They said the evening prayers together, she says, when they heard the Compline bell.'

'And you believe her?'

'Why say it, else?' said Cadfael simply. 'She had nothing to prove to me. She told me of her own will, and had no need to add one word.'

'Well, if true,' said Hugh seriously, 'it speaks for him. It fits with the time he came to us at the castle, and puts him an hour behind Aldhelm on that path. But you realize as well as I that the word of the girl will hardly be taken more gravely for proof than his own, if things are thus between them. However innocent that assignation may have been.'

'Have you considered,' Cadfael asked sombrely, 'that Herluin will surely want to set out for home now he's lost his bid? And he is Tutilo's superior, and will certainly want to take him back with him. And so far as I can see, as the case stands at this moment he has every right to do so. If you had kept him in the castle on suspicion things would have been different, possession is still the better part of the law. But he's here in the Church's prison, and you know how hard the Church holds on to its own. Between a secular charge of murder and a clerical one of theft and deception, on the face of it the lad might well prefer the latter. But as between your custody and Herluin's, frankly, I'd wish him in your charge. But Herluin will never willingly let go of him. The fool child raised his prior's hopes of gaining a miracle-working saint, and then failed to make a success of it, and brought the whole down to a reproach and a humiliation. He'll be made to pay for that tenfold, once Herluin gets him home. I don't know but I'd rather see him charged on a count of which he's innocent, and hoisted away into your hold, than dragged off to do endless penance for the count on which he himself owns he's guilty.'

Hugh was smiling, a shade wryly, and eyeing Cadfael along his shoulder with rueful affection. 'Better get to work in the day or so remaining, and find me the man who really did murder, since you're certain this boy did not. They will surely all leave together, for Rémy and his party are joining Robert Bossu's household, and Herluin's way home takes the same road as far as Leicester – it's why the wagon fell victim there in the first place, and started all this to-do – so he'd be mad not to avail himself of a safe escort and ask to travel with the earl, if indeed the earl does not invite him before he can ask. I may contrive to delay Robert a couple of days, but no longer.'

He rose and stretched. It had been an eventful day, with many mysteries propounded and none of them solved. He had earned an hour or two of Aline's company, and an amiable tumble with the five-year-old tyrant Giles, before the boy was swept away to bed by Constance, his devoted slave. Let lesser considerations, and for that matter greater ones, too, hang in abeyance until tomorrow.

'And what particular responsibilities did he want to talk over with you in private this afternoon?' asked Cadfael as his friend turned towards the door.

'The need,' said Hugh, looking back and weighing words with care, 'for all thinking men in this dead-locked contention to set about finding a means of doing away with factions, since neither faction has any hope of winning. The thing is becoming very simple: how to clamber out of a morass before the muck reaches our chins. You can be giving your mind to that, Cadfael, while you say a word in God's ear at Compline.'

*

216

Cadfael could never be quite sure what it was that prompted him to borrow the key yet again after Compline, and go in to pay a late visit to Tutilo. It might have been the sound of the light, pure voice from within the cell, heard eerily across the court when he came from the last Office of the evening. A faint gleam of light showed through the high, barred window; the prisoner had not yet put out his little lamp. The singing was very soft, not meant to reach anyone outside. but the tone was so piercingly true, in the centre of the note like an arrow in the gold of a target, that it carried on the twilit stillness to the most remote corners of the court, and caused Cadfael to freeze in midstride, stricken to the heart with its beauty. The boy's timing was a little out: he was still singing the close of the Office. Nothing so wonderful had been heard in the choir of the church. Anselm was an excellent precentor, and long ago in his youth might have sounded like this: but Anselm with all his skills was old, and this was an ageless voice that might have belonged to a child or an angel. Blessed be the human condition, thought Cadfael, which allows us marred and fallible creatures who are neither angels nor children to make sounds like these, that belong in another world. Unlooked-for mercies, undeserved grace!

Well, that could be meant as a sign. Or again, what sent him to the gatehouse for the key might have been simply a feeling that he must make one more effort to get something useful out of the boy before sleeping, something that might point the way forward, perhaps something Tutilo did not even realize that he knew. Or, Cadfael thought afterwards, it might have been a sharp nudge in the ribs from Saint Winifred, stretching out the grace of a thought all the way from her grave in Gwytherin, having forgiven the graceless youth who had had the excellent taste to covet her, as she had forgiven the graceless old man who had presumed to suppose he was interpreting her will, just as impudently, all those years ago. Whatever it was, to the gatehouse he went, the entrancing and agonizing beauty of Tutilo's singing following him all the way. Brother Porter let him take the key without question; in his solitude Tutilo had shown every sign of resignation and content, as if he welcomed the peace and quiet to consider his present state and his future prospects. Whatever complex motives had combined to drive Tutilo into the cloister, there was nothing spurious about his faith; if he had done no evil, he was assured no evil would come to him. Or else, of course, being the lad he was, he was lulling everyone into believing in his docility, until they ceased to pay him any careful attention, and let him slide out of the trap like an eel. With Tutilo you would never be quite sure. Daalny was right. You would have to know him very well, to know when he was lying and when he was telling the truth.

Tutilo was still on his knees in front of the plain, small cross on the cell wall, and did not immediately look round when the key grated in the lock, and the door opened at his back. He had stopped singing, and was gazing musingly before him, eyes wide open, and face placid and absent. He turned, rising when the door swung heavily to again, and beholding Cadfael, smiled rather wanly, and sat down on his cot. He looked mildly surprised, but said nothing, waiting submissively to hear what was now required of him, and in no apprehension about it, because it was Cadfael who came.

'No, nothing,' said Cadfael with a sigh, answering the look. 'Just a gnawing hope that talking to us earlier might have started a hare, after all. Some small thing recalled that might be useful.'

Tutilo shook his head slowly, willing but blank. 'No, I can think of nothing I haven't told you. And everything I have told you is truth.'

'Oh, I don't doubt you,' said Cadfael resignedly. 'Still, bear it in mind. The merest detail, something you think negligible, might be the very grain that makes the weight. Never mind, leave your wits fallow and something may come back to you.' He looked round the narrow, bare white cell. 'Are you warm enough here?'

'Once in the brychans, snug enough,' said Tutilo. 'I've slept harder and colder many a time.'

'And there's nothing wanting? Any small thing I can do for you?'

'According to the Rule, you shouid not so much as offer,' said Tutilo, with a sudden sparkling grin. 'But yes, maybe there is one lawful thing I could ask, even to my credit. I have kept the hours, alone here, but there are bits I forget sometimes. And besides, I miss reading in it to pass the time. Even Father Herluin would approve. Could you bring me a breviary?'

'What happened to your own?' Cadfael asked, surprised. 'I know you had one, a little narrow one.' The vellum had been folded many times to make its cramped pages. 'Good eyes you'd need for that minuscule, but then, your eyes are young enough to be sharp.'

'I've lost it,' said Tutilo. 'I had it at Mass, the day before I was locked in here, but where I've left it or dropped it I don't know. I miss it, but I can't think what I've done with it.'

'You had it the day Aldhelm was to come here? The day – the night, rather – you found him?'

219

'That was the last I can be clear about, and I may have shaken it out of my scrip or dropped it somewhere among the trees in the dark, that's what I'm afraid of. I was hardly noticing much that night,' he said ruefully, 'after I found him. What with bolting down the track and across the river into the town, I could have shed it anywhere. It may be down the Severn by now. I like to have it,' he said earnestly, 'and I rise for Matins and Lauds in the night. I do!'

'I'll leave you mine,' said Cadfael. 'Well, best get your sleep, if you're going to rise with the rest of us at midnight. Keep your lamp burning till then, if you like, there's enough oil here.' He had checked it in the little pottery vessel with a fingertip. 'Goodnight, son!'

'Don't forget to lock the door,' said Tutilo after him, and laughed without a trace of bitterness.

She was standing in the darkest of the dark, slender and still and erect, pressed against the stones of the cell wall when Cadfael rounded the corner. The faint gleam of Tutilo's lamp through the grill high out of her reach fell from above over her face as no more than a glow-worm's eerie spark, conjuring out of deep darkness a spectral mask of a face, oval, elusive, with austere carven features, but the remaining light from the west window of the church, hardly less dim, found the large, smouldering lustre of her eyes, and a few jewelled points of brightness that were embroidered silver threads along the side hems of her bliaut. She was in her finery, she had been singing for Robert Bossu. A lean, motionless, intent presence in the stillness of the night. Daalny, Partholan's queen, a demi-goddess from the western paradise.

'I heard your voices,' she said, her own voice pitched just above a whisper; whispers carry more audibly than

220

soft utterances above the breath. 'I could not call to him, someone might have heard. Cadfael, what is to happen to him?'

'I hope,' said Cadfael, 'no great harm.'

'In long captivity,' she said, 'he will stop singing. And then he will die. And the day after tomorrow we ride with the earl for Leicester. I have my orders from Rémy, tomorrow I must begin packing the instruments for safe carriage, and the next morning we ride. Bénezet will be seeing to all the horses, and exercising Rémy's to make sure his injury's healed well. And we go. And he remains. At whose mercy?'

'God's,' said Cadfael firmly, 'and with the intercession of the saints. One saint, at any rate, for she has just nudged me with the seed of an idea. So go to your bed, and keep your heart up, for nothing is ended yet.'

'And what gain is there for me?' she said. 'We might prove ten times over that he did no murder, but still he will be dragged back to Ramsey, and they will have their revenge on him, not so much for being a thief as for making a botch of his thievery. In the earl's party half the way, and far too strong an escort for him to break loose.' She lowered her burning eyes to the broad brown hand in which Cadfael held the key, and suddenly she smiled. 'I know the right key now,' she said.

'It might be changed over to the wrong nail,' said Cadfael mildly.

'I should know it, even so. There are but two alike in size and design, and I remember well the pattern of the wards on the wrong one. I shall not make that mistake again.'

He was about to urge her to let well alone and trust heaven to do justice, but then he had a sudden vision of heaven's justice as the Church sometimes applied it, in

221

good but dreadful faith, with all the virtuous narrowness and pitilessness of minds blind and deaf to the infinite variety of humankind, its failings, and aspirations, and needs, and forgetful of all the Gospel reminders concerning publicans and sinners. And he thought of songbirds caged, drooping without air to play on the cords of their throats, without heart to sing, and knew that they might very well die. Half humanity was here in this lean dark girl beside him, and that half of humanity had its right to reason, determine and meddle, no less than the male half. After all, they were equally responsible for humankind continuing. There was not an archbishop or an abbot in the world who had not had a flesh and blood mother, and come of a passionate coupling.

She would do as she thought fit, and so would he. He was not charged with the keeping of the keys, once he had restored this one to its place.

'Well, well!' said Cadfael with a sigh. 'Let him be for tonight. Let all things be. Who knows how much clearer the skies will be by tomorrow?'

He left her then, and went on up the court to the gatehouse, to return the key to Brother Porter. Behind him Daalny said softly: 'Goodnight!' Her tone was level, courteous, and withdrawn, promising nothing, confiding nothing, a neutral salute out of the dark.

And what had he to show for that last instinctive return to question the boy yet again, to hope for some sudden blinding recollection that would unveil truth like flinging open the shutters on a summer morning? One small thing only: Tutilo had lost his breviary, somewhere, at some time, on the death-day. With half a mile of woodland and two or three hundred yards of Foregate back-alleys, and the hasty rush into the town and back again, to parcel out in search of it, if it was

222

valued enough. A breviary can be recopied. And yet, if that was all, why was it that he felt Saint Winifred shaking him impatiently by the shoulder and urging in his ear that he knew very well where to begin looking, and that he had better be about it in the morning, for time was running out?

Chapter Twelve

ADFAEL AROSE well before Prime, opening his eyes upon a morning twilight with the pearl-grey promise of clear skies and a windless calm, and upon the consciousness of a task already decided upon and waiting for completion. As well make the enterprise serve two purposes. He went first to his workshop, to select the medicines that might be running short at the hospital of Saint Giles, at the end of the Foregate; ointments and lotions for skin eruptions chiefly, for the strays who came to refuge there were liable to arrive suffering the attendant ills of starvation living and uncleanliness, often through no fault of their own. Those of cold no less, especially among the old, whose breath rattled and rasped in their lungs like dried leaves from wandering the roads. With his scrip already stocked, he looked about him for the jobs most needing attention, and marked down duties enough to keep Brother Winfrid busy through the working hours of the morning.

After Prime he left Winfrid cheerfully digging over a

patch for planting out cabbages later, and went to borrow a key from the porter. Round the eastern corner of the precinct wall, at the far end of the Horse Fair and halfway to Saint Giles, was the large barn and stable, and loft over, to which the horses had been transferred from the stable-yard within the abbey court during the flood. On this stretch of road the Longner cart had stood waiting, while the carters laboured to salvage the treasures of the church, and here Tutilo had emerged from the double rear-doors of the cemetery to haul back Aldhelm by the sleeve, and make him an unwitting partner in his sacrilegious theft. And here, on the night of Aldhelm's death, according to Daalny, she and Tutilo had taken refuge in the hay in the loft, to evade having to face the witness and admit to the sin, and had not dared return until they heard the bell for Compline. By which time their danger was indeed past, for the innocent young man was dead.

Cadfael opened the main doors, and set one leaf wide. In the straw-scented dimness within the great lower room there were stalls for horses, though none of them was occupied. At seasonal stock sales there would be plenty of country breeders housing their beasts here, but at this season the place was little used. Almost in the middle of the long room a wooden ladder led up through a trapdoor to a loft above. Cadfael climbed it, thrusting up the trap and sliding it aside, to step into an upper room lit by a couple of narrow, unshuttered windows. A few casks ranged along the end wall, an array of tools in the near corner, and ample stores of hay still, for there had been good grass crops two years running.

They had left their imprint in the piled hay. No question but two people had been here recently, the two snug, hollowed nests were there plain to be seen.

But two they were, and that in itself caused Cadfael to stand for some moments in interested contemplation. Close enough for comfort and warmth, but nevertheless clearly separate, and so neatly preserved that they might have been shaped deliberately. There had been no rumbustious rustic coupling here, only two anxious minor sinners crouching in sanctuary from the buffetings of fate for this one night, even if the blow must fall next day. They must have sat very still, to avoid even the rustling of the straw round their feet.

Cadfael looked about him for the small alien thing he had come to find, with no assurance that it would be here to be found, only an inward conviction that some benevolent finger had pointed him to this place. He had all but put his hand on it when he hoisted the trap, for the corner of the solid wooden square had pushed it some inches aside, and half hidden it from view. A narrow book, bound in coarse leather, the edges rubbed pale from carrying and handling, and the friction of rough sacking scrips. The boy must have laid it down here as they were leaving, to have his hands free to help Daalny down the ladder, and had then been so intent on fitting the trap into place again that he had forgotten to reach through for his book.

Cadfael took it up in his hands and held it gratefully. There was a stem of clean yellow straw keeping a page in it, and the place it marked was the office of Compline. In the dark here they could not read it, but Tutilo would know it by heart in any case, and this gesture was simply by way of a small celebration to prove that they had observed the hours faithfully. It would be easy, thought Cadfael, to fall into a perilous affection for this gifted rogue, sometimes amused, often exasperated, but affection all the same. Apart, of course, from that

226

angelic voice so generously bestowed on one who was certainly no angel.

He was standing quite still, a pace or two away from the open trapdoor, when he heard a small sound from below. The door had been left open, anyone could have come in, but he had heard no footsteps. What had caught his ear was the slight rasp of rough ceramic against rough ceramic, crude baked clay, a heavy lid being lifted from a large storage jar. The friction of a slight movement in lifting made a brief, grating sound that carried strangely, and set the teeth on edge. Someone had raised the lid from the corn jar. It had been filled when the horses were moved, and would not have been emptied again, in case of further need, since the rivers were still running somewhat high, and the season was not yet quite safe. And once again, the slightly different but still rasping clap of the lid being replaced. It came very softly, a minute touch, but he heard it.

He shifted quietly, to be able to look down through the trap, and someone below, hearing him, hallooed cheerfully up to him: 'You there, Brother? All's well! Something I forgot here when we moved the horses.' Feet stirred the straw on the flooring, audible now, and Rémy's man Bénezet came into view, grinning amiably up into the loft, and flourishing a bridle that showed glints of gilt decoration on headstall and rein. 'My lord Rémy's! I'd been walking his beast out for the first time after he went lame, and brought him in harnessed, and this I left behind here. We'll be needing it tomorrow. We're packing.'

'So I hear,' said Cadfael. 'And setting off with a safe escort.' He tucked the breviary into the breast of his habit, having left his scrip below, and stepped cautiously through the trap and began to descend the ladder. Bénezet waited for him, dangling the bridle. 'I

227

recalled in time where I'd left it,' he said, smoothing a thumb along the embossed decorations on the brow and the rein. 'I asked at the porter's, and he told me Brother Cadfael had taken the key and would be here, so I came to collect this while the place was open. If you're done, Brother, we can walk back together.'

'I have still to go on to Saint Giles,' said Cadfael, and turned to pick up his scrip. 'I'll lock up, if you've no further wants here, and get on to the hospital.'

'No, I'm done,' said Bénezet. 'This was all. Lucky I remembered, or Rémy's best harness would have been left dangling on that hayrack, and I should have had it docked out of my pay or out of my skin.'

He said a brisk farewell, and was off towards the corner, and round it into the straight stretch of the Foregate, without a glance behind. Never once had he cast a glance towards the corn bin in its shadowy niche. But the bridle, it seemed, he had reclaimed from the last hayrack. So, at least, he had made unnecessarily plain.

Cadfael went to the corn jar and lifted the lid. There were grains spilled on the rim within, and on the floor round it. No great quantity, but they were there to be seen. He plunged both arms into the slithering grain, and felt around deeply till his fingers touched the base, and the grain slid coldly about his hands and yielded nothing alien. Not hiding something, but recovering it; and whatever it was had a nature and shape calculated to hoist out a few grains with it in emerging. The bridle would have let them all slide back into the amphora. Something with folds that would trap the grains? Cloth?

Or had he simply been curious as to how much was left within? A mere idle thought? People do odd, inconsequent things by the way, digressing without

228

reason from what is currently occupying them. But bear it in mind. Odd, inconsequent things are sometimes highly significant. Cadfael shook himself, closed and locked the heavy door, and went on towards Saint Giles.

In the great court, when he returned with his empty scrip, there was a purposeful but unhurried activity, a brisk wind blowing before a departure. No haste, they had all this day to make ready. Robert Bossu's two squires came and went about the guesthall, assembling such clothing and equipment as their lord would not require on the journey. He travelled light, but liked meticulous service, and got it, as a rule, without having to labour the point. The steward Nicol and his younger companion, the one who had been left to make his way back from Worcester to Shrewsbury on foot, and had sensibly taken his time on the way, had very little to do by way of preparation, for this time their collected alms for their house would be carried by Earl Robert's baggage carriage, the same which had brought Saint Winifred's reliquary home, and was now to be baggage wagon for them all, while the earl's packhorse could provide dignified transport for Sub-Prior Herluin. Robert Bossu was generous in small attentions to Herluin, very soothing to his dignity.

And the third of the three parties now assembled for the journey into one, had perhaps the most demanding arrangements to make. Daalny came carefully down the steps of the guesthall with a handsome portative organ in her arms, craning her slender neck to peer round her burden to find the edge of every step, for Rémy's instruments were precious almost beyond the value he put on his singer. The organ had its own specially made case for safekeeping, but it was somewhat bulky, and since space within was limited, the case had been banished to the stable. Daalny crossed the court, nursing the instrument like a child on her arm and clasping it caressingly with her free hand, for it was an object of love to her no less than to her lord. She looked up at Cadfael, when he fell in beside her, and offered him a wary smile, as if she selected and suppressed, within her mind, such topics as might arise with this companion, but had better be denied discussion.

'You have the heaviest load,' said Cadfael. 'Let me take it from you.'

She smiled more warmly, but shook her head. 'I am responsible, I will carry it or let it fall myself. But it is not so heavy, only bulky. The case is within there. Leather, soft, padded. You can help me put it in, if you will. It takes two, one to hold the bag wide open.'

He went with her into the stable-yard, and obediently held the fitted lid of the case braced back on his arm to allow her to slide the little organ within. She closed the lid upon it, and buckled the straps that held it firm. About them the earl's young men went about their efficient business with the smooth and pleasurable grace of youth, and at the far end of the yard Bénezet was cleaning saddles and harness, and draping his work over a wooden frame, where the saddlecloths were spread out in the pale sunlight that was already acquiring a surprising degree of warmth. Rémy's ornate bridle hung on a hook beside him.

'Your lord likes his gear handsome,' said Cadfael, indicating it. She followed his glance impassively.

'Oh, that! That isn't Rémy's, it's Bénezet's. Where he got it there's no asking. I've often thought he stole it somewhere, but he's close-mouthed, best not question.'

Cadfael digested that without comment. Why so needless a lie? It served no detectable purpose that he could see, and that in itself was cause for further consideration. Perhaps Bénezet thought it wise to attriute the ownership of so fine a possession to his master, to avoid any curiosity as to how he had acquired it. Daalny had just suggested as much. He took the matter a stage further, in a very casual tone.

'He takes no great care of it. He had left it in the barn at the Horse Fair all this time since the flood. He fetched it back only this morning.'

This time she turned a face suddenly intent, and her hands halted on the last buckle. 'He told you that? He spent half an hour cleaning and polishing that bridle early this morning. It never left here, I've seen it a dozen times since.'

Her eyes were large, bright and sharp with speculation. Cadfael had no wish to start her wondering too much; she was already more deeply involved than he would have liked, and rash enough to surge into unwise action at this extreme, when she was about to be swept away to Leicester, with nothing resolved and nothing gained. Better by far keep her out of it, if that was any way possible. But she was very quick; she had her teeth into this discrepancy already. Cadfael shrugged, and said indifferently: 'I must have misunderstood him. He was along there in mid-morning, carrying it. I thought he'd been to reclaim it, he was in the stable there. I took it for granted it was Rémy's.'

'Well you might,' she agreed. 'I've wondered, myself, how he came by it. Somewhere in Provence, most likely. But honestly? I doubt it.' The brilliance of her eyes narrowed upon Cadfael's face. She did not turn to glance at Bénezet, not yet. 'What was he doing at the Horse Fair?' Her tone was still casually curious,

231

as if neither question nor answer mattered very much, but the glitter in her eyes denied it.

'Do I know?' said Cadfael. 'I was up in the loft when he came in. Maybe he was just curious why the door was open.'

That was a diversion she could not resist. Her eyes rounded eagerly, a little afraid to hope for too much. 'And what were you doing in the loft?'

'I was looking for proof of what you told me,' said Cadfael. 'And I found it. Did you know that Tutilo forgot his breviary there after Compline?'

She said: 'No!' Almost soundlessly, on a soft, hopeful breath.

'He borrowed mine, last night. He had no notion where he had lost his own, but I thought of one place at least where it would be worthwhile looking for it. And yes, it was there, and the place marked at Compline. It is hardly an eyewitness, Daalny, but it is good evidence. And I am waiting to put it into Hugh Beringar's hands.'

'Will it free him?' she asked in the same rapt whisper.

'So far as Hugh is concerned, it well may. But Tutilo's superior here is Herluin, and he cannot be passed by.'

'Need he ever know?' she asked fiercely.

'Not the whole truth, if Hugh sees with my eyes. That there's very fair proof the boy never did murder, yes, that he'll be told, but he need not know where you were or what you did, the pair of you, that night.'

'We did no wrong,' she said, exultant and scornful of a world where needs must think evil, and where she knew of evil enough, but despised most of it and had no interest in any of it. 'Cannot the abbot overrule Herluin? This is his domain, not Ramsey's.'

'The abbot will keep the Rule. He can no more

detain the boy here and deprive Ramsey than he could abandon one of his own. Only wait! Let's see whether even Herluin can be persuaded to open the door on the lad.' He did not go on to speculate on what would happen then, though it did seem to him that Tutilo's passionate vocation had cooled to the point where it might slip out of sight and out of mind by comparison with the charm of delivering Partholan's queen from slavery. Ah, well! Better take your hands from the ploughshare early and put them to other decent use, than persist, and take to ploughing narrower and narrower furrows until everything secular is anathema, and everything human doomed to reprobation.

'Bring me word,' said Daalny, very gravely, her eyes royally commanding.

Only when Cadfael had left her, to keep a watch on the gatehouse for Hugh's coming, did she turn her gaze upon Bénezet. Why should he bother to tell needless lies? He might, true, prefer to let people think an improbably fine bridle belonged to his master rather than himself, if he had cause to be wary of flattering but inconvenient curiosity. But why offer any explanation at all? Why should a close-mouthed man who was sparing of words at all times go wasting words on quite unnecessary lies? And more interesting still, he certainly had not made the journey to the Horse Fair to retrieve that bridle, his own or Rémy's. It was the excuse, not the reason. So why had he made it? To retrieve something else? Something by no means forgotten, but deliberately left there? Tomorrow they were to ride for Leicester. If he had something put away there for safekeeping, something he could not risk showing, he had to reclaim it today.

Moreover, if that was true, whatever it was had lain in hiding ever since the night of the flood, when chaos entered the church with the river water, when everything vulnerable within was being moved, when Tutilo's ingenious theft was committed – oh, that she acknowledged – and the slow-rooting but certain seed of murder was sown. Murder of which Tutilo was not guilty. Murder, of which someone else was. Someone else who had cause to fear what Aldhelm might have to tell about that night, once his memory was stirred? What other reason could anyone have had to kill a harmless young man, a shepherd from a manor some miles away?

Daalny went on with her work without haste, since she had no intention of quitting the stable-yard while Bénezet was there. She had to go back to the guesthall for the smaller instruments, but she lost as little time over that as possible, and settled down again within view of Bénezet while she cased and bestowed them with care. The earl's younger squire, interested, came to examine the Saracen *ud* that had come back with Rémy's father from the Crusade, and his presence provided welcome cover for the watch she was keeping on her fellow-servant, and delayed her packing, which would otherwise have been complete within an hour or so, and left her with no excuse for remaining. The flutes and panpipes were easily carried; rebec and mandora had their own padded bags for protection, though the bow of the rebec had to be packed with care.

It was drawing near to noon. Earl Robert's young men piled all their baggage neatly together ready for loading next day, and took themselves off to see to their lord's comfort withindoors, and serve his dinner. Daalny closed the last strap, and stacked the saddleroll that held the flutes beside the heavier saddlebags. 'These are ready. Have you finished with the harness?'

He had brought out one of his own bags, and had it

already half-filled, folding an armful of clothes within it. What was beneath, she thought, he must have stowed away when she went back to the guesthall for the rebec and the mandora. When his back was turned she nudged the soft bulge of leather with her foot, and something within uttered the thinnest and clearest of sounds, the chink of coin against coin, very brief, as though for the thoroughness of the packing movement was barely possible. But there is nothing else that sounds quite the same. He turned his head sharply, but she met his eyes with a wide, clear stare, held her position as if she had heard nothing, and said with flat composure: 'Come to dinner. He's at table with Robert Bossu by now, you're not needed to wait on him this time.'

Hugh listened to Cadfael's story, and turned the little breviary in his hands meantime with a small, wry smile, between amusement and exasperation.

'I can and will answer for my shire, but within here I have no powers, as well you know. I accept that the boy never did murder, indeed I never seriously thought he had. This is proof enough for me on that count, but if I were you I would keep the circumstances even from Radulfus, let alone Herluin. You had better not appear in this. You might feel you must open the last detail to the abbot, but I doubt if even he could extricate the poor wretch in this case. Meeting a girl in a hayloft would be excellent grist to Herluin's mill, if ever he got to hear of it. A worse charge than the sacrilegious theft – worse, at any rate, than that would have been if it had succeeded. I'll see him clear of murder, even without being able to prove it home on someone else, but more than that I can't promise.'

'I leave it all to you,' said Cadfael resignedly. 'Do as

you see fit. Time's short, God knows. Tomorrow they'll all be gone.'

'Well, at least,' said Hugh, rising, 'Robert Bossu, with all the Beaumont heritage in Normandy and England on his mind, will hardly be greatly interested in riding gaoler on a wretched little clerk with a clerical hell waiting for him at the end of the road. I wouldn't be greatly astonished if he left a door unlocked somewhere along the way, and turned a blind eye, or even set the hunt off in the opposite direction. There's a deal of England between here and Ramsey.' He held out the breviary; the yellow straw still marked the place where Tutilo had recited the Office and shared the night prayers with Daalny. 'Give this back to him. He'll need it.'

And he went away to his audience with Radulfus, while Cadfael sat somewhat morosely thinking, and holding the worn book in his hands. He was not quite sure why he should so concern himself with a clever little fool who had tried to steal Shrewsbury's saint, and in the process started a vexatious series of events that had cost several decent men hurts, troubles and hardships, and one his life. None of which, of course, had Tutilo actually committed or intended, but trouble he was, and trouble he would continue as long as he remained where he did not belong. Even his over-ardent but genuine piety was not of the kind to fit into the discipline of a monastic brotherhood. Well, at least Hugh would make it plain that the boy was no murderer, whatever else might be charged against him, and his highly enterprising theft was not such as to come within the province of the king's sheriff. For the rest, if the worst came to the worst, the boy must do what many a recalcitrant square peg in a round hole had had to do before him, survive his penance, resign himself to his fate, and settle down to live tamed and deformed, but safe. A singing bird caged. Though of course there was still Daalny. Bring me word, she had said. And yes, he would bring her word. Of both worst and best.

In the abbot's parlour Hugh delivered his judgement with few words. If all was not to be told, the fewer the better. 'I came to tell you, Father Abbot, that I have no charge to make against the novice Tutilo. I have evidence enough now to be certain that he did no murder. The law of which I am custodian has no further interest in him. Unless,' he added mildly, 'the common interest of wishing him well.'

'You have found the murderer elsewhere?' asked Radulfus.

'No, that I can't say. But I am certain now that it is not Tutilo. What he did that night, in coming at once to give word of the slaying, was well done, and what he could do further the next day he did ungrudgingly. My law makes no complaint of him.'

'But mine must,' said Radulfus. 'It is no light offence to steal, but it is worse to have involved another in the theft, and brought him into peril of his life. To his better credit he confessed it, and has shown true remorse that ever he brought this unfortunate young man into his plans. He has gifts he may yet use to the glory of God. But there is a debt to pay.' He considered Hugh in attentive silence for a while, and then he said: 'Am I to know what further witness has come to your hand? Since you have not fathomed out the guilty, there must be cause why you are sure of this one's innocence.'

'He made the excuse of being called to Longner,' said Hugh readily, 'in order to be able to slip away and hide until the danger should be past and the witness departed, at least for that night. I doubt he looked beyond, it was the immediate threat he studied to avoid. Where he hid I know. It was in the loft of the abbey stable on the Horse Fair, and there is reasonable evidence he did not leave it until he heard the Compline bell. By which time Aldhelm was dead.'

'And is there any other voice to bear out this timing?'

'There is,' said Hugh, and offered nothing further.

'Well,' said Radulfus, sitting back with a sigh, 'he is not in my hands but by chance, and I cannot, if I would, pass over his offence or lighten his penalty. Sub-Prior Herluin will take him back to Ramsey, to his own abbot, and while he is within my walls, I must respect Ramsey's right, and hold him fast and securely until he leaves my gates.'

'He was not curious, he did not probe,' Hugh reported to Cadfael in the herb garden; his voice was appreciative and amused. 'He accepted my assurance that I was satisfied Tutilo had done no murder and broken no law of the land, at least, none outside the Church's pale, and that was enough for him. After all, he'll be rid of the whole tangle by tomorrow, he has his own delinquent to worry about. Jerome is going to take a deal of absolving. But the abbot won't do the one thing I suppose, as superior here, he could do, let our excommunicate come back into the services for this last night. He's right, of course. Once they leave your gates, he's no longer a responsibility of Shrewsbury's, but until then Radulfus is forced to act for Ramsey as well as for his own household. Brother must behave correctly to brother – even if he detests him. I'm half sorry myself, but Tutilo remains in his cell. Officially, at any rate,' he added with a considering grin. 'Even your backslidings, provided they offend only Church law, would be no affair of mine.'

'On occasions they have been,' said Cadfael, and let his mind stray fondly after certain memories that brought a nostalgic gleam to his eye. 'It's a long time since we rode together by night.'

'Just as well for your old bones,' said Hugh, and made an urchin's face at him. 'Be content, sleep in your bed, and let clever little bandits like your Tutilo sweat for their sins, and wait their time to be forgiven. For all we know the abbot of Ramsey is a good, humane soul with as soft a spot for minor sinners as you. And a sound ear for music, perhaps. That would serve just as well. If you turned him loose into the night now, how would he fare, without clothes, without food, without money?'

And it was true enough, Cadfael acknowledged. He would manage, no doubt, but at some risk. A shirt and chausses filched from some woman's drying-ground, an egg or so from under a hen, a few pence wheedled out of travellers on the road with a song, a few more begged at a market – but no stone walls shutting him in, and no locked door, no uncharitable elder preaching him endless sermons on his unpardoned sins, no banishment into the stony solitude of excommunication, barred from the communal meal and from the oratory, having no communication with his fellows, and if any should be so bold and so kind as to offer him a comfortable word, bringing down upon him the same cold fate.

'All the same,' said Hugh, reflecting, 'there's justification in the Rule for leaving all doors open. After everything else has been visited on the incorrigible, what does the Rule say? "If the faithless brother leaves you, let him go." '

Cadfael walked with him to the gatehouse when the long afternoon was stilling and chilling into the relaxed calm of the pre-Vesper hour, with the day's manual work done. He had said no word of Bénezet's bridle, and his visit to the Horse Fair stable, in presenting the mute witness of Tutilo's breviary. Where there was no certainty, and nothing of substance to offer, he hesitated to advance a mere unsupported suspicion against any man. And yet he was loth to let pass any possibility of further discovery. To be left in permanent doubt is worse than unwelcome knowledge.

'You'll be coming down tomorrow,' he said at the gate, 'to see the earl's party on their way? At what hour his lordship proposes to muster I've heard no word, but they'll want to make good use of the light.'

'He'll hear the first Mass before he goes,' said Hugh. 'So I'm instructed. I'll be here to see him leave.'

'Hugh . . . bring three or four with you. Enough to keep the gate if there should be any move to break out. Not enough for comment or alarm.'

Hugh had halted sharply, and was studying him shrewdly along his shoulder. 'That's not for the little brother,' he said with certainty. 'You have some other quarry in mind?'

'Hugh, I swear to you I know nothing fit to offer you, and if anyone is to venture a mistaken move and make a great fool of himself, let it be me. But be here! A feather fluttering in the wind is more substantial than what I have, as at this moment. I may yet find out more. But make no move until tomorrow. In Robert Bossu's presence we have a formidable authority to back us. If I venture, and fall on my nose pointing a foolish finger at an innocent man, well, a bloody nose is no great matter. But I do not want to call a man a murderer without very hard proof. Leave me handle it my way, and let everyone else sleep easy.'

Hugh was in two minds then about pressing him for

every detail of what he had it in mind to do, and whatever flutter of a plume in the wind was troubling his mind; but he thought better of it. Himself and three or four good men gathered to see the distinguished guest depart, and two stout young squires besides their formidable lord – with such a guard, what could happen? And Cadfael was an old and practised hand, even without a cohort at his back.

'As you think best,' said Hugh, but thoughtfully and warily. 'We'll be here, and ready to read your signs. I should be lettered and fluent in them by now.'

His rawboned dapple-grey favourite was tethered at the gate. He mounted, and was off along the highway towards the bridge into the town. The air was very still, and there was enough lambent light to gleam dully like pewter across the surface of the mill pond. Cadfael watched his friend until the distant hooves rang hollow on the first stage of the bridge, and then turned back into the great court as the bell for Vespers chimed.

The young brother entrusted on this occasion with feeding the prisoners was just coming back from their cells to restore the keys to their place in the gatehouse, before repairing, side by side with Brother Porter, to the church for Vespers. Cadfael followed without haste, and with ears pricked, for there was undoubtedly someone standing close in shadow in the angle of the gate-pillar, flattened against the wall. She was wise, she did not call a goodnight to him, though she was aware of him. Indeed she had been there, close and still, watching him part from Hugh in the gateway. It could not be said that he had actually seen her, or heard any sound or movement; he had taken good care not to.

He spared a brief prayer at Vespers for poor, wretched Brother Jerome, seethed in his own venom, and shaken to a heart not totally shrivelled into a husk.

Jerome would be taken back into the oratory in due course, subdued and humbled, prostrating himself at the threshold of the choir until the abbot should consider satisfaction had been made for his offence. He might even emerge affrighted clean out of his old self. It was a lot to ask, but miracles do sometimes happen.

Tutilo was sitting on the edge of his cot, listening to the ceaseless and hysterical prayers of Brother Jerome in the cell next to his. They came to him muffled through the stone, not as distinct words but as a keening lamentation so grievous that Tutilo felt sorry for the very man who had tried, if not to kill, at least to injure him. For the insistence of this threnody in his ears Tutilo was deaf to the sound the key made, grating softly in the lock, and the door was opened with such aching care, for fear of creaks, that he never turned his head until a muted voice behind him said: 'Tutilo!'

Daalny was standing framed in the doorway. The night behind her was still luminous with the last stored light from pale walls opposite, and from a sky powdered with stars as yet barely visible, in a soft blue scarcely darker than their pinpoint silver. She came in, hasty but silent, until she had closed the door behind her, for within the cell the small lamp was lit, and a betraying bar of light falling through the doorway might bring discovery down upon them at once. She looked at him and frowned, for he seemed to her a little grey and discouraged, and that was not how she thought of him or how she wanted him.

'Speak low,' she said. 'If we can hear him, he might hear us. Quickly, you must go. This time you must go. It is the last chance. Tomorrow we leave, all of us. Herluin will take you back to Ramsey into worse slavery than mine, if it rests with him.'

Tutilo came to his feet slowly, staring at her. It had taken him a long, bemused moment to draw himself back from the unhappy world of Brother Jerome's frenzied prayers, and realize that the door really had opened and let her in, that she was actually standing there before him, urgent, tangible, her black hair shaken loose round her shoulders, and her eyes like blue-hot steady flames in the translucent oval of her face.

'Go, now, quickly,' she said. 'I'll show you. Through the wicket to the mill. Go westward, into Wales.'

'Go?' repeated Tutilo like a man in a dream, feeling his way in an unfamiliar and improbable world. And suddenly he burned bright, as though he had taken fire from her brightness. 'No,' he said, 'I will go nowhere without you.'

'Fool!' she said impatiently. 'You've no choice. If you don't stir yourself you'll go to Ramsey, and as like as not in bonds once they get you past Leicester and out of Robert Bossu's hands. Do you want to go back to be flayed and starved and tormented into an early grave? You never should have flown into that refuge, for you it's a cage. Better go naked into Wales, and take your voice and your psaltery with you, and they'll know a gift from God, and take you in. Quickly, come, don't waste what I've done.'

She had picked up the psaltery, which lay in its leather bag on the prayer-desk, and thrust it into his arms, and at the touch of it he quivered and clasped it to his heart, staring at her over it with brilliant golden eyes. He opened his lips, she thought to protest again, and to prevent it she shut one palm over his mouth, and with the other hand drew him desperately towards the door. 'No, say nothing, just go. Better alone! What could you do with a runaway slave tangling your feet,

243

crippling you? He won't leave go of me, the law won't leave go. I'm property, you're free. Tutilo, I entreat you! Go!'

Suddenly the springy steel had come back into his spine, and the dazzling audacity into his face, and he went with her, no longer holding back, setting the pace out at the door, and along the shadowy passage, the key again turned in the lock, the night air cool and scented with young leafage about them. There were no words at parting, far better silence. She thrust him through the wicket in the wall, out of the abbey pale, and closed the door between. And he had the sullen pewter shield of the mill pond before him, and the path out to the Foregate, and to the left, just before the bridge into the town, was the narrow road bearing westward towards Wales.

Without a glance behind, Daalny set off back towards the great court. She had a thing to do next morning of which he knew nothing, a thing that would, if it prospered, call off all pursuit, and leave him free. Secular law can move at liberty about even a realm divided. Canon law has not the same mobility. And half-proof pales beside irrefutable proof of guilt and innocence.

She heard the voices still chanting in the choir, so she took time to let herself into his cell again, to put out the little lamp. Better and safer if it should be thought he had gone to his bed, and would sleep through the night.

Chapter Thirteen

HE MORNING of departure dawned moist and still, the sun veiled, and every green thing looked at its greenest in the soft, amorphous light. Later the veil would thin and vanish, and the sun come forth in its elusive spring brightness. A good day to be riding home. Daalny came out into the great court from a sleepless bed, making her way to Prime, for she needed all her strength for the thing she had to do, and prayer and quietness within the huge solitude of the nave might stiffen her will to the act. For it seemed to her that no one else knew or even suspected what she suspected, so there was no one else to take action.

And still she might be wrong. The chink of coin, the weight of some solid bundle shifting against the pressure of her foot with that soft, metallic sound – what was that to prove anything? Even when she added to it the strange circumstances Brother Cadfael had recounted, the lie about Rémy's harness being forgotten in the outer stable. Yet he *had* lied, and what business, therefore, had he in that place, unless he had gone to recover something secret of his own – or, of course, of someone else's, or why keep it secret?

Well, Tutilo was out and gone, she hoped a good way west by now. The Benedictines had no great hold in Wales, the old, less rigidly organized Christianity of the Celtic Church lingered stubbornly there, even though the Roman rite had prevailed. They would accept a runaway novice, all the more when they heard him sing and play; they would provide him a patron and a house harp, and strip him of his skirts and find him chausses and shirt and cotte in payment for his music. And she, whatever it might cost her, would lift from him the last shadow of suspicion of murder, so that wherever he went he would go a free and vindicated man. And as for his other and lesser sins, they would be forgiven him.

There was an ache within her at his going, but she would not regard it, or regret his leaving her, though he had said in his haste that he would go nowhere without her. Now all that mattered to make her achievement complete was that he should never be recaptured, never subjected to narrow stone walls cramping his wings, or a halter crushing the cords of his throat into silence.

All through Prime she prayed unworded prayers for him, and waited and listened for the first outcry of his loss. It came only when Brother Porter had carried the breakfast bread and thin ale to Brother Jerome, and returned for the like repast for Tutilo, and even then it was hardly an outcry at all, since Brother Porter was not an exclaiming man, and scarcely recognized a crisis when he blundered into one. He emerged quickly from the cell, detached one hand from the wooden tray he was carrying to lock the door behind him, and then, recalling that there was no one within to need the precaution, in recoil not only left it unlocked but flung it wide open again. Daalny, keeping a wary eye on that corner of the court from the doorway of the guesthall, for some reason found this reaction perfectly logical. So did Cadfael, emerging at the same moment from the garden. But in view of this want of surprise and consternation on the custodian's part, it behoved someone else to supply the deficiency. Daalny slipped back to her preparations within, and left them to deal with it as they thought best.

'He's gone!' said Brother Porter. 'Now, how is that possible?'

It was a serious question, not a protest. He looked at the large, heavy key on his tray, and back to the open door, and knitted his thick grizzled brows.

'Gone?' said Cadfael, very creditably astonished. 'How could he be gone, and the door locked, and the key in your lodge?'

'Look for yourself,' said the porter. 'Unless the devil has fetched his own away, then someone else has laid hands on this key in the night to good purpose and turned him loose in this world. Empty as a pauper's purse in there, and the bed hardly dented. He'll be well away by this. Sub-Prior Herluin will be out of his mind when he hears. He's with Father Abbot at breakfast now, I'd best go and spoil his porridge for him.' He did not sound greatly grieved about it, but not exactly eager to bear the news, either.

'I'm bound there myself,' said Cadfael, not quite mendaciously, for he had just conceived the intention. 'You get rid of the tray and follow me down, I'll go before and break the news.'

'I never knew,' observed the porter, 'that you had a bent for martyrdom. But lead the way and welcome. And I'll come. Praise God, his lordship is set to leave this day, if he wants a safe journey Herluin and his fellows would be fools to lose the chance for the sake of hunting a slippery lad like that, with a night's start into the bargain. We'll be rid of them all before noon.' And he went off amiably to free his hands of the tray. He was in two minds whether he should return the key to its nail, but in the end he took it with him, as some manner of corroborative evidence, and followed Cadfael down towards the abbot's lodging, but in no haste.

It was a different matter when Herluin heard the news. He surged up from the abbot's table in his deprivation and loss, bereft now not only of his treasure gleaned here in Shrewsbury, but of his vengeance also, enraged beyond measure at having to go back to Ramsey almost empty-handed. For a short time, even though he himself did not know the whole of it, he had been on his way back a triumphant success, with generous largesse for the restoration, and the immeasurable blessing of a miracle-working saint. All gone now, and the culprit slipped through his fingers, so that he was left to trail home a manifest failure, meagrely re-paid for his travels, and short of a novice not, perhaps, exemplary in his behaviour, but valued for his voice, and therefore also in his way profitable.

'He must be pursued!' said Herluin, biting off every word with snapping, irregular teeth in his fury. 'And, Father Abbot, surely your guard upon his captivity has been lax in the extreme, or how could any unauthorized person have gained possession of the key to his cell? I should have taken care of the matter myself rather than trust to others. But he must be pursued and taken. He has charges to answer, offences to expiate. The delinquent must not be allowed to go uncorrected.'

The abbot in evident and formidable displeasure, though whether with the absconding prisoner, his unwary guardians, or this fulminating avenger deprived of his scapegoat, there was no knowing, said acidly: 'He may be sought within my premises, certainly. My writ does not presume to pursue men for punishment in the outside world.'

Earl Robert was also a guest at the abbot's table on his last morning, but thus far he had remained seated equably in his place, saying no word, his quizzical glance proceeding silently from face to face, not omitting Cadfael, who had shot his disruptive bolt without expression and in the flattest of voices, to be backed up sturdily by the porter, still gripping the key that must have been lifted from its nail during Vespers, or so he judged, and put back again before the office ended. Since such interference with the abbatial orders here on monastic ground was unheard-of, he had taken no precautions against it, though most of the time the lodge was manned, and the whole range of keys under the occupant's eye, and safe enough. The porter excused himself manfully. His part was to see to it that the prisoners were properly fed, if austerely; with the authorities rested the overseeing of their incarceration, and the judgement of their causes.

'But there is still a suspicion of murder against him,' cried Herluin, aggressively triumphant as he recalled the secular charge. 'He cannot be allowed to evade that. The king's law has a duty to recover the criminal, if the Church has not.'

'You are mistaken,' said Radulfus, severely patient. 'The sheriff has already assured me, yesterday, that he is satisfied on the proofs he holds that Brother Tutilo did not kill the young man Aldhelm. The secular law has no charge to bring against him. Only the Church can accuse him, and the Church has no sergeants to despatch about the country in pursuit of its failures.'

The word 'failure' had stung sharp colour into Herluin's face, as if he felt himself personally held to blame for being unable to keep his subordinates in better control. Cadfael doubted if any such significance had been intended. Radulfus was more likely to accuse himself of inadequate leadership than to make the same charge against any other. Even now that might well be his meaning. But Herluin took to himself, while he strenuously denied, every failure that had cropped his dignity and authority, and threatened to send him home humbled and in need of tolerance and consolation.

'It may be, Father Abbot,' he said, stiffly erect and smouldering with doomladen prophecy, 'that in this matter the Church will need to examine itself closely for if it fails to contend against the evildoers wherever they may be found, its authority may fall into disrepute. Surely the battle against evil, within or without our pale, is as noble a Crusade as the contention within the Holy Land. It is not to our credit if we stand by and let the evildoer go free. This man has deserted his brotherhood and abandoned his vows. He must be brought back to answer for it.'

'If you esteem him as a creature so fallen from grace,' said the abbot coldly, 'you should observe what the Rule has to say of such a case, in the twenty-eighth chapter, where it is written: "Drive out the wicked man from among you." '

'But we have not driven him out,' persisted Herluin still incandescent with rage, 'he has not waited the judgement nor answered for his offences, but taken himself off secretly in the night to our discomfiture.'

'Even so,' murmured Cadfael as to himself but very audibly, unable to resist the temptation, 'in the same chapter the Rule commands us: "If the faithless brother leaves you, *let him go*." '

Abbot Radulfus gave him a sharp glance, not altogether approving; and Robert Bossu gleamed into that brief, private, unnerving smile of his, that was gone before any target it might be aimed at could take offence.

'I am responsible to my abbot,' said Herluin, doggedly diverting the argument into a different channel, 'for the novice committed to my charge, I must at least make enquiry after him as best I may.'

'I fear,' said Robert Bossu with relentless sweetness, 'that time is too short even for that. If you decide to remain and pursue this quest, I fear you must resume your journey in less favourable circumstances. As soon as the early Mass is over we muster and leave. You would be wise, all the more as you are now one man short, to take advantage of our numbers and travel with us.'

'If your lordship could delay only a couple of days . . . ' began Herluin, writhing.

'I regret, no. I have malefactors of my own needing my presence,' said the earl, gallingly gentle and considerate. 'Especially if a few rogues and vagabonds like those who attacked your wagon are still making their way out of the Fens into safer fastnesses through my lands. It is high time I went back. I have lost my wager for Saint Winifred, but I don't grudge it, for after all, it was I who brought her back here, so even if she eludes me, I must have been doing her will to the last scruple, and there will surely be a minor blessing in it for my pains. But now I'm needed nearer home. When Mass is over,' said Earl Robert firmly, and made to rise, for it was nearly time, 'I would advise you join us, Father

Herluin, and do as Saint Benedict bids you, let the faithless brother go.'

The valedictory Mass began early and was briskly conducted, for the earl, once roused for departure, somehow conveyed the ardour of his mood to all those about him. When they came out into the early sunlight the bustle of loading and saddling began at once. Out they came to the muster, Nicol the steward and his fellow from Ramsey, attendant on a morose and taciturn Herluin, still very loth to abandon his stray, but even more reluctant to linger, and miss this opportunity of a safe and comfortable passage half the way home, at least and probably a mount for the rest of the way, since Robert Bossu could be generous to churchmen, even to one he cordially disliked.

The grooms came up from the stables with the narrow carriage that had conveyed Saint Winifred's reliquary back to its home. Stripped now of the embroidered draperies which had graced it when it carried the saint, it would now serve as baggage wagon for all the party. Loaded with the earl's belongings, and those of his squires, the alms collected by Herluin at Worcester and Evesham, and the greater part of Rémy's instruments and possessions, which were compact enough, it could still accommodate Nicol and his companion, and not be too heavy a load for the horse The packhorse which had carried the earl's baggage on the outward journey was freed now to carry Herluin.

The two young squires led the saddled horses up from the stable-yard, and Bénezet followed with Rémy's mount and his own, with a young novice leading Daalny's stolid cob bringing up the rear. The gate already stood wide for their passage. All done with competent speed. Cadfael, looking on from the corner of the cloister, had an eye anxiously on the open gate, for things had moved a little too briskly. It was early yet to expect Hugh and his officers, but no doubt the ceremonious farewells would take some time, and as yet the principals had not appeared. In all probability the earl would not think of setting out without taking his leave of Hugh.

The brothers had dispersed dutifully about their labours, but at every approach to the great court tended to linger rather longer than was strictly necessary, to contemplate the assembly of grooms and horses shifting restively about the cobbles, ready and eager to be on their way. The schoolboys were shooed away to their morning lesson, but Brother Paul would probably lose them again at the moment of departure.

Daalny, cloaked and bareheaded, came out from the guesthall and descended the steps to join the gathering below. She marked the balanced hang of Bénezet's saddlebags, and knew the one that held his secrets by the rubbed graze she had noted on its front below the buckles. She watched it steadily, as Cadfael was watching her. Her face was pale; so it was always, she had skin white as magnolia, but now it had the drawn ice-pallor of stress over her slight, immaculate bones. Her eyes were half-hooded, but glitteringly fixed under the long dark lashes. Cadfael observed the signs of her tension and pain, and they grieved him, but he did not quite know how to interpret them. She had done what she set out to do, sent Tutilo out into a world better suited to him than the cloister. To come to terms with her inevitable daily world without him, after this brief fantasy, must cost her dear, there was no help for it. Having made his own plans, he failed to realize that she might still have plans of her own for a final cast, the one thing she still had left to do.

253

One of the young squires had returned to the guest-hall to report that all was ready, and to carry cloak and gloves, or whatever was still left to be carried for his lord and his lord's new retainer, who ranked, no doubt, somewhere among the lesser gentlefolk, well above the servants, but not reverenced like the harpers of Wales. And now they appeared in the doorway, and Abbot Radulfus, punctual with every courtesy, emerged from the garden of his lodging, between the still ragged and leggy rosebushes, at the same moment, with the prior at his back, and came to salute his departing guests.

The earl was plain and elegant as ever in his sombre colourings and fine fabrics, crimson cotte cut reasonably short for riding, and deep grey-blue surcoat slashed to the thigh fore and aft. He seldom covered his head unless against wind, rain or snow, but the capuchon swung and draped his higher shoulder, concealing the hump; though it was hard to believe that he ever gave any thought to such a device, for the flaw neither embarrassed him nor hampered the fluency of his movements. At his elbow came Rémy of Pertuis in full exultant spate, breathing spirited court converse into his patron's ear. They descended the steps together, the squire following with his lord's cloak over his arm. Below, the assembly was complete, for abbot and prior were waiting beside the horses.

'My lord,' said the earl, 'I take my leave, now the time is come, with much regret. Your hospitality has been generous, and I fear very little deserved, since I came with pretensions to your saint. But I am glad that among many who covet her the lady knows how to choose the fittest and the best. I hope I take your blessing with me on the road?'

'With all my heart,' said Radulfus. 'I have had much

pleasure and profit in your company, my lord, and trust to enjoy it again when time favours us.'

The group, which had for a moment the formal look of immediate parting, began to dissolve into the general civility of visitors at the last moment reluctant to go, and lingering with many last things still to be said. There was Prior Robert at his most Norman and patrician, and even his most benign, since events had finally turned out well; certainly he was unlikely to let go of a Norman earl without exercising to the last moment his eloquence and charm. There was Herluin, in no very expansive mood but not to be left out of the courtesies, and Rémy, delighted with his change of fortune, shedding his beams impartially on all. Cadfael, with long experience of such departures, was aware that it would go on for as much as a quarter of an hour before anyone actually set foot in the stirrup and made to mount.

Daalny, with no such assurance, expected haste. She could not afford to wait, and find she had waited too long. She had steeled herself to the act, and dreaded she might not have time to make good what she had to say. She approached as close to abbot and earl as was seemly, and in the first pause between them she stepped forward and said loudly and clearly:

'Father Abbot – my lord Robert, may I speak a word? Before we leave this place, I have something that must be said, for it bears on theft, and may even bear on murder. I beg you hear me, and do right, for it is too much for me, and I dare not let it pass and be put aside.'

Everyone heard, and all eyes turned upon her. There fell a silence, of curiosity, of astonishment, of disapproval that the least of all these gathered here should dare to ask for a hearing now, out of a clear sky, and publicly. Yet strangely, no one waved her away or frowned her to silence and humility. She saw both abbot and earl regarding her with sharply arrested interest, and she made a deep reverence for them to share between them. Thus far she had said nothing to make any man afraid or uneasy for himself, not even Bénezet, who stood lounging with an arm over his horse's neck, the saddlebag hard against his side. Whatever lance she held she had not yet aimed, but Cadfael saw her purpose and was dismayed.

'Father, may I speak?'

This was the abbot's domain. The earl left it to him to respond.

'I think,' said Radulfus, 'that you must. You have said two words that have been heavy on our minds these past days, theft and murder. If there is anything you have to tell concerning these, we must listen.'

Cadfael, standing aside with an anxious eye on the gate, and praying that Hugh might ride in now, at once, with three or four sound men at his back, cast an uneasy glance at Bénezet. The man had not moved, but though his face remained merely a mask of interested but impersonal curiosity, much like all the others, the eyes fixed intently upon Daalny's face were levelled like the points of two daggers, and his very immobility seemed now deliberate and braced, a hound pointing.

If only, Cadfael thought, if only I had warned her! I might have known she could do terrible things for cause enough. Was it what I told her of the bridle that set her foot on this trail? She never gave sign, but I should have known. And now she has struck her blow too soon. Let her be logical, let her be slow to reach the heart of it, let her recall all that has gone before, and come to this only gradually now she has won her point. But time was not on their side. Even the Mass had ended early. Hugh would keep to his time, and still come too late.

'Father, you know of Tutilo's theft, on the night when the flood water came into the church, and how, afterwards, when Aldhelm said that he could point out the thief, and was killed on his way here to do what he had promised, reason could find none but Tutilo who had anything guilty to hide, and any cause to fear his coming, and prevent it by murder.'

She waited for him to agree thus far, and the abbot said neutrally: 'So we thought, and so we said. It seemed clear. Certainly we knew of no other.'

'But, Father, I have cause to believe that there was another.'

She still had not named him, but he knew. No question now but he was looking round towards the gate, and shifting softly, careful not to draw attention to himself, but in a furtive effort to draw gradually clear of the ring of men and horses that surrounded him. But Robert Bossu's two squires were close, hemming him in, and he could not extricate himself.

'I believe,' she said, 'there is one here among us who has hidden in his saddlebag property which is not his. I believe it was stolen that same night of the flood, when all was in chaos in the church. I do not know if Aldhelm *could* have told of it, but even if he *might* have seen, was not that enough? If I am wronging an innocent man, as I may be,' said Daalny with sharp ferocity, 'I will make amends by whatever means is asked of me. But search and put it to the test, Father.' And then she did turn and look at Bénezet, her face so blanched it was like a white hot flame; she turned and pointed. And he was penned into the circle so closely that only by violence could he break out; and violence would at

257

once betray him, and he was not yet at the end of his tether.

'In the saddlebag against his side, he has something he has been hiding ever since the flood came. If it was honestly come by, or already his, he would not need to hide it. My lord, Father Abbot, do me this justice, and if I am wrong, justice also to him. Search, and see!'

It seemed that for one instant Bénezet contemplated laughing at the accusation, shrugging her off, saying contemptuously that she lied. Then he gathered himself convulsively, pricked into response by all the eyes levelled upon him. It was fatally late to cry out in the anger of innocence. He, too, had missed his time, and with it whatever chance was still left to him.

'Are you mad? It's a black lie, I have nothing here but what is mine. Master, speak for me! Have you ever had cause to think ill of me? Why should she turn on me with such a charge?'

'I have always found Bénezet trustworthy,' said Rémy, stoutly enough and speaking up for his own, but not quite at ease. 'I cannot believe he would steal. And what has been missed? Nothing, to my knowledge. Who knows of anything lost since the flood? I've heard no such word.'

'No complaint has been made,' agreed the abbot frowning and hesitant.

'There is a simple means,' said Daalny implacably, 'to prove or disprove. Open his saddlebag! If he has nothing to hide, let him prove it and shame me. If I am not afraid, why should he be?'

'Afraid?' blazed Bénezet. 'Of such calumny? What is in my baggage is mine, and there's no answer due from me to any false charge of yours. No, I will not display my poor belongings to satisfy your malice. Why you should utter such lies against me I cannot guess. What did I ever do to you? But you waste your lies, my master knows me better.'

'You would be wise to open, and let your virtue be seen by all,' Earl Robert said with dispassionate authority, 'since not all here have such secure knowledge of you. If she lies, uncover her lie.' He had glanced for one instant at his two young men, and raised a commanding eyebrow. They drew a pace nearer to Bénezet, their faces impassive, but their eyes alert.

'There is something owed here to a dead man,' said Abbot Radulfus, 'since this girl has recalled to us one most precious thing stolen. If this is indeed a matter that can shed light on that crime, and lift even the shadow of doubt from all but the guilty, I think we have a duty to pursue it. Give here your saddlebag.'

'No!' He clutched it to his side with a protective arm. 'This is unworthy, humiliation . . . I have done no wrong, why should I submit to such indignity?'

'Take it,' said Robert Bossu.

Bénezet cast one wild, flashing glance round him as the two squires closed in and laid competent hands, not on him, but on bridle and saddlebag. There was no hope of leaping into the saddle and breaking out of the closed circle, but the young men had loosed their own bridles to pen him in, and one of the horses thus released was some yards nearer to the gate, standing docilely clear of the agitated group in the centre of the court. Bénezet plucked his hands from his gains with a sob of fury, dealt his startled mount a great blow under the belly that sent him rearing and plunging with an indignant scream, and burst out of the hampering ring. The company scattered, evading the clashing hooves, and Bénezet clutched at the bridle of the waiting horse,

259

and without benefit of stirrups leaped and scrambled into the saddle.

No one was near enough to grasp at rein or stirrup leather. He was up and away before anyone else could mount, turning his back upon the tangle of stamping horses and shouting men. He drove, not directly at the gate, but aside in a flying curve, where Daalny had started backwards out of one danger to lay herself in the path of another. He had his short dagger out of its sheath and bared in his hand.

She saw his intent only at the last instant as he was on her. He made no sound at all, but Cadfael, running frantically to pluck her from under the flying hooves, saw the rider's face clearly, and so did she, the once impassive countenance convulsed into a mask of hatred and rage, with drawn-back lips like a wolf at bay. He could not spare the time to ride her down, it would have slowed him too much. He leaned sidewise from the saddle in full flight, and the dagger slashed down her sleeve from the shoulder and drew a long graze down her arm. She sprang backwards and fell heavily on the cobbles, and Bénezet was gone, out at the gate already in a driven gallop, and turning towards the town.

Hugh Beringar, his deputy and three of his sergeants were just riding down from the crest of the bridge. Bénezet saw them, checked violently, and swung his mount aside into the narrow road that turned left between the mill pond and the river, southwestward into the fringes of the Long Forest, into deep cover on the quickest way into Wales.

The riders from the town were slow to understand the inferences, but a horseman hurtling out of the abbey court towards the bridge, baulking at sight of them and wheeling into a side-road at the same

260

headlong speed, was a phenomenon to be pondered, if not pursued, and Hugh had bellowed: 'Follow him!' even before the youngest squire had come running out from the gates into the Foregate, crying: 'Stop him! He's suspect as a thief!'

'Bring him back!' ordered Hugh, and his officers swung willingly into the byroad, and spurred into a gallop after the fugitive.

Daalny had picked herself up before Cadfael could reach her, and turned and ran blindly from the turmoil in the court, from the sick terror that had leaned to her murderously from the saddle, and from the shattering reaction after crisis, which had set her shivering now the worst was over. For this was certainty. Why else should he run for his life before ever his saddlebag was opened? Still she did not even know what he had hidden there, but she knew it must be deadly. She fled into the church like a homing bird. Let them do the rest, her part was over. She did not doubt now that it would be enough. She sat down on the steps of Saint Winifred's altar, where everything began and everything ended, and leaned her head back to rest against the stone.

Cadfael had followed her in, but halted at sight of her sitting there open-eyed and still, her head reared erect as though she was listening to a voice, or a memory. After chaos, this calm and quietness was awesome. She had felt it on entering, Cadfael felt it on beholding her thus entranced.

He approached her softly, and spoke as softly, and for a moment was not sure she would hear him, for she was tuned to something more distant.

'He grazed you. Better let me see.'

'A scratch,' she said indifferently; but she let him

261

draw back her loose sleeve almost to the shoulder, where it was slit for a hand's-length. The skin was barely broken, there was only a white hair-line, beaded in two or three places with a tiny jewel of blood. 'Nothing! It will not fester.'

'You took a heavy fall. I never thought he would drive at you so. You spoke too soon, I meant to spare you the need.'

'I thought he could neither love nor hate,' said Daalny with detached interest. 'I never saw him moved till now. Did he get clean away?'

That he could not answer, he had not stopped to see.

'I am very well,' she said firmly, 'and all is well with me. You go back and see what is still to do. Ask them . . . Ask them to leave me here a while alone. I need this place. I need this certainty.'

'You shall have it,' said Cadfael, and left her, for she was in command of herself and all her thoughts, words and acts as perhaps she had never been before. He turned back at the door to look at her one last time, and she sat regal and erect on the steps of the altar, her hands easy on the stone on either side, half-open, as though they held the insignia of sovereignty. There was the faintest curve of a smile on her lips, private and solitary, and yet he had the illusion – if it was an illusion? – that she was not alone.

They had unbuckled the saddlebag from its harness, and carried it into the gatehouse as the nearest place where a solid table offered a hospitable surface on which to spill the contents. There were six of them gathered close about the board when Cadfael joined them to make a seventh: Abbot Radulfus, Prior Robert, Sub-Prior Herluin, Robert Bossu, Rémy of Pertuis and Hugh Beringar, freshly dismounted within the gate, and very briefly appraised of all that had been happening here. It was Hugh, at the earl's silent invitation, who brought forth from the bag the modest personal equipment of a valued body-servant, folded clothing, razor, brushes, a good belt, a pair of worn but well-made gloves. At the bottom, but occupying half the space, Hugh grasped by its draw-string neck and hauled forth upon the table a plump, soft leather bag that gave forth an unmistakable chinking of coins settling, as it sagged together and squatted still and enigmatic before their eyes.

One thing at least was no longer secret. Three of them here recognized it at once. At the loud gasp that escaped Herluin even the lower orders, gathered avidly about the doorway, Nicol, and the squires, and the humble layman from Ramsey, drew eager anticipatory breath, and crowded closer.

'Good God!' said Herluin in a marvelling whisper. 'This I know! This was in the coffer for Ramsey, on the altar of the Lady Chapel when the flood came. But how is it possible? It was put on the wagon with the load of timber. We found the coffer at Ullesthorpe, ravaged and empty, everything stolen . . . '

Hugh pulled open the strings of the bag, turned up the soft leather upon the table, and slid out a slithering flood of silver pence, and among the whisper and the glitter, a little bulkier and last to emerge, certain shining ornaments: a gold neckchain, twin bracelets, a torque of gold set with roughly cut gemstones, and two rings, one a man's massive seal, the other a broad gold band, deeply engraved. Last came a large and intricate ring brooch, the fastening of a cloak, in reddish gold, fine Saxon work.

They stood and gazed, and were slow to believe or understand.

'These I know, also,' said Radulfus slowly. 'The brooch I have seen once in the cloak of the Lady Donata. The plain ring she wore always.'

'She gave them to Ramsey before her death,' said Herluin, low-voiced, marvelling at what seemed almost a miracle. 'All these were in the casket I put in Nicol's charge when he left with the wagon for Ramsey. The casket we found, broken open and discarded . '

'I well remember,' said Nicol's voice hoarsely from the doorway. 'I carried the key safe enough, but they had prised up the lid, taken the treasure, and cast the box away . . . So we thought!'

So they had all thought. All this goodwill, all these gifts to a ravaged monastery, had been in their casket on the altar of the Lady Chapel on the night of the flood, high enough to be clear even of the highest flood water. Safe from the river, but not from thieves coming on the pretext of helping to preserve the holy things, while taking advantage of the opportunity to help themselves to what lay temptingly to hand. The key had been in the lock, no need that time to break it open. Easy enough to lift out the leather bag, replace it with whatever offered, rags and stones, to represent the weight that had been removed. Relock the box, and leave it to be transferred to the wagon in Nicol's care. And then, thought Cadfael, his eyes upon Donata's bright last charity, hide the booty somewhere safe, somewhere apart, until the time comes for leaving Shrewsbury. Somewhere apart, where even if discovered it could not attach to a name; but where it was unlikely to be discovered. Bénezet had helped to move the horses from their low-lying stable within the walls. It would take no time at all to thrust his prize to the very bottom of the full corn bin, newly supplied for the few days of the horses' stay. Small fear of their having to remain long enough to expose the alien thing beneath the corn. Safer there than in the common guesthall, where casual overnight travellers came and went, and there was little if any privacy. Even thieves can be robbed, and curious neighbours can find out things that were hidden.

'They never left Shrewsbury!' said Hugh, staring down at the pile of silver and gold. 'Father Herluin, it seems God and the saints have restored you your own.'

'Under whom,' said Robert Bossu drily, 'thanks are due also to this girl of yours, Rémy. She has proved her point concerning theft. Are we not forgetting her? I hope he did her no injury. Where is she now?'

'She is in the church,' said Cadfael, 'and asks that you will allow her a little time in private before departing. She has nothing worse than a graze, as concerning the body, she can go and she can ride, but a while of quietness is what her spirit needs.'

'We will wait her convenience,' said the earl. 'I would like, I confess, Hugh, to see the end of this. If your fellows bring back the thief alive, so much the better, for he has robbed me, in passing, of a good horse. He has much to answer for.'

'More,' said Cadfael sombrely, 'than mere theft.'

He had moved aside the pile of clothes which had covered Bénezet's plunder from sight, and thrust a hand into the depths of the saddlebag, and there was some folded garment still left undisturbed within, put away beneath all. He held it unfolded in his hands, a linen shirt, clean from fresh folds after laundering, and was gazing down at the cuff of one sleeve, turning it about in his fingers with fixed attention. A very self-sufficient man, Bénezet, very orderly in his management of his affairs, needing no woman to wash and furbish for him. But not rich enough to be able to discard a shirt, even if there had been much opportunity, shut in here within monastic walls at his master's pleasure, while Rémy pursued his quest for patronage. He had washed it and folded it deep under everything in his packing, to await its next airing miles distant from here and weeks later. But there are stains not easily washed out. Cadfael extended the cuff beneath Hugh's wondering gaze, and Earl Robert leaned to take up the second sleeve. For about a hand's breadth from the hem they were both thinly spattered with small round stains, no more than a faint but clear pink outline, even fainter pink within. But Cadfael had seen the like before, often enough to know it. So, he thought, had Robert Bossu.

'This is blood,' said the earl.

'It is Aldhelm's blood,' said Cadfael. 'It rained that night. Bénezet would be cloaked, thick black wool swallows blood, and I am sure he was careful. But . . .'

But a jagged stone, raised in both hands and smashed down upon the head of a senseless man, however the act is managed, however discreetly accomplished, and with no great haste, no one to interfere, must yet threaten at least the hands and wrists of the murderer with indelible traces. The worst was trapped under the stone, and bled into the grass after, but this faint sprinkling, this fringing shower, had marked flesh and linen. And from linen, unless it can be steeped at once, it is difficult to erase the small shapes that betray.

'I remember,' said Rémy, dazed and half-incredulous, clean forgetful of himself, 'I was your guest that night, Father Abbot, and he was free to his own devices. He said he was bound for the town.'

'It was he who told the girl that Aldhelm was expected,' said Cadfael, 'and she who warned Tutilo to be safely out of sight. So Bénezet knew of the need, if need there was for him. But how could he be sure? It was enough that Aldhelm, required to recollect clearly, might recollect all too much of what he had seen in innocence. And therefore in innocence he is dead. And Bénezet was his murderer. And Bénezet will never know, and neither shall we, if he murdered for nothing.'

Alan Herbard, Hugh's deputy in office, rode in at the gate an hour before noon.

The party was just reassembling for departure, after Earl Robert's generous delay for Daalny's sake, and Cadfael, self-appointed custodian of her interests, for good reason, had just been requested, very courteously, to go and call her to join the group, if by this time she felt sufficiently recovered. There had been time, also, for all the rest of them to assimilate, as best they could, the flood of revelations and shocks that bade fair to diminish their numbers and change several lives. Sub-Prior Herluin had lost a novice and his revenge for sorely felt abuses, but recovered the treasures he thought lost for ever, and his mood, in spite of sins and deaths and violence, had brightened since his glum morning face almost into benevolence. Rémy had lost a manservant, but secured his future with a very influential patron: a manservant is easily replaced, but entry to the household of one of the foremost earls of the land is a prize for life. Rémy was not disposed to complain. He had not even lost the horse with the man, the stolen beast belonged to Robert Bossu's squire. Bénezet's sedate and aging roan, relieved of his saddlebags, waited now imperturbably for another rider. Nicol could ride, and leave his fellow to drive the wheeled cart. Everything was settling into the ordinary routines of life, however deflected from their course hitherto.

And suddenly there was Alan Herbard in the gateway, just dismounting, curious and a little awed at approaching Hugh in this illustrious company.

'We have the man, sir. I rode ahead to tell you. They are bringing him after. Where would you have him taken? There was no time to hear why he ran, and what he was accused of.'

'He is charged with murder,' said Hugh. 'Get him safe into the castle under lock and key, and I'll follow as soon as I may. You were quick. He cannot have got far. What happened?'

'He took us a mile or more into the Long Forest, and we were gaining on him, and he turned off the open ride to try and lose us among thick woodland. I think they started a hind, and the horse baulked, for we heard him curse, and then the horse screamed and reared. I think he used the dagger . . .'

The squire had drawn close to hear what had befallen his mount. Indignantly he said: 'Conradin would never endure that.'

'They were well ahead, we could only judge by the sounds. But I think he reared, and swept the fellow off against a low branch, for he was lying half-stunned under a tree when we picked him up. He goes lame on one leg, but it's not broken. He was dazed, he gave us no trouble.'

'He may yet,' said Hugh warningly.

'Will's no prentice, he'll keep safe hold of him. But the horse,' said Alan, somewhat apologetic on this point, 'we haven't caught. He'd bolted before we ever reached the place, and for all the searching we dared do with the man to guard, we couldn't find him close, nor even hear anything ahead of us. Riderless, he'll be well away before he'll get over his fright and come to a stay.'

'And my gear gone with him,' said the unlucky owner with a grimace, but laughed the next moment. 'My lord, you'll owe me new clothes if he's gone beyond recall.'

'We'll make a proper search tomorrow,' promised Alan. 'We'll find him for you. But first I'll go and see this murderer safely jailed.'

He made his reverence to the abbot and the earl, and remounted at the gate, and was gone. They were left looking at one another like people at the hour of awaking, uncertain for a moment whether what they contemplate is reality or dream.

'It is well finished,' said Robert Bossu. 'If this is the end!' And he turned upon the abbot his grave, considerate glance. 'It seems we have lived this farewell twice, Father, but this time it is truth, we must go. I trust we may meet at some happier occasion, but now you will be glad to have us out of your sight and out of your thoughts, with all the troubles we have brought you between us. Your household will be more peaceful without us.' And to Cadfael he said, turning to take his horse's bridle: 'Will you ask the lady if she feels able to join us? It's high time we took the road.'

He was gone only a few moments, and he emerged through the south door and the cloister alone.

'She is gone,' said Brother Cadfael, his tone temperate and his face expressionless. 'There is no one in the church but Cynric, Father Boniface's verger, trimming the candles on the parish altar, and he has seen no one come or go within the past halfhour.'

Afterwards he sometimes wondered whether Robert Bossu had been expecting it. He was a man of very dangerous subtlety, and could appreciate subtlety in others, and see further into a man at short acquaintance than most people. Nor was he at all averse to loosing cats among pigeons. But no, probably not. He had not known her long enough for that. If she had ever reached his Leicester household, and been in his sight a few weeks, he would have known her very well, and been well able to assess her potentialities in other pursuits besides music. But at the least, this was no great surprise to him. It was not he, but Rémy of Pertuis, who raised the grieving outcry:

'No! She cannot be gone. Where could she go? She is mine! You are sure? No, she must be there, you have not had time to look for her . . . '

'I left her there more than an hour ago,' said Cadfael simply, 'by Saint Winifred's altar. She is not there now. Look for yourself. Cynric found the church empty when he came to dress the altar.'

'She has fled me!' mourned Rémy, whitefaced and stricken, not simply protesting at the loss of his most valuable property, and certainly not lamenting a creature greatly loved. She was a voice to him, but he was true Provençal and true musician, and a voice was the purest of gold to him, a treasure above rubies. To own her was to own that instrument, the one thing in her he regarded. There was nothing false in his grief and dismay. 'She cannot go. I must seek her. She is mine, I bought her. My lord, only delay until I can find her. She cannot be far. Two days longer . . . one day . . . '

'Another search? Another frustration?' said the earl and shook his head decisively. 'Oh, no! I have had dreams like this, they never lead to any ending, only barrier after barrier, baulk after baulk. She was indeed, she is, a very precious asset, Rémy, a lovely peal in her throat, and a light, true hand on organetto or strings.

But I have been truant all too long, and if you want my alliance you had best ride with me now, and forget you paid money for what is beyond price It never profits. There are others as gifted, you shall have the means to find them and I'll guarantee to keep them content.'

What he said he meant, and Rémy knew it. It took him a great struggle to choose between his singer and his future security, but the end was never in doubt. Cadfael saw him swallow hard and half-choke upon the effort, and almost felt sorry for him at that moment. But with a patron as powerful, as cultivated and as durable as Robert Beaumont, Rémy of Pertuis could hardly be an object for sympathy very long.

He did look round sharply for a reliable agent here, before he gave in. 'My lord abbot, or you, my lord sheriff – I would not like her to be solitary and in want, ever. If she should reappear, if you hear of her, I beg you, let me have word, and I will send for her. She has always a welcome with me.'

True enough, and not all because she was valuable to him for her voice. Probably he had never realized until now that she was more than a possession, that she was a human creature in her own right, and might go hungry, even starve, fall victim to villains on the road, come by harm a thousand different ways. It was like the flight of a nun from childhood, suddenly venturing a terrible world that gave no quarter. So, at least, he might think of her, thus seeing her whole in the instant when she vanished from his sight. How little he knew her!

'Well, my lord, I have done what I can. I am ready.'

They were gone, all of them, streaming out along the Foregate towards Saint Giles, Robert Beaumont, earl of Leicester, riding knee to knee with Sub-Prior Herluin of Ramsey, restored to good humour by the

271

recovery of the fruits of his labours in Shrewsbury, and gratified to be travelling in company with a nobleman of such standing; Robert's two squires riding behind, the younger a little disgruntled at having to make do with an unfamiliar mount, but glad to be going home; Herluin's middle-aged layman driving the baggage cart, and Nicol bringing up the rear, well content to be riding instead of walking. Within the church their hoofbeats were still audible until they reached the corner of the enclave, and turned along the Horse Fair. Then there was a grateful silence, time to breathe and reflect. Abbot Radulfus and Prior Robert were gone about their lawful business, and the brothers had dispersed to theirs. It was over.

'Well,' said Cadfael thankfully, bending his head familiarly to Saint Winifred, 'an engaging rogue, and harmless, but not for the cloister, any more than she was for servility, so why repine? Ramsey will do very well without him, and Partholan's queen is a slave no longer. True, she's lost her baggage, but that she would probably have rejected in any case. She told me, Hugh, she owned nothing, not even the clothes she wore. Now it will please her that she has stolen only the few things on her back.'

'And the boy,' said Hugh, 'has stolen only a girl.' And he added, glancing aside at Cadfael's contented face: 'Did you know he was there, when you followed her in?'

'I swear to you, Hugh, I saw nothing, I heard nothing. There was nothing whatever even to make me think of him. But yes, I knew he was there. And so did she from the instant she came in. It was rather as though it was spoken clearly into my ear: Go softly. Say nothing. All things shall be well. She was not asking so

272

very much, after all. A little while alone. And the parish door is always open.'

'Do you suppose,' asked Hugh, as they turned towards the south door and the cloister together, 'that Aldhelm *could* have revealed anything against Bénezet?'

'Who knows? The possibility was enough.'

They came out into the full light of early afternoon, but after the turmoil and passion this quietness and calm left behind spoke rather of evening and the lovely lassitude of rest after labour and stillness after storm. 'It was easy to get fond of the boy,' said Cadfael, 'but dangerous, with such a flibbertigibbet. As well to be rid of him now rather than later. He was certainly a thief, though not for his own gain, and as certainly a liar when he felt it necessary. But he was truly kind to Donata. What he did for her was done with no thought of reward, and from an unspoiled heart.'

There was no one left in the great court as they turned towards the gatehouse. A space lately throbbing with anger and agitation rested unpeopled, as if a lesser creator had despaired of the world he had made, and erased it to clear the ground for a second attempt.

'And have you thought,' asked Hugh, 'that those two will certainly be heading southwest by the same road Bénezet took? South to the place where it crosses the old Roman track, and then due west, straight as a lance, into Wales. With the luck of the saints, or the devil himself, they may happen on that lost horse, there in the forest, and leave nothing for Alan to find tomorrow.'

'And that unlucky lad's saddlebags still there with the harness,' Cadfael realized, and brightened at the thought. 'He could do with some rather more secular garments than the habit and the cowl, and from what I recall they should be much the same size.'

'Draw me in no deeper,' said Hugh hastily.

'Finding is not thieving.' And as they halted at the gate, where Hugh's horse was tethered, Cadfael said seriously: 'Donata understood him better than any of us. She told him his fortune, lightly it may be, but wisely. A troubadour, she said, needs three things, and three things only, an instrument, a horse, and a lady love. The first she gave him, an earnest for the rest. Now, perhaps, he has found all three.'